Author's Note

Note: Shauna Richmond writes in British English. Therefore, spelling and grammar may differ from American English.

Although it is a Rom-Com, Screw you too! Edges on some harder issues. See Trigger warning list below.

Scew you too! Is the second book in the duology although it links in with another standalone that runs in a consecutive timeline. Jailbait is a darker romance with the men from Screw it! (book 1) and Screw you too! Aiding a wrongly convicted prisoner in her fight to prove her innocence.

All of Shauna's books (fantasy and contemporary) are based in Ireland and/or have Irish protagonists. Some things, like slang, humour et cetera may be lost on some readers.

TRIGGER WARNINGS:

Explicit sexual scenes.

Strong language.

Depression.

To every parent who is constantly overwhelmed, overtired, overworked, and over-caffeinated... me too, we need stronger coffee.

CRAIG

I knew it was bad, but I didn't realise it was this bad. When my jeans screamed in protest, that's one thing— I can blame the dryer. But when my toddler comes in and slaps me on the belly, giggles, and calls me "daddy pig," that's an entirely different story. That pink pain in the arse, Peppa, is officially barred from the house.

It didn't help that I noticed a rip in my jocks, and our little hellion is adamant that I farted and blew a hole right through them. In all fairness, she kind of has a point; we did order out last night— curry is no longer a late-night friend after the age of thirty-five.

"Well?" Lottie calls from the bedroom. As she rounds the doorway, one look at me is all it takes: "That bad?"

"No, not at all." I know I'm being a pouty little shit right now. You would be too if you got called fat before having your morning coffee. "I just stood on the scales, and my phone number came up.

Lottie tosses her hair back and laughs. "You're clearly exaggerating."

"No?" I slap my belly, and just like good old St. Nick, it

jiggles like Mamma June's fat flaps. "Daddy pig, daddy pig, where are you?"

"Craig," Lottie cackles, snorts, and then laughs some more at my expense like the supportive wife she is.

"I haven't seen my dick since Christmas."

She braces herself on the doorframe to stop herself from falling over. "It was cold."

"It's June!" I storm out of the bathroom; that scale is dead to me. "This is your fault."

"My fault?"

"You need to stop baking, babe. It's not a good look on me."

She comes up, stifling a laugh, and wraps her arms around me. "Nothing wrong with a dad bod," Lottie says, standing on her tiptoes, her lips grazing my cheek. "I prefer you this way." Her hand slips down to the band on my boxers.

"Daddy look!" Tilly charges into the room, holding out her Baymax plushie. "He looks just like you!"

How dare she!

"That's it, I'm going back to the gym."

Lottie gives me a sideways grin and asks, "Monday?"

"Today!"

She glares at me with all the frustration of Tilly when we tell her she cannot have chocolate for breakfast, "but we have the barbecue today."

Of course. How stupid of me. More food. Lottie's cheesecake—damn that cheesecake, or as I call it, diabeto. It's good cake. Damn good cake. That should be set right about now.

"This is why I'm chunky!" I wail.

"Ethan Barnes!" Lottie's voice cracks like a whip, and Ethan practically jumps out of his skin, stopping his impression of Stewie Gryphon singing about the cow going moo.

"Sorry, Mam!"

"I told you not to let him watch Family Guy; he's too young." Lottie turns to me, working as much venom into her stare as humanly possible.

"Sorry, love." Our little hellion grabs our attention yet again. Ethan blows his cinnamon hair away from his face and turns to Jamie with an impish glint in his eyes. "What if someone pulls up on you and asks you to help them find their dog?"

"That's easy," Jamie snorts. "You help him find that fucking dog."

"Jamie!" Tiffy, Lottie's bestie, spits venom.

"It wasn't me!"

"At least I didn't let Ethan on TikTok," I shrug, swigging from my beer, noticing Jay turn and scowl at me. *Beer. How I'm going to miss you, my bubbly friend.*

Jay turns to me and growls, "Throw me under the bus, why don't you?"

Yeah, we're in trouble again.

Averting my gaze, I'm suddenly enchanted by the barbecue. My beautiful, albeit cranky, wife stares a hole through me.

Jay's in the middle of getting a bollocking from Tiffy. My eyes flit to the remains of my drink. "Ethan, go inside and get those plates off the counter for me."

"I am down, how much for crack?"

"Ethan!" Lottie whirls around.

He's gone. He's gone, and I'm left choking on a bottle of Miller.

It's not our fault. Lottie had to go to a book signing, and I had to work. Josie was away with George; Kim was on a weekend bender somewhere up north. I had no one to mind the kids, so I had to bring them to work with me.

"Daddy!" my golden-haired princess Ellie—or, as Lottie calls her, demon number two—sprints up to me with nothing but love in her eyes, meaning one thing and one thing only. She wants something.

"Yes, baby?"

"Can we get a cat?"

"By cat... you mean dog, right?"

"No, I want a fluffy pussy."

Sweet baby Jeremiah.

"Mam—" is going to lose her shit if she hears you saying something like, "doesn't like cats."

Ellie's lower lip pushes out in a pout, and she fixes me with a stare that would make puss-in-boots envious. *Don't say it, Princess. Don't say what I think you're about to.*

"But Heather's mam just got a lovely ginger pus—"

"Lottie!" That is the last thing I need right now; I could go the rest of my life without picturing Rita's mousse knuckle.

"Yeah?"

"Ellie wants you."

"But, Daddy!"

"Talk to your mother." Holy shitballs. How inappropriate are my kids? Even when they don't mean to be.

"What was all that about?" Jay swigs his beer.

"Apparently she wants a pussy." I rub my eyes, convincing myself it's hay fever and not an aneurysm.

His beer stops in mid-air. "Don't we all?" he chuckles lowly.

I stretch, feeling my back crack. The joys of life, you work until you creak, and then you die, and I'm already creaking. "Be thankful you don't have daughters," I grumble, turning to watch Ellie argue with her mother.

"Please!" Ellie begs.

"No."

"Please!!"

"No," Lottie says, crossing her arms, and I know she is not about to fold on the cat thing. Better luck next time, kiddo.

"PLEASE!!!"

"Hmm... nope. Not going to happen," Lottie clicks her tongue. Stance unwavering.

"But why?"

Oh, great, here come the crocodile tears.

"Cats smell. They're moody, and I'm not having one in the house, Ellie."

"But, Mam!"

"No."

"If Ethan asked, you'd let him!"

Trying the favouritism card now? God loves a trier. Too bad Lottie isn't going to budge.

"No, I wouldn't and stop trying to play me. It doesn't work."

"Daddy!"

Hey, she's only your mother. I have to live with her. "No, Ellie."

"It's not fair!" Her arms snap at her side, and she retreats into her treehouse to lick her wounds.

"Cry me a river," Lottie growls. Tiffy softens the blow by handing over a WKD blue, an offering Lottie is all over.

"Daddy!" Tilly, our youngest, comes barrelling out of a bush. I don't even want to know. At this rate, she's probably going to ask me to do the truffle shuffle.

"Hey, baby girl," I pick Tilly up, and she looks at the grill, unimpressed that my attention is anywhere but on her.

"Let's play!"

I'll play in a minute, baby. I have to cook first, ok? Go play with James."

There are only three months between James and Matilda. Lottie and Tiffy had each other for their pregnancies, while Jay and I clutched each other for dear life to survive their hormones.

As much as we love the kids, we cannot wait to abandon them and piss them off next weekend.

Every year around the same time, the four of us go back to the place where it all started—for me and Lottie anyway.

I'm looking forward to the extra hour in the morning to sleep in. To not answer fifty million questions a day, and most importantly, to have Lottie to myself for the weekend.

We learned quickly that the more kids you have, the harder it is to squeeze in some alone time together.

Hell, two weeks ago I used my lunch hour to drive home and violate my wife in the tiny window of time we had between the kids being in school and Tilly's afternoon nap.

The school term provides a gap, minus the toddler being at home. This summer will be excruciating. I thought I was being smart last year by signing Ethan and Ellie up for the scouts and summer project.

Yeah. Real fucking smart.

Jay and I were sent away with the kids on the camping trips because the girls don't trust anyone with their babies. The day trips with the rest of the kids from their school... Lottie went on those. So, yeah, that didn't go to plan.

Tilly was our surprise baby. Well, so was Ethan. Ellie was the only one that was planned, and she is the most demanding of the three.

It's my fault. I spoil her. I spoil all the kids, but I'm whipped when it comes to my girls. Ethan milks Lottie for all she's worth, while the girls hit me up anytime they want something.

"Skewers are done." Jay comes out of the kitchen armed with two plates of chicken skewers. Any excuse to escape his wife's wrath.

Lottie takes two and comes over to me. "You ok, Batman?"

"Never better."

Lottie pushes the skewer into her mouth, and I can't pull my eyes away. What is with her and phallic-shaped food?

"What?" Her hand comes up, covering her mouth as she continues to chew on the diced chicken breast.

"I want to trade places with that skewer." She smirks, leans in, and kisses me. Then she holds out the other skewer for me to take. "You wait until I get you back to that hotel, baby."

"Going to break the bed again?" Something sparks behind those sea-green eyes.

"You bet your sweet arse I am."

"Promise?" she purrs.

I bite off a chunk of chicken, trying not to smirk. "How do you feel about boarding school?"

"What?"

"If I don't get between those legs soon, I'm going to start selling the kids."

"What, like a two-for-one?"

"Good idea!"

"It would never work," she says, swigging on her bottle of WKD. "They would be gone for an hour, and we'd be paid to take them back."

"I'd still get the hour in you; totally worth it." I'm done with quickies. I'm sick of them. I don't get a chance to enjoy Lottie anymore.

"You're still upset over what happened two nights ago?"

Too fucking right I'm upset!

The kids finally went to sleep early without me threatening them with chloroform. Lottie met her deadline, and I had an easy day at work.

We got hot and heavy under the covers. Lottie was driving me wild, sucking me hard and slowly, teasing the head with her tongue. She felt amazing. The next thing I know, Tilly charges into the room after having a nightmare, and my birthday blowjob goes out the window.

"I haven't thought about it," I say, tearing off another piece of chicken from the skewer.

"You're a rotten liar," she says as she steps closer to me, running her hand up my chest. "I'll make it up to you soon."

"I'll hold you to that."

I serve up the burgers, and it's like feeding time at the zoo. I'm practically tackled by five kids, only three of whom are mine.

"Tilly, you need to eat something, sweetie." Lottie tries the nice guy approach first.

"No."

"Matilda." Tilly jumps down from her chair, abandoning her plate, and runs to me. "Come on then," I say, hoisting her onto my lap.

Lottie sighs, "Tilly, Daddy needs to eat."

Yeah? Like she gives a rat's arse. Tilly decides my food looks more appetising. "Tastes better off someone else's plate," I shrug.

Lottie gets up, grabs Matilda's abandoned plate, and brings it to me as an offering. "Thanks, babe."

"No!" the little demon snaps.

"Matilda!" Lottie looks as if she's about to lose her reason.

"Mine has onions," Ellie pouts.

Lottie grinds her teeth and hisses, "Pick them off then."

Oh, yeah. There's the steam. She's going to blow.

"What do you call a leprechaun in cement?" Ethan asks around a mouthful of burger.

Jamie cocks an eyebrow and asks, "what?"

"A little hard man."

"I don't get it." Ellie's eyebrows knit together.

I'm getting the snip. Three kids are enough.

Well, that day was interesting. The kids are finally washed, fed, and put to bed. Tilly held me hostage for the best part of an hour, just because— at least she didn't call me fat this time.

Ellie went to bed still begging for a cat, and Ethan thinks he is being smart and that I can't see his night light on. He is currently rebelling by "secretly" reading in his room.

He's quiet; that's all I care about.

Strolling into our room, I catch sight of Lottie changing.

You'd think after eight years together, plus the two extra years added on for living together beforehand, and three kids later, the spark would be gone.

Her body has changed over the years as a result of giving birth to the children. She has silver and purple stretchmarks on her breasts, thighs, and stomach from carrying the three terrors. I don't know why so many women have a problem with stretch marks. I love Lottie's. They're her tiger stripes. Proof of what she endured to bring our kids into the world.

I walk to the bed, pulling her onto the mattress with me. "They're finally asleep." I bury my head in her hair.

"Ellie is not letting up about the cat, is she?"

"Nope. I may have to promise her a pony to distract her." Dropping my lips to her neck, she wiggles closer, letting out a soft moan. "That feels nice."

"Yeah? I can make it feel better, you know."

"Can you now?" Her lips pulled to the side.

"Mmm-hmm." I drop another open-mouthed kiss to the base of her ear and give her breasts a firm squeeze.

"We will have to be quiet." She slides her hands behind her, running her fingertips up my thigh.

"I think we can manage."

Lottie turns her head, and I instantly claim her perfect pink lips. My hands slide down to her thighs, then push up her nightshirt. My fingertips skim up her thighs, and she shudders.

I'm instantly halted by the sound of Tilly crying.

"Urgh." Lottie groans, "do you want to go, or will I?"

"I don't believe this."

"That's my cue," Lottie shuffles out of the bed. I'm left watching her march out and tend to our youngest.

Have kids, they said; it will be fun, they said.

Yeah, great fun being cocked by a three-year-old!

"Daddy!" Ellie yells

I'm not here.

"Daddy!

I'm in my happy place...

"DADDY!

For fuck's sake, what? "Yes, Princess?"

"I can't find my blue shoes." Ellie looks at me as if I should know why this is a problem. She has a wardrobe full of shoes upstairs, some with the price tag still on them.

What's wrong with any of them?

I groan into my hands and say, "You have other shoes."

"I want my blue ones!"

Ironic because that is the colour of my balls thanks to having kids. I've not even had my coffee yet; it winks at me from the other side of the kitchen, taunting me. "I'm sure you have more than one pair of blue shoes, Princess."

"But I always wear my blue shoes when Nanna Josie brings us to Nanna Ellie's grave!"

Seriously? How am I supposed to argue with that? "I'll ask Mam if she has seen them. Go on inside. I'll call you when breakfast is ready."

"Thank you, Daddy!"

Yeah. I'm a fucking saint.

"No, Hotdog!" Tilly screeches from the sitting roo

"But I'm watching—"

"Ethan, turn on Mickey Mouse for Tilly!" Lottie shouts from the staircase.

Sometimes I think Michael, Lottie's psycho ex, should have been forced to look after my kids for five years rather than face a prison sentence for attempting to shish kebab me. Nothing screams rehabilitation like a grown man rocking back and forth in the foetal position because he accidentally gave a toddler the blue cup instead of the red one.

Just kidding, a knife-wielding psycho like Michael would not last five minutes with my kids, never mind five years.

They'd smell his fear and devour him.

"Coffee!" Lottie demands, stomping into the kitchen.

"Good morning to you, too."

"Don't start. I just got the head pulled off me for changing Tilly's nappy."

"I don't call her my little ginger snap for nothing."

"Demon child," Lottie pouts. Now I know where Ellie gets it from.

"Well, she is ours. It's not like she was going to be normal."

"I'm tired, Craig. I'm so tired. I just want to sleep."

"Only a few days left, baby."

"It can't come quick enough," she yawns, tears of exhaustion streaming down her cheeks. "I love them, but I need a break." Her eyes threaten to close as she walks closer to me. I pull her onto my lap, and she rests her head against my shoulder.

"You can have all the naps you want while we're away."

"Mmm, sounds divine."

"Then, when you're recharged, I'm burying myself between those legs."

"Keep talking."

"I'm talking obnoxiously loud, ball-slapping, headboard-rattling sex."

"Ooh, the nasty kind. I like it."

"I'm claiming that fine arse as soon as we get to the hotel room, and you know what I'm going to do with it?"

"What's that?"

"Mam!" Ethan roars.

For fuck's sake! I can't even fantasise about sex without being interrupted.

"To be continued?" Lottie smiles weakly, noting the look of disappointment on my face.

"If we ignore him long enough, he'll go away."

"Craig!" she giggles. I drop my lips to her neck, drawing out a moan.

"Ma— eww!"

If I don't move, he won't see me.

"Gross!"

He cannot see me. I'm invisible.

"What now?" Lottie barks.

"I'm hungry," Ethan grumbles, rubbing his arm and shuffling on his feet impatiently.

And I'm horny, pissed off!

"Dad's making breakfast in a minute. Go inside and wait for it to be cooked," she says, getting to her feet with a grumble.

"He's the first one I'm selling!" I growl, getting to my feet.

LOTTIE

"He's that good then?" Tiffy snorts.

"To say he's snapping is a hideous understatement."

"Jay's the same. James hasn't been sleeping great, so every time we go to try anything, it's like the child has an alarm in his head that goes off and he screams the house down."

"That good?"

"Jay cracked one out beside me the other night because I was too tired to participate." Tiffy flips her ebony hair behind her shoulder like she hadn't just put an image in my head that I'd rather not have there.

"Ok. We aren't that bad, yet."

"We all need time away from the kids for our sanity."

"I can't wait; the peace I'll have."

Her brow raises until it touches her dark hairline. "You remember who we're going with? Jay and Craig are like two big kids."

More like two toddlers on a sugar buzz. "Yeah, but I can deal with that. Come on, you can't say you're not looking forward to having some." I glance at Tilly and James playing on the floor. "Cuddle time."

"Oh, I can't wait for some cuddle time," Tiffy says as she sips from her Costa cup. "A nice long, hard cuddle." Smacking her lips together, Tiffy turns from me to the kids and back again. "What day are we again?"

"I don't even know what year it is anymore."

"Too distracted with the whores trying to poach your husband?"

Urgh, don't even remind me. After Michael's trial, the papers started printing our story; the fact that Craig fought off Michael at knifepoint was front page material—safe to say, his face was plastered everywhere as a hero, and of course, because Craig is a looker, the amount of attention he received afterwards was unreal.

He logged onto Instagram one day and went from 200 odd followers to 25k+. His business is still riding the publicity wave. So many people want their homes done in the hopes that Craig will be the one to show up and work on them.

I was so insecure when we first started dating—it left me as soon as I had Ethan. Craig is my man, my husband. The father of my children, and yet there are still women blatantly out to poach him.

"Don't even get me started on them. They have no shame. They don't care if I'm there with the kids; they still try and come onto him!"

"Kick them in the gooch."

"Tempting. Very tempting."

Tiffy giggles, stifles a yawn, and asks, "So, the big 40. How's he taking it?"

"Grumpier than usual, but that's just because we had to stop during birthday cuddles because of the kids."

"I hate when that happens." Tiffy clicks her tongue. "Jay had me right on the brink of an insane cuddle. Of course, James woke up, decided to scream the house down like a banshee in heat, and demanded to sleep in our bed for the night. I was an antichrist for a good three days after."

"Well, I did spend a small fortune online to make it up to him. Lingerie, toys, and massage oils. I'm going all out."

"Wow, go you! I just bought some crotchless pants and some aerosol cream. That's me, good to go.

"I never thought of getting cream!" Mental note: add that to the shopping cart tonight.

Yikes.

I thought I knew cranky until I saw Craig on a comedown from sugar. It's his first day cutting out junk, and he's practically foaming at the mouth.

Jay is enjoying this a bit too much. He showed up with a box of Krispy Kreme doughnuts and waved them under my husband's nose. It's the equivalent of waving a bag of coke in front of an addict.

"Just get the hoover and suck the fat out that way."

Not helping, Jay!

Craig slams his closed fist on the desk. "Don't you have a house to haunt?"

Jay snorts, lowering himself into the chair on the opposite side of the desk. "We have to study, remember?"

Right. Hence the doughnuts. For once, Jay is actually being considerate and not an arse—a pig must have flown over the house tonight.

After the whole Michael thing, Craig came to me with the idea of private security for women like me. Women who were trying to leave an abusive situation. Women who felt unsafe felt like they were being followed, and unlike me, they lacked a six-foot-four carpenter with a track record of being hostile towards abusive arseholes.

Of course, I was all for it, and as soon as Jay got wind of it, he was all in. So, the boys took up as many night courses as they could on security, criminology, and God knows what else. It feels like they have had a major exam every week for the past seven years.

Leaving them to it, I return to the kitchen. Ellie is staying the night at Nick and Abbie's; she is finally a big cousin and is absolutely loving her little life—I think it's because she can hand the baby back when she's done. Ethan is in his room playing online with Jamie, and Tilly is finally passed out between Mickey Mouse and Elmo. I think I can finally get some work done.

My bare feet pad softly down the hallway, coming to an abrupt stop when I see him at the counter. Nick is making what I can only assume is coffee; his back is facing me. At first glance, I thought I saw a ghost. He looks more like Dad every day.

"Make yourself at home," I call as I step into the kitchen. Nick turns and offers up a tired smile. He has been doing some serious overtime lately. "Hey," he answers in a voice that is thick from exhaustion.

"Please tell me you've finished for the day," I beg. "You look like shit."

He peels away from the counter with his coffee in hand, an eyebrow raised in amusement. "Just finished. "I didn't trust the drive home."

"You did right to stop in. You can have a nap if you want before you head back." I park my arse in the nearest chair and draw a knee to my chest. I hate to ask, but I loathe seeing him like this: "Are you in some sort of trouble? Financially, I mean?"

His eyebrows shoot to his hairline. "What? No!"

"You're sure?"

He snorts, and I follow his movements as he joins me at the table. "Positive."

"Why all the overtime then?"

Nick smothers a yawn behind his hand and then says, "I know you're not waiting on it, but—"

Oh no. Hell no!

"We don't want it back," I interrupt. "Your money's no good here."

"Lottie—"

"No, Nick! If you try to hand us a cent, Craig will impale you. It was a gift. No takebacks." Nick and Abbie tried for years to get pregnant naturally. I've never been so devastated for them when it looked like it was never going to happen. Craig and I are good financially; we are by no means rich, but we are doing well enough that we were able to gift them the money needed for IVF.

Nick tries again, "It was a massive amount of—"

"CRAIG!"

"Yeah?" His gravelly voice seems to reverberate off the walls.

"Nick wants to pay us back!"

Silence.

A long pregnant pause leaves Nick and I staring at each other until his silhouette charges down the hallway. "I'm sorry. I must be hard of hearing. What was that?"

Nick sits back in his chair, glaring at me as if I have just committed the ultimate betrayal.

"He wants to pay us back," I can't help but beam like a Cheshire cat.

Craig walks to the counter, picks up one of his books, and swings it at Nick's head with all the momentum of a baseball player going for a home run. "Cop the fuck on," he snarls, leaving Nick a soggy mess—it's safe to say he's awake now. If the smack to the head didn’t do it, the hot coffee shower definitely did.

"I’m sorry, sir, but your card was declined," I cackle, watching Craig storm out of the room—I've got a funny feeling he is going to use that book against Jay by the end of the night.

CRAIG

"I'm dying. Dying. The wank bank is running low," Jay moans.

"I don't want to know."

"Blue ball syndrome is in full swing. I need to ditch the kids."

"What are you planning on doing? Going to the shop for cigarettes and never coming back?"

"Like that would work. The boys would still find me." Pulling his stash of cigarettes from under the driver's seat of his jeep, Jay holds one between his lips and lights up. "I'm remembering this shit for when they're older. I'm going to cockblock them at every turn for payback."

My head falls back against the passenger seat. I'm wrecked. I'm not sure if it's parenthood or the abrupt departure of sugar from my life, but I feel like I've gone ten rounds with Jean Claude van Damme, "taking the high road, I see."

"This weekend away can't come quick enough," Jay says, taking a long pull from his cigarette. "Charles is taking the boys Thursday night."

"Why can I see them sitting on the step with their bags packed at 6 a.m.?"

Jay chuckles in response. He loves his boys; we all know that. Like the rest of us, he's just exhausted, sex-deprived, and grizzly as hell.

"Josie's taking the kids?" He blows out a white cloud of smoke, cracking open the window to get rid of the evidence.

"Nah, Kim's got them this time. She'll be there early, as usual, and most likely fill them up on sugar and let them away with murder before sending them back."

My phone pings and I pull it from my pocket and see Lottie's name pop up.

LOTTIE

Sorry about this morning, here's something to keep you going for a while ;) xxx

Ah, yes, this morning.

This morning, when I thought we were getting lucky. We woke up before the kids and tried to squeeze in a quickie. The next thing I know, Tilly-thunder-foot comes storming down the hallway. I had just enough time to roll off Lottie before the little demon jumped on the bed and decided to use my stomach as a bouncy castle, all the while demanding I get up and feed her.

Lottie has attached a mirror selfie of her in some barely-there lace underwear.

Hot damn.

I bite back a groan, palming the front of my pants in hopes of readjusting myself, and I realise that *he* is not going away any time soon. Stuffing my phone into my pocket, I jump from the car and march for the office.

"Going somewhere?" Jay calls.

Yeah, going to have a vicious wank. "I need to take a piss."

"Ah. I'm going to get something to eat; do you want anything brought back?"

"Yeah, whatever you're getting is fine."

I come home from work to Tilly running headfirst at my balls. It is safe to say she does not want any more siblings, and after that hit, I don't think I can provide any.

Lottie comes downstairs wearing an oversized T-shirt and a pair of my boxers. I can't help but admire that fine arse going about the house.

Don't get me wrong, it's not a total dry spell; we do have sex —quickly and quietly in the little windows we have.

I don't want quick and quiet. I want to hear her moan. I want to hear her cry out. I want to strap a saddle on her back and ride her into battle. At the rate I'm going, the only way I'm getting laid is if I crawl up a chicken's arse and wait.

"You're home early." Lottie tosses her strawberry-blonde hair over her shoulder. Leaning on the counter, she scowls at her laptop.

"Not much to do today—for me anyway. Jay is flat out." Walking up to her, I snake my arms around her waist and kiss her cheek.

"Eww," Ethan grimaces from the doorway.

How much trouble would I get into for throat-punching my eight-year-old? "Go out and play."

"It's boring outside," he protests.

"Stay, and you'll have to watch me kiss Mam again."

Ethan cringes but does not budge.

"On the lips."

He's gone.

Hallelujah.

"I didn't say which lips," I smirk, nuzzling her neck.

"Not the time to tease me, Batman," Lottie tenses. "Tilly won't eat for me; we've had another screaming match."

I walk to the kettle and flip it on. "Who won?"

"Considering I was the one crying first, I believe she won this round." She offers me a tight smile. The kettle whistles behind me as I take in the sight of her. Beautiful. Exhausted.

"Ouch." Spinning her by the hips, our lips fuse, and I can feel her relax. "I'll sort her out." I brush her hair and a stray tear away from her face. Turning to the kettle, I prepare her coffee. My girl deserves more than a coffee break, but sadly, this is all I can provide her with right now.

"Thank you."

"We're missing one." I notice one of our little hellions has yet to show her face.

"She's out on the climbing frame," Lottie sighs, lowering herself into the chair and clutching her coffee like it's the holy grail.

I sigh, trying to psych myself up for a possible screaming match with our youngest. "Ah right—Tilly!"

No reply.

"Tilly?"

Not even a cricket chirp.

"Matilda?"

Christ, when she goes quiet like this, I worry. She's probably got a match and is about to burn the house down. I better go investigate.

"Boo!" She jumps out of her toy box like some deranged Jack-in-the-Box. Of course, I play along or risk getting hit in the nuts again. "You scared me!"

She giggles like an evil mastermind.

"Come on, Mammy said you didn't eat your dinner."

"No."

"Tilly, you have to eat."

"No."

"Tilly—Oh, look, it's a hotdog!" She turns to hear the Mickey Mouse Clubhouse intro music, and I shove a spoonful of food into her mouth. She is by no means impressed, but the mouse is on, and only one of us can get her full attention.

I shovel another spoonful in, and she stops protesting, deciding that the food is probably not laced with arsenic after all. She must decide she quite likes it because she opens willingly for the next round.

Three-year-olds. They could take over the world if they weren't so easily distracted.

I leave the minion to watch Mickey Mouse look for his gooey fish and strut back into the kitchen like I'm in the next Bond movie.

"Any luck?"

"She ate the majority of it." I tilt Tilly's bowl to show most of the contents are gone.

"My hero," Lottie says as she tosses her arms around my neck, pulling me down for a fiery kiss.

The wrong thing to do to me right now.

I toss the bowl on the table and then pull her flush against me. My hands slip down, gripping her arse. She lets out a low, approving moan. Picking her up, her legs wrap around me and I move for the counter, sucking on the curve of her neck.

"Tilly's in the next room," Lottie pouts.

"Come on." I pull away, grab her hand and head for the stairs. Sneaking a peek in the sitting room, Tilly is happily bouncing on her trampoline around watching her shows. She'll be fine for ten minutes.

LOTTIE

Craig's hands are everywhere. On my legs, sides, and breasts. He's gone feral. I love it when he's like this—so raw, hungry, and so damn sexy.

I palm the bulge in his pants, and he growls, biting down on the whorl of my ear. Craig kisses my shoulder, tugging at the material, trying to reveal some bare skin.

Reaching into his pants, I run my hand up and down the length of him. As I close my fingers around his cock, my mouth waters. I'm aching for him. I want to taste him.

Craig growls, his eyes darkening with desire, I hold his gaze while lowering myself to my knees. He braces his hand on the door, his eyes never leaving mine.

"DADDY!"

No. No. No.

Craig's eyes widen, and he bites back a curse.

"DADDY!" Tilly yells again; I can hear her stomping around downstairs in her search for Craig.

"I'll be down now!" He growls, biting on his lower lip, eyes laced with disappointment.

"Go on, Batman!" I sigh, rising to my full height.

Craig grumbles, adjusting himself and muttering under his breath about eBay, chloroform, and a rubber mallet.

LOTTIE

"Did you brush your teeth?" I ask the room. Ethan barely sticks his head over his book long enough to tell me he did.

"Yes, Mammy," Ellie says as she sulkily dresses her LOL doll. She's still pissed about the cat thing.

"No," Tilly says, bouncing on her trampoline like a little kangaroo.

"Where is your toothbrush?"

"No."

"Tilly!"

"No!"

I'm going to kill this child.

"Do you want to go to Nana Josie's?"

"Yaaaay!" She looks like I offered her the keys to Willy Wonka's chocolate factory.

"Then do your teeth."

Her face drops. "No."

Why? Why must this be so difficult?

Two out of three ain't bad? Yeah, right, Meatloaf forgot to mention that the third is Satan's minion.

People say it's the secondborn who doesn't give a damn

about anything. Compared to Ethan, they might be onto something. Tilly, on the other hand, out of my three womb gremlins, is by far the most difficult.

I don't live with a toddler. I live with a three-foot-tall dictator.

"Matilda!" Craig's voice cracks like a whip. "Do as your mother says."

"No," her little happy head continues to bounce about to Mickey Mouse.

"She's like a broken record." Scouring the room on my hands and knees, I eventually find her toothbrush under the couch. Rinsing it down, I find the minion and present it to her. "No!"

"Tilly, you either brush your teeth like a big girl or I'll brush them for you!"

"N—"

I've had enough.

Pulling her onto my lap, I wrestle with her. She puts up a fight, but eventually I get the toothbrush in, and she starts to laugh. "There, all clean."

Craig is leaning on the doorjamb with a smirk on his face. "Coffee?"

"No," Tilly says. She sticks her nose in the air and returns to her trampoline.

"I was asking mammy," Craig sighs, brushing a hand through his dishevelled hair.

Tilly is not impressed; how dare he pay even the slightest bit of attention to me when she's around? "No. Me!"

Craig laughs and says, "You're not getting coffee."

"Why?"

"Because you're already bouncing off the walls as it is."

"No."

Craig pinches the bridge of his nose, and his head tilts down as if to stop a nosebleed. "Go watch Hotdog."

"No," Tilly's eyes spark, the same grey eyes as Craig's. The same mischievous glint shines when she's up to something.

"Tilly," Craig rolls his eyes, spotting our two other gremlins behaving for once.

"No. I want coffee."

"Tough."

She bats her lashes and pouts. He's a goner. Craig can never say no to his girls. Bless him; he tries, but he's whipped.

"Please, Daddy, please."

"No, Tilly."

"I'm your girl!"

Oh, she's good. She's very good.

"You are my girl, but you're not getting coffee."

"But I want some."

"No, Tilly," his arms cross over his broad chest. Hmm, he's holding out this time.

Tilly starts with the crocodile tears.

"Fine. Fine! I'll make you some coffee!"

"Yay," the baby kangaroo says, returning to her happy dance.

I spoke too soon.

Following Craig into the kitchen, I see him pulling out the hot chocolate and filling a cup for Tilly.

"Wow, you almost made it that time," I snort, watching him fumble with the sachet.

He spins so quickly that I take a step back, "Don't start."

Ethan is like a bloodhound; as soon as the hot chocolate is poured, he appears in the kitchen like some crack-addicted phantom.

"Thanks, dad!" He's gone with Tilly's cup, leaving Craig standing with the milk in mid-air, watching a miniature Captain America flee the room to get his chocolate fix.

"Where did you get that?" Ellie's voice echoes from down the hall.

"Looks like you're making two more cups." I strangle a

laugh, and Craig responds with some colourful curses under his breath.

While the kids are distracted, I use the opportunity to go to the bathroom in peace. My rear barely hits the porcelain when I spot something that makes my blood run cold.

A shadow passes under the door, and I watch in horror as a finger slowly crawls under the crack, then another. Soon Tilly's hand is under the door, feeling for me. "Mammy?"

They will find you. It doesn't matter how quiet you think you are or how distracted they might appear. They will always know when you are left alone for two seconds, and they will hunt you down.

"Be out in a second."

The handle starts to rattle; thank God I locked it.

"Mammy?"

"Two minutes, Tilly."

"MAMMY!!"

"Mammy's going wee-wee!"

"MAMMY!" The hand slides back under the door.

"Tilly, look... coffee!" Craig shouts from the floor below.

Tilly responds with, "I don't like coffee!"

I can hear Craig grumbling. The hand disappears, and the thunderous shaking of the bathroom door stops.

She's sniffed out her next victim.

When I come downstairs, Craig is sitting in the armchair in the sitting room, with Ellie on the floor at his feet. He braids her hair with bobby pins sticking out of his mouth. He secures the braid into a golden halo atop her head.

It took him a while to learn how to work the girls' hair, but he got it in the end. He did a good job; Ellie's hair looks perfect.

Tilly's hair has been tied into pigtails with a bow on either end. Like butter wouldn't melt.

"Daddy?"

"Yes, Ellie belly?"

"Sarah is going to her nanny and grandad's this weekend." Ellie's eyes scan the family pictures on the wall.

"Ok?"

"How come I don't have a grandad?"

Craig's throat bobs. An innocent question, but how do you explain this to a six-year-old?

I try to save Craig from the explanation. "My daddy is in heaven, baby. That's why."

"Oh. And is your daddy in heaven with Nana Ellie?" She turns to Craig, fixing him with her best doe-eyed gaze.

"He will be if I ever get my hands on him," Craig mutters, getting to his full height.

Ellie cocks her head like a confused puppy. Craig inhales deeply, looking at each of the kids as he thinks of how to approach this subject.

He always swore that he would never lie to them; perhaps it would have been easier to break that rule just this once.

"My daddy," Craig says, clearing his throat. "He was not a very good daddy. That's why Nanna Josie raised me," he says as he crouches beside Ellie, placing a hand on her shoulder.

"He a naughty boy?" Tilly asks, running over with her Mickey Mouse plush toy clutched to her chest.

Craig nods with a weak smile and says, "Very naughty."

"Oh! I hate naughty boys!" Tilly stomps on the floor. "He's a bold daddy!"

"He was," Craig smirks, shifting to rise to his feet once again.

"I kick him!" Tilly declares, causing Craig to laugh.

He hunkers down to her height and boops her on the nose. "That's why you're my girl," he winks.

Tilly squeezes him tightly and says, "And you're my daddy."

She grins, scaling him like a little spider monkey. "You need sweets."

"Is that so?"

"Sweets!" Tilly demands.

And just like that, our sweet little cherub is gone, and the dictator is back.

CRAIG

We wrestle to get the kids dressed, and by kids, I mean Tilly.

Their bags are packed, the kids are fed and watered, and Lottie is in the shower. "Nanna!" Ethan cries, jumping from the couch and running to the hallway.

What? Already?

I glance at the clock; it's just gone ten. She's not supposed to be here for at least another hour. Josie comes bounding up the garden, arms out wide in greeting, saying, "Hello, darlings."

"Nanna!" Ellie squeals, pushing Ethan out of her way to be the first to receive a Josie hug.

"Dozie!" Tilly shrieks from the sitting room. It's not long before she charges into the garden.

I can't help but beam at her and say, "Josie, my auld flower, what are you doing here so early?"

"Oh, you know, we were up, and since I only have the kids until five, I figured why not get a head start?" Her enormous handbag hangs from her shoulder; she means business. The kids are not going to want to go to Kim's if Josie spoils them.

"Ready to go?" George calls over Tilly's cheering as he steps out of the car to help strap the kids in.

The kids yell in unison, "They are beyond ready to go, and I'm ready to be rid of them."

"Let's go!" Tilly is the first one in the car. I have to hand it to George; for a pensioner, he can move when he wants to. I turn into the house for the bags and carry them to the car.

"Is that everything?" Josie asks after closing the door on the three demons, sealing them in. There's no turning back now.

I close the booth and grin, "Yep. Everything to keep Kim sane for three days."

Tilly bangs on the glass and says, "Bye." In other words, "piss off, dad."

"You guys be good for Nanna Josie and Nanna Kim, ok?"

Ethan grins, "We will!"

Ellie gives me an innocent smirk, "Yes!"

Tilly rolls her eyes and bangs on the glass. "Go away!"

Well, that's me told.

I turn to Josie, dropping my voice, and say, "Watch out for the little one; she bites."

Josie lets out a musical laugh and climbs into the car. "Enjoy yourselves!"

"Thanks, Josie. Call us if there are any problems, yeah?" I say that, and I'm already tempted to switch my phone off for the weekend.

"Will do, love, bye!"

"Bye, Dad!" Ethan calls, waving me off before the car has even started.

"Bring me back presents," Ellie demands as the engine starts up.

"Let's go!" Tilly insists. The car pulls off, and I walk back into the house, switch off the TV, and am greeted by the sweet sound of silence.

Then I remember the hot little number up in the shower.

There is no one here. No one to interrupt us. No kids are

hammering the door down or screaming because they cannot find the cookie they ate earlier today.

Happy fucking birthday to me!!!

I'm up the stairs in a heartbeat. Clothes get discarded somewhere between the downstairs hallway and the bathroom. Note to self: Get Josie a big gift basket when I come back.

Opening the bathroom door, Lottie is wet, naked, and soapy under the steamy shower. Her lashes flick in my direction and she bites her lip once she realises what's about to happen.

"The kids?" she queries.

I smirk, "gone. Josie came early for them." Stepping into the shower, I pull her body against me. "We have the house to ourselves."

Our lips meet with startling urgency. I catch her in a hungry, possessive kiss. Lottie sucks in my bottom lip, and I slam her up against the tiled wall. "What are you planning on doing to me, Barnes?"

"You know what they say: dildos are great, and vibrators are fun, but nothing can beat the almighty tongue." My frantic fingers pluck and pinch her nipples, then I draw her breast into my mouth. I suck hard enough to leave a mark. Lottie moans, her hands clawing at my hair. I sink to my knees and pull her leg over my shoulder.

She whimpers as my tongue coasts across her sensitive little bud, and I skim a finger along her entrance. My hands travel to her breasts, fondling them as my lips meet her sweet pussy.

Lottie lets out a sound that is like music to my ears. We don't have to be quiet. The kids are gone. I want more than her gasps. I want her to scream.

I mapped out the pleasure points of her body a long time ago. I know where to hit and when. By stroking her clit with my tongue, I coax the bud from beneath the hood. "Craig."

"That's right, baby, call my name." Just hearing her is turning my blood to molten ore. I find the spot where she needs me most and tease her towards orgasm.

"Fuck, Craig!" Her legs begin to tremble. I keep Lottie pressed against the wall as she pulses against my tongue.

Standing, I toss her over my shoulder, turn off the water, and proceed to our room while smacking her delicious derriere.

I want to draw this out. I want to keep her on the brink for hours and have her beg me to let her come. It will have to wait until the hotel. Right now, I'm craving that nasty, obnoxiously loud, ball-slapping sex I've been dreaming about for months.

After I toss Lottie onto the bed, she gets on all fours, and I bury my face in that arse. She gasps, her legs still trembling uncontrollably, as my tongue flicks over her opening. I press the finger inside her, and her hips buck. "Craig."

I smack her hard on the rear, delighting in the sight. Then crawl over to the nightstand and pull out the lube. It's been a while since we did this; time to prep is not something we are usually blessed with. I'm not passing up the opportunity to take her now.

I slip a finger in her, then another, while I make myself slick for her. I just made my girl moan; now I'm going to make her scream.

LOTTIE

I feel Craig move behind me, positioning himself. He sinks his cock into me, and my mouth waters. My eyes roll into the back of my head as he presses in, inch by delicious inch.

"God, I missed this," he groans. His hands bite into my hips as he starts to move.

He thrusts forward, and I brace myself on the pillows in front of me. His left hand snakes around, rubbing my clit as he thrusts deep inside me.

Craig pulls me back against him, both on our knees; he's going hard, so hard that I need to reach for the headboard to steady myself. "Craig!"

"Yes, baby, let me hear you."

Oh God, I've lost control of my body. My legs are shaking. I can't stop them. I feel like they'll give out at any minute.

I grip his arm as he drives into me. I can't think of anything but his touch, his kiss, and his impossibly large cock pounding into me.

Feeling a vibration at my thigh, I glance down and notice Craig has my bullet in his hand and is slipping it between my legs.

"Craig, I can't take it. I can't—fuck!"

Pulling my head around to meet his, Craig's lips claim mine in a hot, messy kiss.

He pulls away grinning, his lips falling to my neck. "You know I love hearing you moan, baby." His teeth graze my neck, his hot breath grazing my ear as he says, "I want to hear you come for me, Lottie."

Raking my nails across the back of his neck, his arms, his thighs—anywhere I can grip him—I'm hit by a warm, blinding wave of ecstasy. "Fuck, Craig!"

He leans back, angling his hips, and growls, "Yes, baby. Yes!"

I'm still riding out the high of my orgasm, Craig thrusts faster and deeper. His grip tightens, his breathing raspy: "You're so fucking sexy when you come, Lottie." He cries out, sounding like a man possessed, his grip on me never wavers.

Collapsing on the bed in two boneless heaps, the only noise

other than our staggered breathing is the light buzzing from my bullet.

Craig laughs, reaches down and turns it off. He rubs his eyes to clear his vision. "Now, that was sex."

I laugh, curling into him. We both needed that.

That's the great thing about our marriage—it doesn't matter if it's slow and tender or fast and filthy, the passion is always there. It's just much better when we can make love without holding back.

I glance at the clock and have to do a double-take. "Holy crap, is that the time?"

We've been going far longer than expected. Jay and Tiffy will be here in half an hour.

Craig moans in protest. "Do we have to move? The kids are gone; let's just stay here." He gives me a boyish grin and rolls onto his side, watching me scramble from the bed to clean up and get dressed. "You're beautiful, baby, stunning."

"You're not so bad yourself, Batman." Pulling on a maxi dress, I crawl up the bed and kiss him passionately, drawing out a low moan. "Get dressed."

"Do I have to?"

"I'll give you a free pass for the hotel if you get dressed," I smirk, catching his reflection in the mirror as I climb from the mattress.

He cocks an eyebrow. "Anything I want?"

"Anything you want, Batman."

He's up.

He jumps into a pair of jeans, pulls on a t-shirt and says, "Let's get that juicy ghetto booty into the car and to the hotel. I have some exceptionally lurid plans for that arse."

CRAIG

What did I ever do to deserve this?

Usually, the girls' hit up 80s stuff on these road trips. Today they've decided on Eminem all the way.

Tiffy may very well be mixed-race but right now she sounds like the whitest, white girl to ever try and rap. Meanwhile, I keep forgetting how well Lottie raps Eminem songs. It's all down to where you grow up, I suppose. Lottie is from a working-class background while Mrs Tiffany Singh, as she is known in the legal world, is from a more privileged background.

When Lottie starts rapping about putting anthrax on a Tampax, I can legitimately see her following through with that —or at least, laughing at it happening to someone she hates. When Tiffy does it... well—kind of hard to take any threat seriously from someone brought up in Foxrock.

Other than the howlers in the car, this weekend is already off to a great start. I had hot, dirty sex with Lottie before we got picked up, and to top it off, Jay brought snacks. This is my happy place.

Lottie is sucking the ever-loving shit out of a lolly. I know she knows I'm watching her. She's doing it to get a rise out of me, and it's working!

"Keep doing that and pretty soon you'll have something else to suck on."

Jay chokes on his can of coke.

Tiffy shoots around, her eyebrows lost behind her dark fringe, but her eyes are wide enough to tell me she's affronted, "Craig!"

"Don't even start," I point a finger directly in her line of sight. "I saw that couple's toy set in the boot. Didn't think you'd be one for butt plugs."

Jay is forced to pull into the hard shoulder and turn on the hazards. He's laughing so hard that he can't see straight.

Lottie bites back a laugh, "Craig, behave."

I snort in response and stare out the window, feeling Lottie placing her hand on my knee while Jay composes himself and pulls back onto the motorway.

Lottie's hand begins running up and down my leg in slow strokes.

Tiffy glares in the side view mirror at me and asks, "What's wrong? No sex this morning?"

"Not enough."

Lottie's hand slams down on my leg, "hey!"

"What?" I turn to meet her scowl. "It wasn't. I haven't had my fill of you yet, baby. I doubt I ever will."

Lottie's gaze softens just as I hear Tiffy scoff, "Thanks for that image."

"Ah, shag off and worry about your gimp over there."

"Hey!" Jay glares at me in the rear-view mirror.

"That butt plug is probably for him anyway."

"Keep it up and I'll shove it up your hole!" Jay warns.

I turn to catch him glaring at me, I offer up a wicked smirk, "Got lube?"

Tiffy clicks her tongue, "bollocks, I knew I was forgetting something."

"Too bad," I snort, grip Lottie's hand and squeeze before placing it back on my thigh. How dare she move it without consulting me first.

"It's fine," Jay indicates to take the upcoming exit. "I'll just spit on it."

Lottie snorts, scraping her nails along my leg, "That's what she said."

"How old are you?" Tiffy demands.

"I'm the youngest in this car so suck my dick," Lottie retorts.

Jay raises an eyebrow, "you got one now?"

"It's called pegging," Tiffy declares.

My head snaps in Jay's direction. "Ha! I knew that plug was for him!"

My beautiful, sexy wife keeps rubbing up against me and all I want to do is to throw her down and mount the shit out of her.

This is the one weekend a year that we get to act like horny teenagers in a no holds barred fuckathon as we did eight years ago when we first got together.

The best weekend of my life.

I craved her. I wanted Lottie from the moment I clapped my eyes on her. I waited four years for her and then Nick's wedding happened.

A one-night stand turned into a weekend of hot, passionate sex and by the time we checked out, I was a full-blown addict. I needed another hit ASAP. I needed more of her, and I didn't give a damn if that ruined my friendship with Nick. Lottie was more important to me; she always has been.

The now thirty-six-year-old beauty is now thick as fuck after having our children, and I love every inch of that goddess.

She complains about needing to diet, to lose weight—to lose that arse? Those tits? Is she insane? Hell no!

I don't want any stick-thin ruler as a wife. I've dated girls like that in the past. Aesthetically pleasing? Yes, but they haven't got a tit to their name and their arse is practically non-existent. I was always left looking like I fought off a horny chimp. I was covered in bruises from grinding on bone. Those girls are best suited for those who are into vanilla sex, as for me, no. No chance. It just couldn't work. You can keep Kendal Jenner; I always did prefer Ashley Graham.

We turn down a familiar country road, and I know we are nearly there. I deliberately look at Lottie's tits bouncing as we go over uneven road. I'm tempted to bury my head in her cleavage, but she'll most likely slap me for it.

Maybe I can squeeze them?

"Hey," she bats my hand away.

"Hey yourself, they're my tits."

"Since when?" she demands.

"Since that ring went on your finger."

She gives me a mischievous grin, "In that case," her hand lands on my crotch and squeezes.

I jump on instinct, "touché."

Jay looks in the rear-view mirror and barks, "Don't make me put you on a time-out."

"Shut up and drive the car."

"I'll turn this car around!"

I meet his amber gaze, "You really want to miss out on more sex?"

He's quiet for a second, turns his attention back to the road and mumbles, "Shut up."

When we arrive, Jay and I check us all in while the girls wait at the bar.

"All set?" Tiffy asks when she spots our approach.

Jay stuffs the key card in his pocket and says, "All set. Dinner is at seven tonight."

Lottie downs the remainder of her cocktail and asks, "What's the plan?"

Jay reaches out, pulling his wife against him, "Don't even come looking for us for at least an hour."

Lottie groans and locks pleading eyes on me, "Please tell me we are not in neighbouring rooms again!"

"No!" I stuff my wallet in my pocket. "Not after last year."

I'm still haunted by the things we heard through the walls.

Jason grabs their bags and turns for Tiffy, "You, upstairs, now."

Tiffy slaps her hands on her hips, "Or what? You gonna spank me?"

Christ, not in the lobby.

"Are you talking back to me, brat?" Jay takes a step closer to Tiffy who averts her gaze and mumbles, "No, sir."

"You two can piss off if you think that I'm witnessing this shite. Get in the elevator and bollocks off."

Thankfully, they walk away, and I take my place at the bar next to Lottie.

I'm, by no means, into vanilla sex. I'll order it on occasion but at the same time, the BDSM world is not something I'm particularly drawn to either. I'm a happy medium.

Jason, on the other hand, is a proud dom. I was not at all surprised to find out that Tiffy is a brat. I'm sure Lottie would wear the crown when it comes to brats in that world, but she's my brat.

"Excuse me?" I turn to the melodic voice. "Are you Craig Barnes?"

I glance at Lottie whose face is already sour. She hates this, and I don't blame her. If the tables were turned, I'd probably be snapping necks by now.

"Yes, I am."

Keep it short. Boring. Maybe then she'll piss off.

"Oh my god, I knew it," the randomer flips her orangey-blonde hair over her shoulder. "I'm such a big fan."

Fan? I'm not a fucking actor.

"Err," *awkward*. "Thanks?"

"What are you doing here?" I can smell her fake tan developing as he inches closer.

Look to your left, she's two minutes away from beating you upside the head. Probably knock that bird's nest right off.

I reach out for Lottie, hauling her against me, "I'm here with my wife."

The girl looks at me and then at Lottie, "Hi!"

"Hi," I'm pretty sure she's baring her teeth right now.

"You're so lucky to have a guy like him!"

"Don't I know it," Lottie's hand slides up my chest, gripping my shirt, she hauls me down, claiming my mouth.

I don't know why she feels the need to put on a show for these people—I'm not complaining. If I'm honest, it's kind of a turn-on.

Lottie's tongue delves into my mouth, and I grin. If it's a show you want to put on, baby, then it's a show we will give them.

My hands find that delectable derriere and I pull her closer, grazing her bottom lip with my teeth and drawing out a soft moan.

When I pull away, the girl has gone, and I'm left panting.

In truth, these women show me so much attention because they heard about my fight with Michael and assume I'm some sort of hero. I'm nothing of the sort. A hero will step up and defend anyone at any cost. If that had been anyone bar Lottie I was dating and some knife-wielding psycho ex showed up, I would have bailed. Bollocks to that. I'm not risking being shanked for a shag.

But it wasn't a random girl. It was Lottie. My Lottie. If anyone wants to get near her, they're going to have to get through me first. She's the only woman I'd risk being skewered for.

"Ready to go, Batman?"

"You bet your sweet arse I am."

As soon as we enter the room, Lottie rises onto her toes and our lips connect. She pushes her tongue in my mouth and wraps her arms around my neck as I kick the door closed.

"You little minx," I dip and lift her, feeling Lottie close her legs around my waist. "Good thing we're alone now, baby because I've been having filthy thoughts all day."

"I need to feel you inside me," her teeth tug on the whorl of my ear."

"You dirty bitch," I claim her already swollen lips. "Get on the bed." I don't give her much choice; I step for the bed and throw her onto it.

Pulling my shirt overhead, I toss it aside. Noticing Lottie's eyes raking over me approvingly, she bites her lower lip as I step out of my jeans and crawl up the bed to her.

I shimmy down her pants and toss them aside.

Lottie drags me up for a kiss that sucks the breath from my lungs. With my hands on her knees, I push her legs apart, and glance down, "crotchless panties!" My favourite. My mouth waters just looking at her, I have to taste her.

Sliding my hand between those soft, pillowy thighs, I slowly push a finger into her, and she throws her head back, moaning. "I love it when you touch me like that," she gazes at me through lowered lashes.

"You like that, baby?"

"Yeah."

"What about when I do this?" lowering myself to her

entrance, I spread her and take her into my mouth. Her hands run through my hair as I suck and flick her clit with my tongue.

Lottie moans approvingly, instinctively opening her legs wider for me and I push two fingers inside her, increasing the pressure and speed.

"Yes, Craig. Yes," I glance up to meet her gaze, her cheeks are flushed, and I grin up at her, loving the way she watches me feast on her. "Right there, just like—oh God!"

I pinch her swollen bud between my thumb and tongue, flicking relentlessly until her legs tremble and her body convulses. I hear her scream.

Her legs tighten around me, squeezing me as she pulsates against my tongue, and I lap up her juices.

LOTTIE

Craig sits back, grinning victoriously. He sucks on his fingers and then runs his tongue over his lips.

Grabbing my legs, Craig pulls me towards him, placing my legs on either side of his torso.

Pushing him backwards, he throws an arm back to catch himself. His thick, swollen member greets me as I crawl forward.

"I believe I owe you a birthday gift," smiling up at him, I wrap my fingers around his cock and begin stroking him.

Craig's gaze is darkened by desire. His mouth forms an O as I continue to pump him.

He groans lowly as I lick him from base to tip, flicking my tongue over the head just to watch him twitch.

I love having this power over my man. I love how desperate

he becomes to claim me, how his eyes spark dangerously when he's aching for release.

I want him feral.

I let my tongue dance over the head once more, then push his entire length into my mouth.

"Fuck, Lottie!" His hands are covering his face, and his head tips back as I stroke him in and out of my mouth, increasing the tempo as he moans.

His hips buck, pushing his length into the back of my throat with each thrust. I increase the pressure, licking the base with my tongue every time his hips jerk.

His fist tangles in my hair, "I'm going to come if you don't stop." He leans down, shaking my shoulder. I glance up at him, refusing to let up.

His hands are back over his face, he knows I'm going to make this happen. I'm not going to stop until I do.

"Ooh—" Craig grabs my hair, holding me steady as he starts to pump his hips. "You're going to forget your name when I'm done fucking you tonight." His thrusts are harder. He lets out an animalistic growl as he takes control. "You look so sexy with your lips wrapped around me like this."

I tighten my lips around him and hear another low rumbling growl. My eyes flit up to look at him. His chest glistens with sweat, and his scorching gaze looks directly at me as he demands, "Keep that pretty little mouth open to me when I'm fucking it."

I hum around him, a move that pushes him over the edge. I feel his hot seed spill into my mouth. I love the taste of him.

When he's done, I pull away, wiping my mouth with the back of my hand and gifting him a wicked grin.

Craig's mouth is ajar. His breathing is heavy. He sits back, pulling me on top of him, his tongue invading my mouth while his fingers pinch my nipples.

I feel him twitch beneath me and gasp. *There is no fucking way.*

CRAIG

Lottie's long fingers wrap around my cock, confirming her suspicions. She's surprised that I'm ready to go again.

I guide myself into her and she bites down on my shoulder, her nails clawing into my back.

Uncontrollable desire takes hold.

I grab her by the hips and move her over me, sliding into her a little deeper with each bounce.

Pressing her hips against mine, I push her back to the mattress, staying seated inside her as we change position.

Hooking my arms under her thighs, I drive deeper.

"Craig," she moans, "I want to feel all of you inside me. Give me all of you," her tongue licks up the column of my neck.

This is unbelievable. She is unbelievable. I feel like I'm losing my damn mind.

I give my girl exactly what she wants, and soon her walls clench around me, her pending orgasm coming in strong.

Grabbing her wrists, I pin them to the mattress, "You don't get to cum until I tell you to."

I slow down; she looks like she could slap the shit out of me for it.

"Craig," she growls, "keep going!"

"I want to hear you beg me," I pull out, almost fully, then slam back inside. I do it again three more times before she concedes, "P-please, baby, please don't stop. I need you to—oh God yes! Just like that."

I give her what she wants and more, slipping my thumb over her clit, I gladly send her into oblivion.

Lottie claws at my back, hard. I feel her coming all over my cock and that pushes my pleasure forward. I follow mere seconds after her.

Pressing my forehead to hers, I attempt to pull out, but she doesn't let me. Instead, I collapse on top of her. Still buried in her.

"Oh. My. God," she pants.

We both laugh, and my mouth finds hers under the tendrils of hair sweeping across her face.

Before I know it, we fall asleep in a naked embrace, right there in the centre of the bed.

About an hour later, I blink the sleep from my eyes to find the source of the ringing.

Crawling to the end of the bed, I find my jeans and pull out my phone, "yeah?"

Jay's voice booms over the phone, "Still alive?"

"Barely."

He chuckles lowly, then says, "Tiffy wants to go down to the pool before dinner, you up for it?"

"Yeah," I rub my eyes, glancing back at the goddess sleeping soundly on top of the sheets. "Yeah," I repeat. "Just give us about half an hour."

"Grand, see you then," he hangs up.

I crawl up the bed next to Lottie and nuzzle her awake.

"Five more minutes," she groans, grabbing onto my arm and wiggling closer.

"Wake up, gorgeous."

"I don't wanna."

"Well, I want to see that gorgeous arse in a bikini."

She peels her eyes open, casting a suspicious glance over her shoulder, "Tiffy?"

"Yep."

"When?"

"Half an hour."

She pouts.

Lottie loves the pool, but she loves her comfort more, and right now, she's not going to budge.

"Coffee?" I ask, placing a chaste kiss on her forehead.

"That's a start."

"Are you sore?"

I know I can be a bit rough at times. Hell, I've never lost control with anyone the way I do with her, but she thrives on that. Still, I have rubbed her raw on occasion, and I want to make sure my girl is ok.

She yawns and shakes her head dismissively. "Wait for me to wake up and I'll want seconds."

I grin down at her, "I am more than happy to service you whenever you want me, baby."

"I'll hold you to that."

Climbing off the bed, I switch on the kettle while Lottie forces herself up on the bed, "love you, Batman." She smiles, yawns again and then steps from the bed, draping herself around me.

"Love you too, baby."

"I'm going for a quick shower, want to join me?"

"Always!"

Lottie steps for the bathroom and I hear running water soon after.

Stepping away from the kettle just as it boils, I follow my wife into the shower.

If this is only the start of this weekend, I can't wait to see what else is in store.

CRAIG

The girls lounge in the hot tub while Jay and I swim laps in the pool. It's evident already that everyone is much more relaxed than when we set out this morning. It's amazing how some time away to just be adults can reset a person.

Tiffy is beaming, divulging God only knows what to Lottie. I thought the light bruises on my wife's legs were bad until I saw Tiffany's wrists. She wears her marks like a trophy.

Glancing at the hot tub, I notice two guys zoning in on our girls. I'm just guessing, but they look to be in their early thirties. Lottie, though four years my junior, looks younger again. Most people estimate her to be in her late twenties.

"Jay," I nod in their direction. Jason has the same idea as me, *run them.* He is out of the pool and in the hot tub before you can say man-whore. I follow behind, my gaze fixed on the guy who is looking at my wife like a snack.

Pushing my way past him, I sit down and pull Lottie onto my lap. I couldn't care less about their grumbling.

The guys sit across from us, not taking the hint to retreat and the taller of the pair continues eye-fucking Lottie. I'm tempted to drown the bastard.

Following his gaze, I realise her nipples are threatening to poke a hole through her bikini top.

"Craig!" she blushes, trying to push my hand away. *Not a hope in hell, love. If I've to resort to wrapping my mouth around them right now, I'll do it.*

"Get in the pool," I demand, she looks affronted as she asks, "what?"

"The deep end," I subtly pinch her nipple between my fingers and her eyes widen in understanding. Lottie stands and walks out of the hot tub; I'm left staring at the balls of her arse in the barely there bottoms she has on.

Fucking hell, I can't tell if she's trying to kill me or have me arrested.

I'm up, following her and blocking her from prying eyes.

I jump in the pool after her, water sloshes around us on all sides. She grabs the bar, her legs floating upward as I take my place between them. Reaching out to grip the wall to stop me from going under, I have her trapped.

She bites her lower lip and mumbles, "I didn't know."

"I know."

She looks flustered.

I pull myself closer to her, "that's what you have me for."

"To protect my modesty?" she blushes.

"The only one allowed to start eye-fucking you, doll, is me," I lean in, kissing her. Lottie lets out a soft moan the instant our tongues meet.

I'm fully aware that we are being watched and I really don't care.

I pull away and catch Lottie glancing over my shoulder at the clock. "I should go back to the room. It will take me a while to shower and get ready for dinner."

"Want me to come with you?"

"No, stay with Jason. You'll be bored in the room if you come back now."

"Fine, I'll walk you through," I'm still trying to decide what side of her I should cover when she gets out. I decide to walk ahead and cover her front until we reach the hot tub, and then I nudge her ahead and cover that juicy rear.

Tiffy spots Lottie leaving and follows, Jay has the same idea as me, keeping her covered until she's got her robe on.

"So," I start, watching the girls leave the pool area. "A bit rough then?"

He chuckles in response, "the wrists you mean? Yeah, I guess I might have been," he rubs at his neck and then turns, his amber gaze meeting mine. "You should try it sometime."

"I'm good thanks."

Jason pauses, takes in our surroundings, and then demands, "what have you got against it?"

"I'm not into pain or causing it... unless someone is trying to poach my wife, then I'll happily start shattering kneecaps."

Jay gifts me a crooked grin, "agreed."

"Plus," I continue, "the crying—Nah, I'd rather ruin her lipstick, not her mascara. If I ever saw her crying, I'd turn into a limp noodle in a heartbeat."

Jason snorts, "Yeah, so that's SM gone for you, but what about the rest?"

"Huh?"

"Come on, Craig. You can't think the entire BDSM community is just about causing pain."

"Eh," I rub at my neck, suddenly uncomfortable.

"Christ," Jay looks like he could punch me for that. "BDSM," he says a bit too loudly, we're now receiving some quizzical looks. "BD, bondage and discipline," he raises one meaty finger, quickly followed by another as he starts listing off the meanings. "DS, domination and submission," the last finger practically smacks me in the jaw. "SM, sadism, and masochism. I've got a feeling you've been doing one of the other two without realising it."

"Hmm," I think about what he's said. He's right. I have. "Good point."

"I'm Tiffy's Dom in the bedroom, we both know I'm her bitch when it comes to everything else. With her career, and the kids she needs to be badass. Behind closed doors, she likes to relinquish that dominance and leave things to me."

I say the only thing that comes to mind, "I'll think about it."

Retreating to the room a short time later, I find Lottie wearing one of my shirts and nothing else while she does her makeup.

I'm tempted to grab her and ram her up against the table but I've come to learn that when she does her eyeliner and I ruin it, she'll smash my head into the wall.

I'm only allowed to ruin her makeup at the end of the night.

"You look," I stop to take in every delectable curve. "Delicious." Gripping her hips, I spin her to me. She looks incredible, then again, she always does. When she does her makeup like this, she still looks like my Lottie just with enhanced features. I love that.

Those big green eyes sparkle back at me. I tilt her chin up and brush my lips against hers, "you taste like the sweetest of sins."

"I'm glad you approve," she smiles up at me, then with the tip of her makeup brush, points towards the bathroom. "Go on, we need to leave within the hour."

"I'm going, I'm going."

We set off on time despite Lottie's insistence that I'd make us late. Unfortunately, as soon as we park our arses at the table, several eyes are on us—or should I say, on me. I spot the flash of a phone or two and groan into the menu.

"For fuck's sake, who do they think you are? George Clooney?" Jay teases, trying to keep the mood light but it's a hindrance. I'm tempted to say fuck it and just order to our room when a familiar face approaches our table, arms open wide and a massive smile on his otherwise stoic face. "Craig Barnes, what the hell are you doing here?" Shit. AJ. This could get awkward. AJ is a blast from the past—unlike Jay and I, he escaped having a criminal record at a young age. He's one of those friends that you call if you need to do something illegal but would never invite him around otherwise. It doesn't help that Tiffy has crossed paths with him on several occasions, though she never was able to get charges to stick.

Evidence has a way of mysteriously disappearing where AJ is involved.

"About to jump out the fucking window, you?"

AJ turns and spots several people speaking in hushed tones. "Ah," he clicks his tongue and snaps a tattooed finger at the waiter, beckoning them over.

"What can I do for you, Mr Quinn?"

"You can escort my friends here to a private room, they would like to enjoy their meal in peace," he brushes a hand over his light-brown hair, fixing it in place as he turns back to us, gifting me a devilish smirk.

"You don't have to—"

"Nonsense, what are friends for?"

There's that word again, *friends.* The problem with AJ is he doesn't have friends, he has puppets. I suppose Jason and I would be the closest thing to friends he would have, we did teach him how to fight back in our MMA days. We occasionally see him around. The scrawny kid we took under our wing is now a multi-millionaire, a dangerous one at that.

"Thank you," Lottie offers a warm, somewhat forced smile,

while Tiffy scowls at the man standing before us in his six-thousand-euro suit. Tiffany has recently caught a case or two with AJ's known associates, safe to say that she knows what kind of man he is, but she keeps her mouth shut. No point pissing off a mob boss on his own soil.

"You," AJ turns his attention to Lottie, his grey eyes sparkling as he takes her in. "Must be Charlotte," he reaches for her hand and brings it to his mouth, placing a chaste kiss on her knuckles. "A pleasure to finally meet you."

After a long moment, the waiter comes back and guides us into a small function room. AJ apologises that he cannot stay and chat, before he leaves, he insists that we eat and drink for free and I'm not about to argue with him. Neither is Jason for that matter, in fact, he's already ordered three bottles of 1988 Domaine Leroy Vosne-Romanee Les Genaivrieres costing over three-thousand-euro a bottle.

I'm sure AJ won't mind... right?

LOTTIE

Waking around eight the next morning, Craig is lightly snoring beside me. His breath stirring my hair, I can't help but smile and shimmy closer, tucking my head under his chin.

This is nice, waking up on my own accord and not being trampled on by hungry kids.

My eyes drift to Craig's hands, his knuckles are red and insidious from knocking some pervert on his back last night. I left the function room to use the bathroom, and, on my way there some scumbag grabbed my arse. Safe to say Craig was anything but impressed when I told him.

Craig's dominating nature is not for everyone, and I understand that. I have some friends like Shannon and Katie for example, that if their other half promised to break someone's neck for going near them, they'd run. It would be too intense for them.

It's not that Craig is in any way abusive at all, he's far from it. I have my freedom—as much as the kids will allow. I can get up and talk and dance with guy friends and not have to worry about him going off on one, but if he senses a threat, if he thinks that there is even the slightest chance of me being hurt, that is when he is at his most dangerous.

It's not just with me either, oh no, the kids... well... Ethan was being bullied at school, he never told us until one day he came home bruised and tattered. That was sorted pretty damn quickly, although I'm not 100% certain how Craig put a stop to that one. I can only assume. Ethan was enrolled in martial arts the following week.

Then there was Ellie. Craig bet me to that one... again.

Ellie came home crying that a boy in her class had hit her and pushed her down. I was livid but Craig already had his keys in hand and was out the door in a heartbeat.

I heard from one of the mams on the school run that

Craig showed up on the offender's doorstep, waited for the dad to answer and clobbered him. He told him that every time his son hit Ellie, he would come back and hit the dad ten times harder.

Safe to say the bullying stopped immediately.

That's Craig though, he guards those he loves jealously. Maybe it's because his mam died when he was Ethan's age and his dad walked out soon after which has him all caveman-like.

Whatever the reason, he is my caveman, and I wouldn't trade him for the world.

I drop my lips to his neck, his jaw, and finally his lips. His eyes open reluctantly, and he smiles up at me lazily, "Fucking hell, it's the Hamburglar."

I chuck a pillow at him, "you're such an arsehole!"

He chuckles lowly, squeezing me tightly. I knew I forgot to take my makeup off last night, but it can't be that bad, can it?

Pushing myself up, I turn to face the mirror, "Christ on a bike!" I've dark circles down to my cheekbones, yikes! "I look like one of the ugly stepsisters."

"First of all," Craig yanks me down, pinning me against his chest. I think he's trying to hide the ugly. Let's face it, I've seen better days. "You are not and will never be ugly. You do, however, look like you've been dragged through a hedge backwards."

"That's your fault," I mumble against his chest. He tugged on my hair that much last night I'm surprised I don't have a bald patch.

"I can't argue there," Craig stretches out his long limbs, then claws his way to the edge of the bed in search of his jeans, or more precisely, his phone.

"Breakfast in half an hour?" he asks, tapping away at the screen.

"Perfect."

CRAIG

Dragging myself from the bed, I pop the kettle on and stick my phone on charge. I can hear Lottie moving about behind me, most likely looking for the nearest exit. Our first night here and I got in a fucking fistfight. That, and I did go at her like a savage afterwards, she's probably sore. I feel a twinge of guilt hit me. I need to do something to make this up to her, we came away to relax, not so Lottie would worry about me getting arrested... *again.*

I saw red when she told me what happened. There is no way in heaven or hell that I am allowing some arsehole to harass my woman like that.

"Do you want—" I stop dead, too distracted by the sight of her kneeling on the bed with my open shirt barely covering her breasts to finish my sentence.

"Craig?" she looks tired, still half asleep. She's not even

doing this on purpose. This is her not seducing me and I'm already three positions in in my head.

"Huh?"

"Want what? She presses.

You on my face. "C-coffee," I clear my throat. "Do you want coffee?"

"Are you ok?"

I'd start with the left tit, then the right, then—

"Craig?"

"Huh?"

"Are you ok?" her brow furrows, and she's looking at me like I've lost it.

"Yeah—no. Not at all. Not in the slightest," I step towards her. She still looks concerned.

"What's wrong?"

"That shirt," *I'm going to shred it.* "It doesn't suit you at all. You should remove it."

Her brow furrows, and she looks down at the flimsy material, "Oh?" It takes a second for her to look up at me and grin. "Ooh, is that what you think?"

"Yeah, off now. It's hideous, burning my eyes."

"That bad?"

"Rip it off, baby."

She moves slow, painfully slow.

Peeling one arm free and then the next. The shirt falls to the bed exposing her magnificently curvaceous body.

"Better?" she asks innocently, I'm on the bed in two long strides, pulling her flush against me.

She giggles, squeals, and moans as my mouth descends on her nipple.

"This morning is all about you, doll," dropping to the mattress, I position Lottie so she's sitting astride my chest.

LOTTIE

"Craig," I gasp as he runs a finger through my folds.

"You must be sore after last night, let me kiss it better," he shuffles under me until my sex is positioned directly over his face.

Craig growls and licks in long, eager strokes. His hands grip my thighs and then slide around, kneading my rear as his tongue dances around my sensitive flesh in a deliciously wicked waltz.

My hands pull mindlessly at his hair, I can feel my orgasm beginning to build already. He has such a talented tongue, and he knows exactly where I need him.

I groan, rocking my hips above him and he responds with one of his own. Craig sucks my clit between his lips, allowing his teeth to graze my oversensitive pearl. A jolt of pleasure shoots through me.

I look down at the man devouring me like I'm his last meal, "you like that, baby?"

An answering moan from him is followed by him pushing two fingers inside me, "I could spend all day between your legs, doll."

His fingers disappear, and he grabs my hips, pulling me onto his face, his tongue delves and swirls inside me. I hear another moan as one of his hands comes off my hip and the other slides to my breasts, pinching each nipple between his thumb and index finger.

Glancing back, I see him stroking himself while he continues to feast on me.

Fuck, that's hot.

He kisses the inside of my thighs, and then his tongue delves back inside me, "Craig!"

He pulls away, snarling. I can feel his movements as he continues to pump himself. "The other guests can hear you, doll." Craig kisses and nips at my inner thighs hard enough to leave marks. "Tell them who you belong to."

He runs his tongue through my folds, and I feel my legs quake, "you do."

"Say my name, doll," he sucks my clit between his lips, and I'm seeing stars.

"Craig!"

"Do you want anyone else, baby?" his tongue swirls and flicks, making me shudder.

"No! Oh God," I fall forwards, he keeps bringing me right to the edge but refuses to let me come. "I'm yours, Craig, only yours."

He continues to lick and nip my flesh, to the point where I'm shaking over him. I claw at the sheets, at his hair. I need release, I need it so much it hurts, "my body belongs to you, baby."

"Good answer!" I feel him wrap his lips around my clit and suck hard. His tongue rubs my sensitive pearl until I cry out.

I'm flipped onto my back, chest heaving, and I'm still dazzled from my high. Craig pushes my legs open, kneeling between them, his swollen length clutched in his hand, I watch mesmerised as he pumps himself over me.

His calloused hand slams down on the mattress at the side of my head, and he hovers over me, gaze darkened, dropping his mouth to my lips, neck, and breasts.

I can tell by his grunts and the increasing speed that he's close.

"Where do you want it, baby?"

"All over my chest," his favourite spot. As soon as the words pass my lips his mouth slants over mine, muffling his moans.

"Fuck, Lottie—I'm—" Craig roars, his hand fisting the sheets as he decorates my stomach and breasts in hot spurts.

He drops to the mattress, panting, and laughing. His hands slide over his face as he tries to catch his breath.

"I hate to break it to you, Batman," I glance at the clock. "But we need to get dressed for breakfast."

"I just ate."

I slap him lightly and he chuckles lowly into the pillow.

I move out from under him and go for a quick shower. When I come out, I find Craig exactly where I left him, naked and snoring.

I take a moment to admire him. To admire the play of light on the broad expanse of his bare chest. I hate to wake him, he looks so handsome, but we have five minutes to get our butts downstairs before Tiffy comes knocking.

"Craig."

"Mmm?" he doesn't bother opening his eyes.

"Come on, we need to go."

"Meh," is his only response. Still no movement. Crawling onto the bed, I kiss him, he still tastes like me. "Come on," I shove him lightly.

"They've nothing on the menu I want," he protests.

"You don't know that."

"I do. Nothing they have can tempt me like you do."

"Well, at least come down for a coffee?"

"Kettle is over there," he rolls onto his side, refusing to budge.

Right, if that's the way you want to play it, "those guys from the pool might be there."

His eyes flash open, and he's up and jumping into his jeans at record speed.

We leave the room with two minutes to spare. Craig, acting as my unofficial bodyguard, guides me down the hallway with his hand on my lower back.

CRAIG

Warm croissants, homemade jams, and fine coffee. The air smells like a seaside daydream.

For all the wonderful aromas from the breakfast and coffee, it is Lottie's eyes that I love the most. I could rest in them forever.

Lottie's breakfast consists of soft pancakes and berries with maple syrup threaded on top. I follow the fork's journey from her plate to her mouth, "oh my god," she moans. "It's like an orgy in my mouth."

"That good?" Tiffy asks.

"Try it!" Lottie insists and Tiffy stretches across the table for a forkful.

"Oh my god!" Tiffy lets out a moan of approval, grabbing Jason's attention, who announces, "I'll be ordering a stack of those to the room later."

It's a warm day outside, so we all set off for the beach after breakfast.

The sand is soft and golden with just the right soothing warmth, matched with the sunshine-filled sky. I stretch out both arms and fold them behind my head, my grin grows slowly into a broad smile. The only marker of our time today is the sun above, the moment savoured by the waves that wash sands in white lace.

Lottie and Tiffy splash about the water and, as usual, my little ginger ninja is beginning to burn.

Pushing myself from the sand, I stride into the water. Lottie spots me coming, runs at me, and leaps into my arms. I catch her easily, spinning as she giggles into my chest.

"Where are you taking me?" she looks up, shielding her eyes with her hand.

"It puts the lotion on its skin or else it gets the hose again."

"Ah," she clicks her tongue at my Hannibal reference, glances at her reddening skin and says, "good call."

Falling onto the beach towel, taking Lottie with me, I look through her bag until I find the sun lotion.

She gasps as the liquid hits her back, "that's fricken cold!"

"Woman up!" Rubbing the lotion into her back, shoulders, and neck, she moans and tips her head back.

"Not in public," Jay warns, peeking over his sunglasses and giving us the dad brow.

Lottie snorts, "quiet you, you filthy little beast."

"Ooh," Tiffy approaches, her gaze drifting to the car park, "ice cream." She grabs Lottie by the hand and they both take off like toddlers to the van.

When they return, it is obvious that they forgot about me and Jay—they look content with themselves as they devour their 99s.

"Thanks for that," Jay growls, looking from his wife to the van in the car park and debating if he should get up or stay put.

"Get your own," Tiffy scoffs, turning her back on him.

When Lottie sits down, I lean in, taking a slow bite of her ice cream. My eyes are fixed on hers the entire time.

"If you weren't so pretty, I'd kill you for that," she growls. I offer her up what I hope is a dazzling grin. My tongue darts out, cleaning up any stray drops on my lips.

"So," Tiffy begins once she's down to mostly all cone. "What's the plan later?"

We always spend at least one night with just our partners on these trips away. We all feel that it's important to have some time for just the couple.

"We're going to that Thai place in town," Jay announces, his eyes daft to the car park once again, he's still debating if he should get himself some ice cream.

"The one we found last year?" Tiffy asks.

"The very one."

"Great, what are you two up to?" Tiffy's chocolate gaze falls on us.

"Steakhouse or Chinese. What do you think, doll?"

"Steak!" Lottie demands, barely lifting her mouth from the cone.

"That was easy," I lean back on my elbows, watching the waves push and pull their way to shore.

"And after?" Lottie presses.

"You'll have to wait and see."

"I hate waiting."

"Tough titties."

Tiffy clears her throat, "her name is Titseanna Boobereeny."

Lottie snorts, then adds, "and my husband is Craven Moorehead."

"Yeah, I am!"

"Oh sure, we get the blame on the kids coming out with inappropriate shit, what about you two?" Jay pushes himself to his feet. I'm assuming he's about to make a beeline for the ice cream van.

"Bottom bitches don't talk back, Jay," Lottie cocks an eyebrow watching as Jay's hulking frame abruptly stops and spins to face her.

"You what?" his best brat tamer eyebrow raises like he's Dwayne Johnson. "You're lucky you're not my brat, Lottie."

"She would ruin you, Jay. You couldn't handle her," I chuckle, watching him stomp off.

"That's right, switch bitch," Lottie moves closer to me.

"Keep it up," I warn, I know her answer before the words pass her lips.

"That's what she said!"

A cacophony of laughter breaks out around our group, the passers-by look at us, some looking at our surroundings to see if we're day drinking.

Nope. We're not. We don't need to drink, we're bad enough sober.

Josie gave me a word of advice before I proposed. *How you got her, is how you keep her*, in other words, never stop dating your spouse. Never stop trying, even if it's just a cheap bunch of supermarket flowers on the way home from work one evening. It's harder to do as the years go on and the kids total up, but we have managed to keep the spark, even if it's something small like movie nights in when the kids are in bed.

We head back to the hotel to get ready, and I get a phone call from Tilly deciding to give out to me because Nanny Kim ran out of the big cookies.

Lottie looks incredible, as usual. I'm a lucky son-of-a-bitch. I have this hotel to thank for the free bar at Nick's wedding. If we hadn't been so plastered that night, we might not have crossed that line from friendship to this. I was hooked from the very first night. Hell, if I'm honest, I was hooked before then. it just took that one night of hot drunken sex to make me a fully-fledged addict.

Lottie dresses in a simple red bodycon dress, she straps on her heels and asks, "ready?"

"Ready," taking her hand in mine, I lead her to the elevator and out into the open world.

Two bottles of wine and a three-course meal later, I bring Lottie back to the hotel, much to her disappointment.

"What's wrong?" I ask, taking out the key card and waiting for the green flash on the door before opening it.

"I thought we'd be out a bit longer."

Tossing my jacket over the chair, I scroll through my phone and admit, "I don't want to share you tonight."

Finding the playlist I set up earlier, I hit play and *I see the light by Mandy Moore and Zachary Levi* comes on. Lottie lights up instantly.

I wasn't at all surprised that she picked a Disney song for our wedding. To be honest, I was kind of surprised it wasn't Moana considering how much she made me watch it.

"Our first dance," she looks at me with sparkling eyes.

"It was, wasn't it... huh... it slipped my mind. What a coincidence."

Taking Lottie's hand in mine, I pull her in close and we begin to move around the room. I spin her, dip her, lift her and it's like our wedding day all over again. Be it a room full of our friends and family, or a hotel room with just the two of us, she is the only thing I'm focused on.

Those gorgeous eyes, her bright smile, her snorting laugh. Everything about her is perfect.

As the song ends, I draw her back into me, her head leaning on my chest until the music fades away. She raises her head and presses those delicate pink lips to mine.

A knock sounds on the door, and I know it's the champagne I ordered earlier.

Pouring two glasses, I go into the bathroom and prepare a bath. I spent a small fortune on candles and rose petals for this, hiding it was the difficult part.

I must admit, I didn't do a bad job at staging this. Plus, I love this hotel, their baths are designed so I don't get stabbed in the back with the tap if Lottie decides to take up one end.

Shrugging out of my shirt, I open the door to find her fighting with her dress.

Scooping the hair from her back, I tug on the zipper, kissing her shoulder as she is slowly freed from her confines. "Ready?" I press my lips to her neck.

"Maybe?" she turns, beaming up at me.

Lifting her, I carry her into the bathroom, and she gasps at the sight of two dozen flickering candles surrounding the bathtub.

Lottie steps out of her lingerie, and I help her into the bath before climbing in after her. She pushes forward, sliding onto my lap and dominating my mouth with hers.

When she pulls away, I reach for the champagne and hand her a glass.

"You did good, Batman," she squeals. "You did very good."

"I'm glad you approve," I hear Ed Sheeran's Perfect playing from my phone in the adjoining room.

"To alcohol," Lottie raises her glass and giggles. "The cause of... and solution to, all life's problems."

"Well said, Homer."

She giggles again, takes a sip of champagne then offers me a warm smile, her eyes sparkling in the candlelight, "to the best husband and friend a girl could ask for."

"To the big cookies for keeping Tilly remotely sane," I quip, watching Lottie snort into her glass. I down the contents in mine and then top us back up. "To the only woman worth a shanking. The mother of my beautifully demented children, my best friend—"

"Don't say that in front of Jason or I'll be skewered," she laughs.

I reach for her hand, bringing her knuckles to my lips, "to the love of my life."

"Aww, baby," she looks as if she might start crying. Inhaling deeply, she gazes at me and declares, "let's go for number four!"

"Let's not."

Our booming laughs reverberate off the walls. The water sloshes around us as Lottie continues to move into different positions, undecided if she wants to straddle me or be spooned by me.

The night is still young, but it's not about having a piss-up with our friends or rattling the headboard and having reception call asking us to keep it down... ***again.*** It's about spending the tiny window we get together, to actually be together.

No phones, kids, or friends. No distractions. Just us. I plan on taking full advantage of that tonight.

I top up the glasses for the third time and realise we're all out. I'm going to need to order more champagne. I have plans for tonight and cheaping out is not going to cut it.

LOTTIE

Back to reality today after an amazing three-day break.

I pack up our things, the rock candy for the kids, a jawbreaker for Tilly, though I have a feeling that won't last half as long as we expect it to.

We ran into the shops yesterday and got Ethan some new Diary of a wimpy kid books to add to his collection. Ellie got some new dresses, and our little terror got a new Mickey Mouse toy.

"That's everything," I sigh, slamming the suitcase shut and zipping it closed.

"Won't be long," Craig's muffled voice comes from the bathroom. I walk to the half-opened door to spot him shirtless, with his toothbrush dangling from his mouth when he spots me watching.

Wrapping my arms around his waist, I rest my head on his shoulder, inhaling his scent. Savouring the last few hours of alone time before we're back to being mammy and daddy.

CRAIG

"Pass the pringles," I pull my eyes from the rolling hills and turn in the direction of the little raccoon sitting next to me. Lottie's cheeks are stuffed to the brim, she tilts the tub my way, and I try and fail to get my hand down the tube. "Your hands are smaller, stuff them in there and grab a handful."

Her cheeks expand, and she fights back a laugh but obliges me.

Jay glances at his phone which keeps lighting up with messages from Dylan and the other lads at work. He grumbles something under his breath that I don't quite make out before asking, "so, who's checking your one out tomorrow?"

Meaning he really isn't arsed about going and is hinting at me to go and meet with the new client instead.

"I suppose that will be me," I concede, shoving a handful of pringles in my mouth, the calories don't count until I get home.

When we get home, we just have enough time to get in and unpack before the kids come barging through the door.

Ellie spots me first, her little cherub face lights up, "Daddy!"

Ethan, of course, ignores me and makes a beeline for Lottie, "Mam!"

"Presents!" I hear Tilly before I see her.

Ellie makes a run for me, I pick her up and spin her, and she clutches my neck and laughs. Meanwhile, the demon appears and runs headfirst into my bollocks.

Safe to say, we are not having any more kids.

Lottie barks out a laugh, then composes herself as she looks down at me and asks, "are you ok?"

I can't answer, I try and instead, bellow like a wounded boar. I'm going to be sick.

"Dad?" Ethan cringes, it takes a hit to the balls before that child acknowledges I even exist, thanks kiddo.

"Here, baby," at first, I think Lottie is talking to me. How foolish of me to think she would come to my aid. Lottie is blatantly ignoring me and is instead, handing over presents to the kids who are now all pretending the middle-aged man curled up on the floor doesn't exist.

"Wow, thanks, Mam!" Ethan beams at Lottie and takes his books, stepping over me as he heads for the stairs.

You're welcome!

"Me?" Ellie asks with excitement in her eyes.

"Here you go," Lottie hands her the dresses. That child usually puts me on a pedestal when shiny things aren't getting handed to her.

"Thank you!"

Seriously?

Ellie turns and bends down, dresses in hand, and kisses my cheek. "Thank you, Dad."

"You're welcome, Princess," I manage to grunt out, while I push myself from the floor with great effort.

Tilly pushes forward, with her hands out. "Gimme!"

"Tilly!" Lottie barks. "What do we say?"

"Now."

"Tilly!"

"Just give it to her before she hits me in the nuts again."

Lottie hands over a Mickey Mouse clubhouse set that we picked up along with the jawbreaker. I'm kind of regretting that purchase now, it is rock candy shaped like a ball, and that could end badly for me.

"Yay!" Tilly proceeds to do her happy dance.

"What do you say?" Lottie presses yet again, hoping to find some manners in the child.

"Mine!" Matilda grabs the box and runs off.

"That one is yours," I point in the direction the little strawberry-blonde blur ran off in.

Lottie sighs, waiting a moment before turning to me and asking, "so where is this house you're going to tomorrow?"

"Hmm? I'm still busy adjusting myself to a hopefully more secure position. "Oh, Foxrock."

"Ooh, the other snob hill," Lottie giggles.

"Yeah, that's why Jay's not too fond of going," he hates dealing with the upper classes. He'd be happier going out to Ballymun and fighting off the junkies trying to steal the tools from his jeep.

"You would think that he would be used to it dealing with Charles. I mean look who his in-laws are."

"You'd think that, but no. It's most likely some barrister or doctor or someone living it up. I'll go but if they start trying to talk down to me, I'll walk out."

Lottie snorts and turns for the kitchen, "it's still a better approach than Jason threatening to fleece them or burn the house down."

I hear the demon make a run for us and pull Lottie in front of me. When it comes to being headbutted in the nether regions, I'm all for chivalry.

"Open!" Tilly shoves the box at Lottie.

"Say please!" Lottie growls.

"P-lease," Tilly demands more than asks. She watches Lottie open the box with a particularly bitchy look stamped on her little face—*definitely gets that from her mother.*

I know a father's job is to protect his daughters but if Tilly keeps this attitude up, I don't think I'll ever have to worry about her. If anyone gives her any hassle, she'll just thump the head off them.

"Hurry up!"

"Matilda!" Lottie is beginning to lose her reason.

"Tilly, don't speak to your mother like that!" I warn. The

hellion turns to me, looks me dead in the eye and demands, "I want the Mickey!"

Forget what I said, I'll definitely have to worry about her.

I've one child moaning because she wants a fluffy pussy and the other demanding the Mickey. I'm fucked.

Glancing at the clock, I see it's just gone half-four. Is it too early to start drinking?

Lottie finally pulls the toy free of the box, and turns to me, grinning, "did you hear that?"

"She's your daughter, you sort her out."

LOTTIE

The kids are finally gone to bed, Ethan, as usual, is "sneak" reading.

Going to the bathroom, I find my period has come a few days early. Great timing! At least I got the weekend to enjoy before it hit.

Stepping into our bedroom, I find the drawer housing my Bridget Jones pants. I pull on one of Craig's t-shirts and I'm all set.

Craig comes into the room, only to spot me and step back, sniggering, "what are you wearing?"

"My granny panties," I beam, emerging from behind the door of the bathroom I just hid behind so I could grab a pad. Slapping my hands on my hips, I raise an eyebrow at him, "do you still fancy me?"

He stifles a laugh, "what?"

"Do you still fancy me in my big pants?" I make a point of wiggling about in front of him.

Craig catches himself on the doorjamb, laughing. "I saw you practically wearing a nappy after giving birth. The big pants are hardly going to make me flaccid."

"I should hope not!" I pull back the covers and slide into bed when I hear a little voice ask, "what's flaccid?"

I peek past Craig to see Ellie standing behind him in the hallway.

"Your dad!"

"I'm not!" he spins to face Ellie. "And you should be in bed."

"I'm thirsty!"

"Ellie," there is a warning bite to his tone.

"Please."

"Come on then," Ellie follows him downstairs. I hear him opening and closing the fridge, all the while Ellie keeps pestering him about what flaccid means. "Some kind of hay."

"I don't get it."

"You don't need to," Craig insists, his head appearing on the landing once again. "Now, off to bed."

I watch as she steps for her room, smiles, and then spins for him, "story?"

"I already told you a story!"

"Please," she begs. "I missed you when you were away."

Craig looks in at me as if to say, *can you believe this shit?* "Breaking my heart, she is," he sighs, nudging her into her room.

I hear Craig telling Ellie a story in her room, Tilly demands that he puts on different voices for the characters. The little shit was pretending to be asleep.

After about fifteen minutes, I hear Ellie, "goodnight, Daddy."

"Night, princess."

"Night, stinky!" Tilly calls.

"Night, Satan!"

"Craig!"

He comes back into our room, grinning, "what?" I watch him strip before he climbs into bed. "It's good to be home."

I turn into him, finding my own personal Craig nook. "Mmm hmm, I missed them."

"Me too," I feel his lips touch my crown.

"Daddy!" Matilda roars.

"Your turn!" Craig instantly moves for his side, pulling his pillow over his head.

CRAIG

Well... I glance around the lavish house; the garage is bigger than my bloody house. It looks like Mariah Carey threw up in here.

This place could rival Charles' place. Fucking hell, I was expecting to pay an entrance fee when I pulled up here.

AJ doesn't live far from here, maybe I'll hit him up later? Find out if I'm gonna pull up a dead body while working here or if this one is good to go without a trip to the shrink.

The girl... woman... girl... person that owns this place looks like she's not long finished puberty. How the hell does a girl this young own something like this? Only fans maybe? Jay would love that.

"Just in here," she flips her long bleached-blonde hair over her shoulder, the kind that costs hundreds a month to maintain —you have girls, and you learn some things, don't judge!

I follow Jessica down the hall, around a corner, down another hallway and eventually, I'm in the kitchen.

The place is pristine white, hard dark-oak floors that cost a small fortune, definitely not the cheaper laminate, click-in stuff. Two obsidian chandeliers hang from the ceiling over the kitchen island.

This place doesn't need to be touched. What the hell?

"So," I clear my throat, trying to figure out the best way to ask if she has more money than sense. "What is it exactly you want me to do?" When I turn back to face her, I realise she's been staring at me the whole time with a somewhat deranged smile on her face.

"I was thinking of redoing it," she begins. My face must say *what the fuck,* because she continues, "It's beautiful but my mum designed it. I'd like to put my own stamp on it."

Ah. A family home. That explains it.

"Ok," I drag the word out. "What do you have in mind?"

She's still smiling at me, studying me. I'm getting freaked out. "Erm... maybe marble floors and some white cabinets?"

"White cabinets?" I can't keep the question, *are you insane* from appearing on my face. The cabinets are already white!

"More modern," she insists. Keep the white but just... yeah... not so... classic?"

"That's doable. I don't do tiling myself, but we have a few guys on the roster that can do it," I'm trying to remain professional here. "Do you have any pictures or anything for reference?"

"Uh, yeah!" she pulls her eyes from me long enough to grab her phone. Her thumbs are going nuts, dancing across the screen. She is obviously googling an image. Not at all prepared. This is weird. "Here you go..." she slides the phone to me, and I scan the image.

"Yeah, we can do that. It won't be cheap though, especially for the marble. It lasts but it comes with a hefty price tag."

I doubt that's a problem for someone who lives here.

"That's fine," she beams, walking to the kettle, "tea? Coffee? Lemonade?"

Woah, what were you snorting? Calm down.

I hear a casual footfall before I can answer, "Jess?" a male voice calls. *My saviour!*

"In here!"

He freezes when he sees me. I'm debating if I should introduce myself or pretend, I don't notice him.

Stepping to me, he offers me a warm smile, "hi, I'm Danny. Jessica's boyfriend."

Not interested, calm down.

"Craig," I extend my hand to meet his when he freezes. The smile on his face fades fast.

"Craig Barnes?" he asks, eyebrows disappearing into his cinnamon hairline.

"Danny," Jessica growls in a warning.

"Is there a problem?" I ask, feeling defensive.

"No!" Jessica insists.

"No, none," the smile is back again, this time forced as he turns to his girlfriend and asks, "can I talk to you for a minute?"

She nods, goes to the fridge, and pulls out a can of coke, sliding it to me with an apologetic grin, before following him from the room.

My hearing may have become sensitive since having kids, or it could be that a house this size has its own echo, but I'm picking up on parts of the conversation.

Are you nuts?

No! I'm not! What's wrong with hiring him?

You're asking for trouble!

Maybe I should have sent Jason. I kind of feel like threatening to fleece the place now.

You don't know what you're talking about.

Why did you do it?

We need the kitchen done. He does kitchens!

You wanted to meet him.

So? Is that such a crime?

You're impossible!

Jessica curses him out, then stomps back into the room.

"Look," I spin from the counter to look at her. "I'm clearly not wanted here. I can pass on a number—"

"No!" She practically jumps at me. "Don't mind him. He doesn't even live here. He's paranoid."

"Paranoid?"

"Men!" she huffs, then turns to me. "No offence."

"None taken."

"I want you to work on the kitchen, please. I'll pay double!"

I'm getting a bad feeling about this. "That's very generous but—"

"Do you have kids?"

"Three."

I look at the can she left out for me. I'm afraid to drink it in case it's spiked.

"I love kids!" she beams.

For breakfast? "Yeah, they're great."

"Umm... you're married, right? I saw a story online about you from a few years back."

Oh shite. Cyberstalker. "Yeah. I'm married."

"Aww, childhood sweethearts?" she presses.

It puts the lotion on its skin or else it gets the hose again. *I'm ending up in the hole, aren't I?* "Not exactly."

"Jess," the boyfriend snaps. "Stop interrogating him!"

"I'm not!"

"You are. You're freaking me out, never mind him!"*Him has a name.*

"Oh gosh!" she turns to me wide-eyed. "I didn't mean—"

"It's fine, I get asked about it a lot." She's just an overeager reader, Craig. Don't worry, it happens. Deep breaths and when she's not looking, run like hell.

"So, you can transform this place for her?" the boyfriend asks.

"Yeah, it shouldn't be a problem."

Jessica jumps in, "when can you start?"

"Eh..."

"Oh!" she snatches her purse from the island. "I can give you the deposit now or would you rather be paid in full before—"

"Eh..."

"Jess!" Danny snaps.

"What?"

"We don't take full payment until the job is complete," I say, mapping out the closest exit in my head. I'm two seconds away from bolting through a window. "Do you want us to source the materials for you or are you getting them yourself?"

"I'd love for you to do it. I trust you," her eyes are huge, she's gotta be snorting something.

"Great, well... erm," I clear my throat and pull out my phone. "Let me make some calls, work out a price and get back to you. If you're happy then we can take it from there."

"Perfect!"

"Great, well," I step away from the counters, slowly backing away from the sharp objects. "I'll get going and ring you when I have something to go on."

"Thank you," she chirps, practically jumping the counter as she insists, "I'll walk you out."

Shit, am I about to get bludgeoned?

I make it outside alive and unwounded.

Jessica waves me off with a slightly psychotic smile.

I dial Lottie's number before I pull out of the drive. She answers on the third ring, "Hello, handsome."

"Baby, I'm scared!"

"What happened?"

"The girl is nuts!"

"How nuts is nuts?"

"Coo Coo for coco pops nuts!" I flip the indicator and tear arse towards AJ's, he might have some information on Lizzy Borden.

"What happened?" Lottie presses.

"She's full on. She had nothing prepared and googled an image last minute to show me."

"That happens from time to time though," Lottie reasons, trying to calm my nerves.

You weren't there, babe! If you were you would have seen the level of crazy behind those eyes. "Yeah, but she started interrogating me as soon as I walked in!"

"How so?"

"Asking if I'm married. She said she saw our story online. Then there was a weird discussion I overheard with her boyfriend."

"Oh?"

"I don't know, just weird."

I stop at a red light and check my mirrors, half expecting to see Jessica chasing me down like Cruella De Vil.

I hear Lottie moving about, a quick silence before she asks, "want me to go over there and punch her?"

"You'd do that for me?" I can't help but grin.

"I'd happily assault anyone that comes for my man."

I stifle a laugh and check my surroundings again before I pull off. The more distance I put in, the better I feel. "Love you!"

"Love you too! Are you heading back to the office?"

I'm not about to tell her that I'm heading to AJ Quinn's house, but I'm not about to lie to her either. So, I say, "I'm going to make a will in case I go missing!"

"It would never happen," I hear her snort. "Tilly would sniff you out in a heartbeat."

"Ooh, send Tilly!"

"So she can sniff you out?"

"So she can headbutt Jessica in the gooch!"

Lottie's booming laugh comes over the phone, "you're not being followed?"

"No," I double-check for good measure. Seeing an unmarked garda car outside AJ's house and inspect it to see if it's Nick in there... *no, not Nick.* "I'm safe."

"Well, I'm not," Lottie moans. I hear Tilly in the background roaring for her mother.

"There's my little demon child!"

"I gotta go, I'll see you when you get home!"

"Ok, love you—" she's gone. Well, excuse me. She'd feel bad if I were abducted by Mad Madame Mim. I have to remind myself that my wife works from home and around Tilly, I have no idea how she manages it. That's two full-time jobs in one.

I buzz into AJ's, his house puts Jessica's to shame, yet I feel safer here, in the house of the Isles' most notorious hitman, than I did with that fresh-faced rich kid.

CRAIG

Boxes come flying from the shelves like a deliciously processed rainfall, "that's for Tilly," Jaffa cakes, "that's for Tilly." Oreos, "that's for Tilly." Twinkies—wait, how much? I didn't realise I was fucking paying for the airfare!

Lottie spins, she has her blinkers on. She has joined me on this stupid weight loss journey, apparently, it's not so funny when she can't get her jeans to fit. I told her to buy a size up, she told me to shut my face, it's all about compromise. "Tilly, stop throwing junk in the trolley!"

Does Matilda listen? Of course not, this is my child we're talking about, she tosses in a few packets of bourbon creams for good measure and announces, "ooh, that's Tilly's too."

"Craig!" Lottie turns to me, pleading. Sorry, baby, can't help you there. The Viennese swirls are calling me, unfortunately, I'm not out of the woods yet, I'm still in my stretchy pants.

"There's no point in arguing with her, we're going to lose anyway," I sigh, mentally waving goodbye to everything I love in the confectionary aisle.

Lottie spots our youngest making a move for the chocolate, "Tilly, you can't do that!"

"Why?" she asks, tiny hands still reaching for the pack of Wispa.

"Because you need to think of everyone in the family, not just Tilly," Lottie reasons.

"Oh," Matilda pauses for 0.2 seconds before turning her head ever-so-slightly to the share pack of Maltesers, "that's for Ethan." She moves to the left, mauling the jelly babies, "that's for Ellie." She backtracks for the Viennese whirls, "that's for Daddy."

"Thanks, baby!" fuck it, I have to eat them now—that's what I'm going with, don't start!

"Welcome," Tilly skips towards me, beaming.

Tossing her hands in the air in defeat, Lottie moans, "unbelievable."

"Craig?" a too-chipper voice calls from the end of the aisle. My balls retreat as the realisation hits, "Oh, cock."

"Who's that?" Lottie asks, lowly.

I turn to her with pleading eyes, I was willing to take a knife for you, woman, now it's payback time, "hello Clarice," I say lowly so only Lottie can hear.

"Oh," Lottie's eyebrows shoot to her hairline. I pull her directly in front of me. She can fight that nut off, I've every faith in her.

What the hell is she even doing here? We don't live anywhere near Foxrock. We're ninety minutes' drive away on a good day.

We left Dublin because we hate people. I distinctly built our house down the sticks, so I'd only need to interact with the cows and pigeons.

"Craig, hi!" Jessica makes a beeline for me. She's way too happy to be shopping at Tesco. Am I the only one to see that this girl is clearly a crackhead?

"Hi, Jessica," *baby, get her. Throat punch her. At least punch her in the tit,* if my only fans theory is correct, it should deflate, cause a scene, possibly make her cry and we can run.

"Ooh, I know who would like that," Tilly distracts me momentarily.

"Who?" Lottie groans, turning to face our little hellion.

"Me!"

"Wow, this is a surprise," Jessica adjusts her bag on her shoulder, I'm assuming the bag costs as much as a one-bedroom apartment in Dundrum. "What are you doing here?"

I nod to the shopping trolley, stating the obvious.

"Of course," she giggles, "why else would you be here."

What the hell are YOU doing here, that's what I really want to ask but I can't force the words out.

"Hi, I'm Jessica," she shoves her hand at Lottie, who smirks and shakes her hand firmly while she introduces herself. Why is she being so damn nice? *Come on, woman, show her how crazy you are.*

"Daddy?" Tilly squeaks.

"Wow, you have a keeper here. She's beautiful," Jessica turns to me, beaming.

"I know, thanks."

"Daddy!"

Jessica turns to look at Matilda, "and who is this?"

Safe to say Tilly has lost her reason, "scuse me, I'm talking to you!"

I turn to face the demon child, "what, Tilly?"

"I want a Donald's."

"We'll go to McDonald's when we're finished shopping."

"I want the burger, not nuggets."

"Noted."

Another squeak grabs my attention, but this one isn't from Tilly, "oh my gosh, she's gorgeous."

"Thank you," Lottie beams, like the proud mama bear she is.

Jessica hunkers down to Tilly's level, "hi."

Tilly screams, drawing the eye of several shoppers, "stranger danger!"

Good girl, I taught her well.

"I gots my own sweets!" Tilly insists, scarpering for my leg. Good woman. She can order the entire menu in McDonald's if she wants.

Jessica stands, still smiling. It's not normal for anyone to be this happy, "are they all for you?" her giant eyes are locked on my daughter. *Good luck trying to rob her, she's a biter.*

"No," Tilly huffs, looking at her mother and then me to gauge our reactions to the newbie. "For Ethan, Ellie, and Daddy." She then points to the top half of the trolley, "those are mine."

"Oh, wow!" Jessica says with sickening enthusiasm.

"I'm not sharing!"

"I don't blame you," Jessica giggles, "what's your name?"

Matilda looks at me, grins, then turns back to Jessica and announces, "Satan."

"She's adorable."

"She bites," I receive an elbow in the gut from Lottie for that one.

Jessica takes a step closer, and I pull Lottie back by the hips until she's pressed against me.

"Well, it was lovely to see you. I best be off; Danny will be looking for me."

"Bye!" Tilly half waves her off, all the while she claws open a pack of Skittles that I didn't even see her take from the shelf.

"Bye," I mumble, refusing to release my wife until there is a good distance between us.

"Wow," Lottie pulls her chin to her shoulder, staring back at me. "She's stunning."

She's alright. Attractive in the influencer sense. Fake hair, eyelashes, tan... I doubt she's eaten a carb this year.

"She doesn't seem that bad," Lottie continues. I usually trust her judgement but the lack of junk food on our behalf is clearly putting her crazy metre on the fritz.

"You don't find it the least bit strange that she's out here?"

"Not really," Lottie shrugs, grabbing the trolley and pushing it towards the checkout. "I mean we are right by the motorway. They could have pulled off to stretch their legs."

Perhaps there's a tracking device on my van? I'm going to have to check for that and possible explosives.

"I'm not going to that house alone," I insist.

"Craig," Lottie sniggers. "You're an ex-MMA fighter. Do you honestly think a little thing like her could hurt you?"

"Just because she's rich doesn't mean she cannot be a criminal. It just means she has money for bribes and plentiful spots to hide a body!"

Lottie frowns, taking my measure, "she really makes you that uneasy?"

"There's just something about her that feels... off."

"Ok," she stops the trolley and reaches for my hand. "Trust your instincts and send someone else in your place to do the work if you do take her on as a client."

I wish I could, but we're all booked up. Unless one of the lads finishes a job early. It has to be me that goes, I'm the only chippy left on the roster.

Lottie must realise this because she demands, "take Dylan or Jason."

"I plan to," I shift on my feet uncomfortably. AJ knew sweet fuck all about the girl. She's not into shadier business or I would have known. There isn't a soul on the streets doing something unlawful that AJ doesn't know about. He was a smart kid, he used his body as a weapon to make his millions, and his mind keeps him on top. I should take some sort of solace in the fact that she's a complete unknown to the likes of Aiden, but my gut is screaming at me that something is very wrong. "I just need to make a call, I'll catch up at the checkout, yeah?"

"Go ahead," Lottie continues with Tilly at her heels, munching away on colourful balls of sugar.

Walking to the entrance, I spot Jessica getting to her car and memorise the reg plate. I watch her drive off while I wait for Nick to answer the damn phone.

"Hello?"

"I need a favour," I'm wasting no time with this one.

"Which would be?"

"Get a pen."

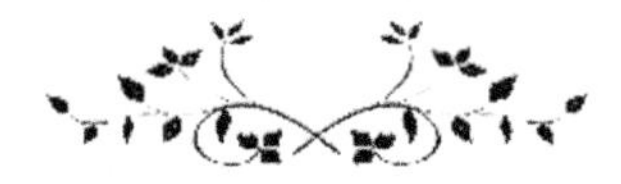

LOTTIE

Tiffy almost chokes on her coffee, "he had Nick run a background check on her?"

"Yeah, I know," I've never seen Craig this on edge before. I blame the diet change—the last time he was in pursuit of abs, he turned into a raging arsehole. He was always tired, constantly hungry and had absolutely no libido.

I've distinctly told him, he is not going extreme this time, I don't believe in divorce, but I do believe in an alibi. But I think this girl has really shaken him up.

I glance at the paper on the table, a picture of Éabha Ryan on the front page. She should have had an alibi the night her ex was killed. I followed the case with Tiffy—it's always best to have the inside gossip when your brother and his friends are gardaí and your best friend is a prosecutor. The entire conviction made absolutely no sense to me.

"What does he think he's dealing with?" Tiffy presses.

"No idea, but she has him unnerved. He said he doesn't necessarily think she's dangerous, just that something about her is off."

"Maybe she triggered PTSD from the Michael incident?" Tiffy says, my heart sinks, and when her eyes flit to me, she panics. "I don't mean—"

"It's fine," I lie. It's not Tiffany's fault, she is only trying to figure out Craig's mindset. It does make sense that the girl triggered something in him. I just hate the thought that he got a disorder because of me. If I had never dated Michael... I can't change it now.

Craig never acted strangely, no nightmares, skittishness or any of the usual signs. I thought we got away with it but now, looking at things, he may very well have the disorder.

He calls me his queen. The love of his life, but I'm second to the kids. They've done more to shape their father than I ever did. They're his greatest achievement.

"I honestly don't know," I admit. "It could be, maybe see if Jason can get it out of him?" Craig's other love.

Cannot forget Jason.

"Does she look like a psycho?"

"Well, no, but they never do," I smirk, and nod at Tilly who is building blocks for James to knock down, the pair are practically laughing themselves out of their nappies.

Tiffy beams, then turns back to me, asking "how old is she?"

"I don't know. About twenty-five-ish."

"It could just be her nature," Tiffy shrugs. "You've seen the younger crowd, they're not as paranoid as us. She could just be one of those people who wants to be your best friend."

"First of all, younger crowd?" I growl. "Screw you too. I'm thirty-five not dead!"

"Thirty-six in October."

"Still far from the nursing home, love." Oh my God, I sound like Craig. "I trust Craig's instincts on this. If he thinks something is off, then something is off."

"But?" She leans over the table, brows raised.

"I really don't peg her for the violent type."

"What could it be?"

"Maybe another person that saw his story and developed a crush?"

"Or read your book and slid off their chair," Tiffany cackles. "Honestly, the way you wrote those scenes... thanks for that. Really needed to know that much about your sex life."

"Don't even start."

"Mr fucking battering ram, could not look at him the same for weeks," Tiffy snorts, then reaches for her bag under the table and starts to rummage.

"It's a nice—" I stop myself, remembering the kids in the room.

"Oh, I know. We all know," she pulls out a compact mirror, giving herself a quick once over before deciding to top up her makeup. "Jeez, if he smacks you across the face with that, he'd break your jaw."

"Tiffy!"

"What? You wrote it!" Pressing a finger to the side of her eye, she runs her kohl-black eyeliner against the faded line on her lid.

"I did. Craig is a bonafide," I clear my throat, "and I'm the bumbling Disney fan whose only real hobby or interest is food."

"Stop reading reviews! Some people are arseholes.

There is a way to tell people you don't like their stuff without being rude about it. Look at the amount of people who reach out to thank you for making their day and cheering them up with that book. Screw the critics."

"I'd rather screw Craig."

"Of course, you would."

CRAIG

I desperately fight with my phone to get the bastard out of my pocket. When I finally get it, I hit the little green phone on the screen, "Well?"

"I got nothing," Nick confesses.

"Nothing?" *Every serial killer has to have their first victim, I suppose that's me.*

"Not so far," I hear Nick stuffing his face with God knows what. He must be on his lunch. "No convictions, not so much as a parking ticket or penalty point."

"Really?" I want my mam. I really could use that woman right about now. They say time heals all wounds, it's bollocks. It still hurts like bitch knowing that she never got to meet her grandkids. That she wasn't around for the wedding. I've gone longer without the woman than I ever had her. Even thinking of it now feels like I've been hit by a bulldozer.

"Her mother is a psychiatrist," Nick explains.

Oh, the irony.

"Her father is in IT. She has an older brother and that's roughly it. The entire family is squeaky clean."

"Keep digging," I pull out the pack of cigarettes from my desk and light up. "Look into the parents too."

"I will do."

"Thanks," I hear Nick saying bye as I hang up the phone.

Inhaling a toxic cloud of smoke, I notice that I'm bouncing my leg under the desk. *Shit, my nerves are gone.*

I glance at the phone again. Jason rang earlier to say he sourced the materials for the job in Jessica's, we actually worked it close to the estimated price we tallied up the other day, it helps to know some guys—AJ Quinn to be exact, he knows everyone, and of course, most fall over themselves to stay in his good books.

It's a long shot, possibly my last opportunity to end this before I have to go in there. Picking up the phone I text Jessica to say the price is now double the estimate we gave her the other day and that I understand if she doesn't want to go ahead giving the cost.

My phone buzzes almost immediately with her response.

JESSICA

That's no problem at all, I'm happy to pay :)

Who in their right mind would not argue about the price of their kitchen doubling in a matter of days?

That settles it. She's nuts.

CRAIG

Fucking hell, where did that rain come from? I only moved from the van to the front door, and I'm soaked. I barely get the front door closed when Lottie comes thundering down the stairs in her sports bra and leggings.

"Out of the way!" she knocks me into the wall and races into the kitchen. As I shrug off my jacket, I hear the backdoor open, followed by her colourful vocabulary floating back into the house.

Ah, I see what's going on here. Pulling open the dryer door on my way to the kitchen, I watch her sprint by me, soaked to the bone as she hurls a bundle of clothes inside the machine and switches it on.

"Typical," she snaps, red-faced. "Sunny all day and as soon as I put clothes on the line, the heavens open."

"You look good wet," I admire the tight, revealing clothes. The water droplets running down her chest, her messy hair and her flushed cheeks. *Who owns you? Oh, that's right, I do! Gimme.*

Lottie pouts and crashes into me, I scoop her up and carry

her into the back room, dropping her on the couch. I follow soon after.

"I'm wrecked," she admits. "I went a bit overboard on the exercise bike today, think we can have a nap without the kids finding us?"

"Only one way to find out," I reach for the blanket on the back of the couch and pull it over us. I recline and Lottie wastes no time in scaling me and seeking out her comfy spot.

"Craig?" she tilts her head to look at me, eyebrow raised.

"Hmm?"

"Are you honestly poking me in the leg right now?"

"I've no control over that. You came down those stairs in tight, wet clothes and you really expect him not to react?

Worse fool you," I snort, then add. "That wiggling doesn't help, either."

"Your belt buckle is digging into me," she protests.

"Take it off then."

Lottie reaches down, popping open my belt and yanking it off with impressive speed, and then she lowers her head to my chest.

"Better?" I stifle a yawn and bury my face in her hair.

"Much," her hands run over the expanse of my chest before she finds her sweet spot and settles into it. "I need to shower, but I don't want to move," she groans.

Grabbing a handful of the blanket, I pull it up, sealing us in like a little cocoon, "we'll shower later, naptime first."

"Ethan is upstairs reading. The girls are having a Disney marathon in the sitting room," she offers up the information before I can ask. Besides the rain beating off the windows, the house is blissfully quiet.

Lottie traces circular patterns over my chest, and I soon find my eyes drifting close. Her fingers continue tracing intricate patterns under my t-shirt, slowly gliding, down, down—I'm awake.

"Is it my birthday again?" I grin, watching the blankets move about. Her delicate hand grips me and starts to pump.

Her kiss comes hard and heavy, sucking the air out of my lungs. Then she straddles me. "You've been on edge lately," she offers me another heartbreakingly sexy grin and I realise that I don't own her. I'm her bitch. I'll wear it like a badge of honour. *Do what you want to me, mama, I'm yours.*

"I guess," pulling my arms behind my head, I watch her work me with both hands. "I've been a little stressed."

I really want to tell her to use her mouth, that I'd do just about anything to watch her lips wrap around me right now. But I don't want to fuck this up so I'm keeping my trap shut.

As if reading my mind, Lottie leans in, suckling the head.

This is why I married this woman. Fucking hell, that mouth is a godsend. I bite down on my knuckles, stifling the moan she's dragging from me.

I want nothing more than to tear off her clothes, throw her down on the couch and have my way with her. But I can't, not for a few days. I can't touch her. I hate it.

"Just like that," I grab a fistful of her hair, encouraging her to destroy me. She takes me all the way in, relaxing her throat, and my hips jolt up. She pulls back. *Bollocks.* Someone needs to tie me down right now because I can't hold still where that mouth is concerned.

She goes back in, grinning. Her head bobs up and down in my lap, she's toying with me. Making sure I don't choke her by becoming overzealous.

Her tongue flicks around the base, I feel the head hit the back of her throat again, it takes everything in me to strangle a moan and stay still.

"Again," I beg as she pulls away, I frame her face in my hands, I don't know if I should kiss her or fuck her senseless. "Please," I run my thumb over her swollen lower lip. Pushing myself up, I claim that gorgeous mouth, and I feel her fingers wrap around my length and begin to pump.

Pulling away, I watch as precum spills onto her hand, "please, baby," I kiss her lips, jaw, and neck. I will get on my hands and knees and beg if I must.

She brings her hand to her mouth, keeping her eyes fixed on me as she sucks her fingers clean. I almost explode right there. "Please?" she echoes, drawing her lower lip between her teeth and biting down.

"Please, baby," she doesn't move. "Lottie," her sea-green eyes glisten back at me. "Charlotte. Mistress. Wife. Devil woman!"

She laughs lowly, deciding to grant me a small mercy and give me what I'm aching for.

She hums around my cock, increasing her suction as she takes in every inch.

"Oh, fuck!" my hands tangle in her hair, "harder." I don't remember closing my eyes. I'm not sure if I've even closed them or if they just rolled into the back of my head, "just like that, baby. I'm going to fucking—"

"DADDY!" Matilda's voice booms from the hallway.

"Shit!" we jump apart, and I stuff myself back inside my jeans before the door bursts open. "What's wrong?" I ask breathlessly.

"Fucky!"

"What?" there is no way she could know what we were just doing and I sure as hell didn't teach her that word.

"I can't find fucky!"

Lottie swipes at her mouth and points to the little bastard that cost me my happy ending, "he's over there."

"Oh, Forky!"

"That's what I said!" Matilda snaps.

"I'll go check on Ethan," Lottie declares, hurrying from the room.

I toss the blanket back on the couch and stand on wobbly legs.

"What's that?" Tilly points at my crotch. I'm still bulging despite my best efforts to conceal it. "Sweets?" Tilly demands more than asks.

"I've no sweets," I step around her, half expecting her to kneecap me.

"Gimme!"

"It's not sweets, it's my phone!"

"Oh," thank God that halted her advances before she tried to search me. "I want sweets."

And I want your mother to finish that blowjob. "After dinner."

"Now."

"No."

"Daddy!"

"Satan."

"Please."

"No."

She runs from the room "crying" in hopes Lottie will see her and cave.

She doesn't.

After dinner, Satan gets a giant cookie, and the Disney marathon continues. Ethan and I hide upstairs, watching Batman and avoiding princess makeovers.

My eldest opens a packet of minstrels and pours them into his bowl of microwave popcorn. He's exactly like his mother.

"You should be the Riddler this year, Dad!" he has cheeks like a beaver right now.

"I don't know. I think Matilda would look better as a villain."

Ethan's hand stops on its way back to the bowl, "she's crazy."

"She's just like your mother," I snort.

"I'm going to tell her—"

"I'll buy you a new batman suit if you keep your mouth shut."

"Deal," Ethan grins, shoving in another mouthful of popcorn and melting chocolate. "Hey, Dad?"

"Yeah?"

"You're not going to get hurt again, are you?"

I sit up, my eyes locking on his concerned gaze, "what do you mean?"

"I heard you and Mam talking. You don't want to go to work, are you being bullied?"

My lips pull to the side, "no, buddy. Nothing like that."

"But you did get hurt before. That's why those people know you," he pushes away his snacks and looks about ready to cry.

He's referring to Michael, try as we might, we can't stop the stories, people talk. Mam's talk, kids hear, kids talk more. Some kids at Ethan's school think I'm an actual superhero.

"I told you, buddy. Mam was being bullied and I put a stop to it. A lot like what happened to you and Ellie."

"But you didn't get arrested for us."

"Well, no. I wasn't really arrested, I just had to tell Uncle Nick what the bully was doing to Mam."

"But he hurt you?"

"Not much," I can see his lower lip quiver and think of the best way to put his mind at ease. "You've seen me training with Jason, yeah?"

"Yeah," he wipes at his eyes.

"Well, it was kind of like that. When you're sparring in your matches, you get a little hurt, right?"

"Yeah!" he chirps up. That's my boy. *No need to worry about your old man. I'm still here, buddy.*

"Well, that's all it was. Nothing to worry about."

"Good, I don't want you to get hurt.

"I won't."

The snack bowl is pulled back in, and he swipes another mouthful. "If Tilly is the Riddler then who is Two-Face?"

"Jay!"

"Good one," he snorts. "And Jamie can be the Penguin," another mouthful of popcorn goes in with a crunch. "Mam can be Catwoman."

Now there's an idea.

"And you?" I ask, swiping a handful of popcorn while there's still some going.

"Batman," he says matter-of-factly.

"Then who am I?"

"Robin."

Damn, that was cold.

My phone rings and I spot Josie's name flash on the screen. "What can I do for you, my little lambchop?"

"A barbecue at mine on Saturday," she demands.

"No beating around the bush with you, is there?"

"Never. You're cooking."

"I guessed as much."

Ethan edges closer, "is that Nan?"

"Yeah."

"Hi, Nan!"

"Hi, Sweetie!"

"We're watching Batman!"

Josie gifts him a musical laugh, "again?"

"Yeah, Dad said he'll be Robin this year."

I said no such thing!

"Matilda is the Riddler because she's a looney," Ethan

continues. I'm completely left out of this conversation, so I just hand him my phone and leave him to it.

Ripping out the old counters and the floors, I have Dylan load up the skip outside with the debris. It's been two weeks since I sent her that text about her kitchen doubling in price, and yet, here I am.

When I'm finished in the kitchen, Dylan gets started with installing the new sink, and David gets a move on with the tiles.

Jason is upstairs, so I rip up the floors in one of the bedrooms to make it easier for him to rewire the kitchen. I'm hiding out with him, so Jessica doesn't find me.

"I think you were right about her," Jay grunts, searching his toolbox for God only knows what.

"Meaning?"

"She cornered me at the skip, and start asking about you," he gives me a look that says he thinks I'm going in the hole.

"Asking what?"

"Nothing too invasive, mostly general crap, like how long we've known each other. What you're like, yadda yadda yadda."

"Why would she—"

"No idea," he shakes his golden head, and large amber eyes meet my gaze. "Maybe she has a crush?"

"She's met me once! Twice if you count the supermarket."

"I don't know what to tell you," Jay says as he lowers a cable into the room below.

My phone rings, and once I see Nick's name, I practically put my finger through the screen answering his call, "hey!"

"Hey, what's up?"

"You called me."

"Yeah, I know," he groans. He doesn't sound right.

"Are you ok?"

"Yeah, no... I mean—"

"Nick?"

He loosens a breath, seemingly steadying his nerves before asking, "where are you?"

"In Jessica's, working on the house."

"You're there now?" I think his balls just dropped.

"Yeah, why?"

"Leave!" he demands, I hear rustling in the background like he's making a beeline for the nearest exit.

"What?"

"Get out!"

"What the hell, Nick? What's wrong?"

He pauses, and I hear him suck in a breath. My muscles are tensed, like I'm about to make a run for it. "I found something when I dug further, something you're not going to like," Nick admits.

CRAIG

"Craig? Craig, are you there?"

Something I'm not going to like? That can be anything! She's a stalker? She went all Éabha Ryan and went snap-happy on someone with an axe? She likes Justin Bieber's music? "What the hell is going on?"

"Just trust me ok!" Nick begs. I hear him open a car door and shut it quickly after him. He's on the move. This can't be good.

She's met my wife, my daughter—*calm the fuck down*, if she was a threat to them Nick would have said by now. "Is she dangerous?"

"No. No, but—" I hear the engine roar and the tires scream as he tears arse out of the carpark. "I'm not doing this over the phone, man. Just trust me, get out of that house, and go home. I'll meet you there, ok?"

"Ok," I hang up. I need to move, but my feet are fixed to the floor.

Jay's on his feet, concern etched on his face, "what's wrong?"

I shove my phone into my pocket and force my legs to

move, I need to pack up my tools and haul arse. "Nick," I spin, and locate my measuring tape and hammer. "He found something."

"Shit, what is it?" Jay looks as unnerved as I feel.

"He won't say, not over the phone. He's going to meet me back at the house." Slamming my toolbox shut I seal it and pick it up, still trying to make sense of what was said to me.

"Are you alright to drive?"

"Yeah, I'll be fine," I nod, loosen a breath and make my way downstairs.

I hear Jessica's voice halfway down, "you can't be here. I'm getting work done in the house, it's not safe."

"Nonsense. I had to come and see if you were ok. I haven't heard from you all week."

I freeze on the steps. There's something familiar about that voice—

"Daddy, you have to leave. I'll come by tomorrow, I promise."

"Fine. Call your mother, she's worried about you."

"I will!"

"Bye, pumpkin."

"Bye!"

I start to move, not wanting them to think I was eavesdropping. My hackles are raised, something about that voice—

I hear a gasp behind me, at the same time Jay comes bounding down the stairs, "Craig! Your wallet!" I turn to Jay, stopping when my eyes fall on the man at the end of the hall.

The colour drains from his face when he sees me, which is ironic given the fact that every drop of blood in my body seems to rush into my eyes. My surroundings, including the people around me, are blood red.

Jason is down the stairs, shoving my wallet at me, I'm not sure if I want to throw up or smash a body through the earth.

"Craig" it talks. It fucking talks. It knows my name.

My lips pull back from my teeth in a snarl, "William."

Noting the venom in my voice, Jay turns to the man rooted to the spot at the end of the hallway. "You two know each other?"

"You could say that," I snatch my wallet from him and shove it in my pocket.

Jessica chews her lip, her eyes are filled with anxiety and genuine remorse, "Craig, I—I didn't want you to find out this way."

"Craig, what's going on?" Jay presses. "Who is he?"

"Jessica's father," I turn for the door, yanking it open.

Jessica backs away with tears spilling down her face, "Craig, please!"

I charge for the van, almost pulling the door from its hinges as I toss my toolbox in the booth before I completely lose it and start searching for the hammer.

"Craig!" I feel a hand clutch my shoulder and I swing on instinct, Jay dodges, attempting to restrain me.

"Talk to me, man," Jason begs, he has me boxed in against the van. Ok, I can do this. I can do this. I'll explain why I have to leave; it hasn't registered with Jason yet, and he's worried. I'm going home to my wife and—

"Craig!" I turn to the husky voice. *I'm gonna snap your fucking neck you prick!*

"Who is he to you?" Jason demands.

"A sperm donor."

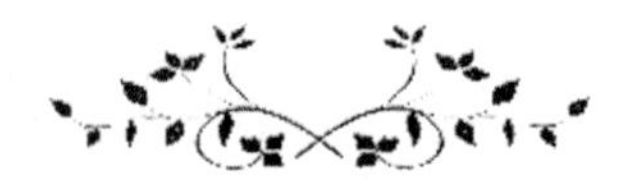

JAY

Craig is gone. The bastard's too fast to keep caged in for long. I've to jump a hedge to intersect him as he sprints towards Jessica's father. There's no doubt in my mind that he's going to fucking kill this man.

What the hell did he call him? Sperm donor, but that would make him—

"Fucking hell, Craig!" Christ, it takes both me and David, our tiler, to catch him and drag his arse back to the van.

Tossing his arms in the air in surrender, Craig paces between the van, me, and David. He looks like a predator circling its cage. Waiting for the right moment to pounce.

Jessica's father steps closer, reaching for him, this fucker has a death wish.

"Don't touch me. DO NOT FUCKING TOUCH ME!" Craig roars like a mountain lion.

Right. New tactic, fuck restraint, I need to get him in the damn van.

"I know you're angry," William reasons.

"Angry!"

Oh shit.

"You think I'm angry?"

Mate, angry is when he's on a diet. This isn't angry, this is homicidal.

"I never meant to—"

Craig swings, and I catch his arm. He yanks it free of my hold, ducks under David's outstretched arm and tries again. "Will you ever stay the fuck away from him!" I roar, trying my best to haul my brother back to the poxy van.

"I'm sorry!"

"Sorry?" Craig whirls around.

Please God, let Tiffy get his case, she'll accept a plea deal.

"You're sorry? Oh, you'll be fucking sorry!"

He's gone over the bonnet! Crap. I nearly had him that time.

I give chase, thankful for Dylan coming out and tackling Craig to the ground. "What the hell is going on?" Dylan asks as he struggles to keep Craig restrained.

Jessica sniffs and points to William, "he's my father."

"Why does Craig want to kill him?" David demands.

William steps forward and I swear I'm two seconds away from shanking him with the screwdriver in my toolbelt, what part of *stay away from Craig* does this man not get?

"I couldn't handle it. I ran, I'm sorry—"

"You bastard!" Craig snarls, writhes, and kicks to be free of us as we drag him to the van.

"She was my wife!" William argues.

Craig's reply is filled with thirty-two years of hatred, and heartbreak. ***"She was my mother!"***

Part of me wants to set Craig free. His so-called father deserves every excruciating second of it. What arsehole abandons their kid two months after their mother dies from a long battle with cancer? Craig will carve him up, I know he will. Which is why I'm not letting him go. I'm not having him getting banged up. Not allowing him to be taken from his children. We aren't blood, but we are family all the same and I'm not letting this prick take my brother from me.

"Craig," William begs.

Craig pulls free, "get the hell out of my way before I mow you down," he pulls open the van door and jumps inside.

Luckily, I have his keys. I snatched them in the scuffle. Pulling open the door, I nod to the passenger seat, "move. You're in no shape to drive."

I jump in next to him and start up the engine. Before I pull off, I see Dylan turn to Jessica, "if he's Craig's dad, that makes you—"

She nods, her face serious. And suddenly I can see it—the slightest resemblance in her face, "His sister."

LOTTIE

Jason rang to say he's bringing Craig home. I got a brief explanation from him about what happened, Nick was good enough to fill in the blanks and insisted on taking the kids for the night.

I've no idea what to expect when Craig gets home. How the hell do you prepare for something like this?

The man he ran into today is the same one that walked out on him after his mother died. He abandoned Craig at the age of eight and Craig has not heard a thing from him since. Craig has made it his mission to be as much of a helicopter parent as possible, he wouldn't miss the kids sneezing. He is all in, totally involved with the kids because he knows what it's like to be the kid that wasn't wanted. He makes up for the hurt with his quick wit, better to be known as the funny one than the victim. If there is anything he loathes more than anything it's pity.

I hear the van pull up and my nerves are already gone. What walks in the door is cold and lifeless, a walking shell of the man that left here this morning for work.

"Craig?" He doesn't even look at me.

I don't think he even sees me; he just floats up the stairs like a phantom.

Jason steps up beside me, watching Craig until he disappears out of sight. "In almost thirty years, I've never seen him like this."

I swallow the lump in my throat, my heart breaks for him, I can't even begin to comprehend how devastating this has been for him, "how bad?"

"He threw up a few times on the way back. He broke down, as you would, given the circumstances, then got angry again and kicked two litres of shit out of the dashboard, so the front of the van is in pieces."

"I don't care about the van."

"It's bad, Lottie," Jay brushes a hand over his face. "Real fucking bad."

"Has he said anything?"

"Not to me, nothing at all in about an hour," Jay looks at the staircase again, "do you want me to stay?"

"No, I'll handle it. Thank you for being there for him.

He won't be in work for a few days, at least."

Jason swallows, nodding his head slowly as he says, "understandable. I'll sort it out, don't worry." He turns for the door, hesitates, then spins back to me, "if you need anything."

"Thank you," I force a smile that I hope comes across as thankful because I am unbelievably grateful for Jason. When the door clicks shut behind him, I take a breath, steadying my nerve before I go in search of my husband.

I find him hovering between the kids rooms, "Craig?" he leans his shoulder against the doorjamb in Ethan's room. I slide my arms around his waist, and rest my head on his back, waiting for him to thaw and come back to me.

After a pregnant pause, Craig says, "he said he's sorry." His voice is low, and hoarse. "Like that changes a damn thing." He shifts, turning to stare into Ellie's room. "I couldn't do it, Lottie. I couldn't—" his voice breaks on a sob.

"I'm here," I reassure him, allowing him time to gather himself.

He wipes his eyes, turning to me so I'm looking right at him. "I thought about it a million times on the way back. I thought of every tortuous scenario that I could possibly think of, and I couldn't do it. I'd never be able to abandon my kids."

He becomes a blur and I realise I'm crying with him. For him.

I'm going to slice that prick from his throat to his ball sack for doing this to him. "You're not him," I say, placing my hand on his tear-stained cheek. "You never were."

Craig buries his face in the crook of my neck, I can feel warm droplets soaking through the fabric of my blouse and streaming down my back.

I hold him for as long as he needs, until his staggered breaths begin to level out and he pulls away from me.

Placing a chaste kiss on his jaw, I ask, "what do you need, baby?"

"I need this day to be over," he grumbles. "The kids?"

"Staying with Nick tonight," grabbing his hand, I lead him to the bathroom and turn on the shower. Craig stands in the doorway watching the water cascade from the showerhead.

I strip him and guide him under the water.

Craig braces a hand on the wall, leaning into the downpour. I strip, mirroring my actions in the hallway, I come behind him and wrap myself around him like a human security blanket.

I don't know what to say. There is nothing I can possibly say to fix this mess, so I do the only thing I can do, I wait with him under the rush of water and hold him for as long as he will allow—for as long as he needs me.

Craig eventually turns, dropping his head to my neck and nuzzling in close. He says nothing, but I feel his body begin to relax. "I love you," I kiss his shoulder and feel his lips twitch against my bare skin. It's a quick smirk but it's better than nothing.

Reaching for the body wash, I create a lather in my hands and work it around his chest and back. Craig lifts his head from my neck and instead, presses his forehead to mine. He watches my movements, all the while remaining silent.

As I reach to turn the water off, Craig's lips fuse with mine. He kisses me fiercely, possessively. There is a spark behind his eyes when he pulls away.

"I really want to hurt someone right now," he confesses.

"I know," I grin, not because he wants to exhaust himself in the ring and leave someone a bloody pulp. But because it's the first hint of him coming back to himself.

"You never ran from it. From me."

"And I never will," I know what he's hinting at. Not the time when I got majorly hormonal in my late pregnancy and thought he was dumping me, so I left him first—I still haven't forgiven myself for that.

I never ran from him. From the real Craig. My Craig.

He has a temper, a fierce one. Hell, anyone who read my debut book can tell you that—or anyone who followed Michael's court case for that matter.

There is a reason he fights in the ring, along with Jason and Dylan and a few others. It's their way of venting that aggression, a healthy outlet, so to speak.

I've known about his temper long before we ever got together. It never frightened me. Craig would never do a damn thing to hurt me or the kids, he hasn't got it in him. Outsiders, on the other hand, are another story.

I know who my man is. I know the worst things he had ever done, and I stay because I love him in spite of it. He's mine, and that bastard that calls himself a father is to blame for all of this.

I'm surprised that Craig didn't bludgeon him, though, I

suspect Jason is to thank for my husband not being locked up right about now.

"You must be starving," I hold his face in my hands, watching the warmth come back into his gaze.

"Not really—"

His stomach growls loudly.

"I know you might not want to, but you need to eat something."

He sighs and rakes his fingers through his hair, "ok."

"Go inside and dry off. I'll be up soon," Grabbing a towel, I wrap myself up and head to the kitchen.

CRAIG

All I want is for the bed to grow a mouth and swallow me whole.

I dry off and pull the covers back, I'm not in the mood for food but my stomach growling is telling Lottie another story, and I better not argue.

She comes upstairs with sandwiches and a cup of tea. Thank God she didn't put the dinner on because trying to eat with the way my stomach is feeling right now is a chore in itself.

Lottie crawls behind me, splaying her legs open. As soon as I recline, her legs wrap around me like a python. She's not about to let me go and, to be honest, I don't want to move.

Everyone has this weird notion that I'm Lottie's knight in shining armour. They think that she depends on me and that's it. They're wrong. Lottie is my personal security blanket. When shit hits the fan, she is the only one who I want to be near.

Even now, she knows that I don't want to talk about what

happened. Instead, of prying, she just lets me recline against her. Her arms and legs practically pin me in place once I'm done eating.

I can hear her heartbeat as I rest my head on her chest. She runs her fingers through my hair, and I melt to her touch.

I did this.

Me.

I started my own business. I got the girl of my dreams and made her my wife. I made three beautifully psychotic children with her. I built our house, and I worked my arse off for the life I have.

I did it all without William. I didn't need a father.

I don't need a father.

I have everything I could ever want.

The biggest part of my world is engulfing me as I lie here thinking about it.

Turning, I kiss her again, then nuzzle into my spot on her chest. She continues to play with the damp tufts of my hair and it's remarkably relaxing. I'm feeling less vindictive already.

Perhaps Tilly is more like me after all?

"I have a dream, I hope will come true," I don't know why but the lava song is stuck in my head right now. Lottie knows it immediately and joins in.

"That you're here with me, and I'm here with you."

I can't help the dopey smile that crosses my face.

"I lava you!" Lottie screeches, and the smile turns into fully-fledged laughter. "If I knew it was that easy to cheer you up, I would have sung it as soon as you came through the door!"

I crawl up to kiss her. "I love you, baby."

"I love you too, Batman."

"You're lucky you're pretty because you haven't got a note in your head."

"Meh," she shrugs.

I kiss her again, "thank you."

"For?"

"Being my Lottie."

"I'm yours and I always will be," she smiles, squeezing me between her thighs.

"What time is it?"

She pulls her phone from under her pillow, "just gone five."

"Is that it?"

"Yep," she kisses my forehead. "Rest, we can get takeout tonight. Have the rest of the day in bed."

"Sounds good," I don't know what I'm going to do

about work or with the information I found out today. Right now, I don't care. I have my Lottie. Nothing else matters.

LOTTIE

I suppose you could say it was a rough night of sorts. Craig didn't really sleep much, he remained taciturn and morose for the best part of the night, but the house was not turned over, so that's a plus.

I told the kids that daddy didn't go to work because he is not feeling well and now—well, he can't shake Tilly.

She comes into the room armed with a spoon and a bottle of squeezy honey, "mesin," she declares, and Craig looks like he's about to jump out the window.

"I don't need medicine, baby."

"Mesin," She shoves the spoon of honey into his mouth, and he has no choice but to swallow it. "Bed!"

"I'm not sleepy."

"Bed!" she shoves the spoon at me, along with the bottle of honey before turning back to her father.

"Tilly—"

"Now!" she interrupts his protests and marches him upstairs. She is determined to look after her father even if he does not want her help.

Matilda forces him into bed and then climbs onto his lap.

"Mickey Mouse will help you feel better," she insists, shoving the remote at him.

Ethan peeks around the door, "Dad?"

Matilda's head snaps around, and her face contorts into a scowl. "Out!"

Ethan ignores her, stepping into the room, he looks at Craig with his large doe eyes and asks, "Dad, are you ok?"

"Get out!" Matilda roars.

Craig rubs at his temples, snarling, "Matilda!"

"You sick, go for a nap," she insists. I don't know why he gives her that death stare, she's immune.

Craig's eyes flit to Ethan, and he forces a smile for our son's sake, "I'm fine, buddy. Just feeling out of sorts."

"Nap," Tilly demands, then turns back to her brother and demands he gets out.

I manage to avoid stepping on the numerous Lego pieces scattered about the landing, "Matilda, don't talk to your brother like that."

"My daddy," she pouts, locking onto Craig's arm with all the strength she can muster as if she's half expecting someone to swoop in and take him away.

"He's my dad too!" Ethan barks.

"No, mine."

"Ok, calm down, guys. Leave daddy alone to rest."

"Nap time," Tilly pushes Craig's head against the pillows and pulls the blankets up and over them both.

I'm not getting her out of there without a SWAT team, am I?

If she were not such a dictator this would be a really cute moment.

I take Ethan downstairs and make him and Ellie pancakes before they go out to play with their friends.

When they are done, I clean up the kitchen and debate working on my new book, calling Tiffy, or dare I say, calling Aidan Quinn and taking a hit out on that prick William.

Craig has told me several things about the man in the past few weeks—mainly since after our run-in with him at the hotel, I've been asking a lot of questions. For research purposes, obviously. I'm drifting towards darker romance and I'm thinking AJ has all the promise of the perfect book boyfriend.

Apparently, the papers have it wrong. AJ does not dabble in narcotics, that's not how he made his fortune. He took a more sinister route, and, from what I've heard, there isn't a shred of evidence that links him to his alleged crimes.

Then again, he is one person I'd happily cheer on. From my understanding, he *"allegedly"* takes down the scum of the earth. Rapists, woman beaters, paedophiles, those types who beat the system—they don't beat Quinn.

As Craig said, the man just does what the law can't. He stops them. I wonder if he'd be willing to add deadbeats to the list?

I go upstairs to find Craig and Tilly asleep in our bed. Tilly is holding onto Craig's hair and neck. She may be a terror, but when it comes down to it, she's a daddy's girl to her core.

The doorbell rings, and I go to see who it is.

"Josie," my face lights up. Thank God for this woman. "You have a key."

She smiles back at me, quirking an eyebrow, "I've learned to always ring the bell first," she lets out a musical laugh while she follows me into the kitchen. Setting her handbag on the counter, she looks around and then frowns. "How is he?"

"Tilly has him under house arrest, he's asleep at the moment—hi, George."

He strolls into the kitchen, looking about anxiously, "hello, darling," he reaches for my hand, placing a firm kiss on my knuckles.

Josie chews on her lip, "he's asleep at this hour?"

"He didn't really sleep last night," I admit. Popping the kettle on and pulling down three mugs.

Josie's eyes flit to a picture of the kids and Craig. Tilly is about ten months old, sitting on his shoulders and smiling brightly, showing off her two bottom teeth. Ethan is sticking his tongue out at the camera while Ellie is hugging her father's legs. "Understandable," is all the woman manages to say.

"He is better than I thought he'd be," I reassure her. "Only—"

"He's still bad," Josie nods in acknowledgement.

"Yeah," I sigh. Hearing the kettle click, I fill two mugs of tea and a latte for me. I need caffeine in an IV drip at this rate. "He's confused," I blow into my mug before taking a sip. "Angry, upset... all the above."

"My poor boy," her voice wobbles. If this woman starts crying now, she'll break me. Nothing is more heartbreaking than a Josie cry. I've seen exactly one in the entire time I've known her, and I'd pay out the nose to never witness it again.

"He's strong. He'll get through it; it was just a shock."

"He's been through far worse and made it out the other side," Josie gifts me a tight smile. "I can't believe that wanker would have the gall to show up after all this time."

"From what Craig told me, I don't think it was planned," I swallow a mouthful of coffee to muffle a groan. "It sounds like Jessica somehow found out that she had a brother, tracked Craig down, and I guess in trying to know him better—"

"Shit hit the fan," Josie nods.

"For lack of a better term."

"What's going on?" Craig's sleepy voice asks from the hallway. He wipes the sleep from his eyes as the pads of his feet slap on the cold wooden floor. "Hey, Josie," leaning down, he kisses her cheek and then steps around the counter.

"Great timing, the kettle just boiled. Tea, coffee?" I pull out another mug and set it down awaiting his reply.

"Coffee, please," he stretches across the counter and leans on his forearms.

"Coming up!"

Josie places her mug down, reaching for Craig's hand and giving a squeeze, "how are you, love?"

"I feel like I've been hit with a freight train," Craig sighs, leans down, and runs his hands over his hair.

George takes a hesitant step forward, "do you need us to do anything?"

Craig stands up, stretching his back, "no, thank you. I'm fine." Craig reaches for his mug and takes a sip. "Thanks, baby."

"Daddy!" Ellie bursts through the door, running to her father who puts on a brave face for her. "You're up."

Craig gives her a toothy smile, picks her up and swings her about before sitting back down. "Princess."

She lets out a happy squeal, then looks at him with hope-filled eyes and asks, "are you feeling better?"

"A little," he hunkers down to meet her at eye level. "You know what would make me feel much better?"

"What?"

"Mammy's cookies," he gifts her a conspiratorial smile, and she takes the bait immediately.

Ellie spins for me, "can we make cookies for daddy?"

My eyes flit to Craig who pushes out his lower lip in a pout, *damn him.* "Sure, we'll make them a little later, ok?"

"Ok!" she sprints out of the room.

"Cookies," I turn back to meet his gaze as he gets to his full height. "You're lucky you're cute."

"I'm adorable," he sniggers.

"I can't argue there."

Matilda thunders downstairs, "Scuse you!" she appears in the doorway, her hands planted firmly on her hips. "Who told you to get out of bed? Get back to bed, mister!"

George chuckles into his mug. "There is no messing around with her, is there?"

I see Matilda opening her mouth, ready to start a rant. I cut in before she can get another word in, “Matilda, Daddy is having a drink. You’ll have to wait.”

“But he’s sick!”

“He’s feeling better.”

She turns to Craig and asks, “did you take your mesin?”

“Yes.”

“Five minutes.”

“Yes, boss.”

Matilda turns her sights on me, “Mammy, I want a drink too!”

“Here’s some juice,” I pass down her sippy and she stomps off into the sitting room for a minute. “Two going on thirty that one.”

“She’s headstrong, didn’t lick that trait off the floor, you know,” Josie nudges Craig with her arm and smiles.

Craig snorts, “don’t know why you’re looking at me like that for?”

Josie cocks a quizzical eyebrow. “Oh, no?”

“No.”

“The barbeque?”

“We’ll be there,” Craig takes a mouthful of coffee,

hearing the little prison warden stomping back in at high speed. “Times up, back to bed!”

“Can I at least finish my drink?”

“Hurry up!”

Matilda guards our room for the rest of the day. That girl is better than a pack of guard dogs. Nobody is getting through her.

She barks orders at me to bring up drinks and treats and to tell me to change her wet nappies. That’s about it. I’m not allowed to sit with Craig, the only way Ellie got into the room was to bribe Tilly with cookies after we made them. Ethan went in fully armed with his lightsabre to fight Tilly off should she attack, even then, she still made him sit at the end of the bed.

"Night, stinky."

"Goodnight, baby."

"I check you tomorrow, ok?"

"Ok."

I bring Tilly to bed and tell her a story, when I come back into the room Craig is out of bed aiming for the stairs.

"Escaping already?"

"Nick and Jay are coming over."

"Drinks?"

"Yeah."

"That's fine. I'll just grab a book and get out of your hair. Make sure you eat something beforehand, yeah?"

"I will."

"I'll throw on a pizza to be safe."

"Don't trust me to eat?"

"Nope and you're no spring chicken anymore, Barnes.

The hangover will not be good to you."

"You don't mind."

"Not at all, but be warned, if you guys wake up Tilly, you're dealing with her."

"Noted."

CRAIG

Alcohol is anaesthetic. It puts one's primitive self in command, and right now, my primitive side is itching to spill blood.

The whisky smells like anger and bruised male ego.

Perfect.

Do I care that my sperm donor has been living it up with his new family for years, playing the role of a doting father to my half-sister and brother? No. I don't because I know it's an act. I know what he is—a fucking wanker.

I cut Nick off before he could divulge any more information because I will call AJ. I am seconds away from going Goodfellas on my sperm donor's arse. I can imagine it now, *get in the fucking trunk,* of course he'd cry and beg and then Jay would just smack him over the head with a shovel and everyone wins.

"Another," Nick demands, grabbing the bottle of J.D from the cabinet.

Jason side-steps him and reaches for the tequila instead, "shots,"

That's true friendship for you, they'll never let you go through it alone. Instead, they'll sacrifice their liver just to sit with you and wait out the storm—unlike some people who run the second things get hard. Oh, there's the anger again. I better swallow it, "bring it."

Jason pours three shots of tequila, and we down them in record time.

"I don't need that prick," was that a slur? I better slow down.

Jason wipes his mouth, "you never did. Fuck him."

"I'd rather fuck Lottie," I snort into my glass that I don't remember picking up.

"Hey!" Nick stretches the word out for all it's worth. "That's my sister."

"My wife."

Jason snorts, stumbles, and catches himself on the table, "hate that for you." He gives us a look that demands we forget we just saw that, then adds, "he's sticking it to her regularly, you know."

"Stop," Nick's hand comes up to cover his mouth.

"Please, stop."

Jason turns to me and announces, "I'll be your daddy."

I never want to hear him say that sentence again, "no thanks, I'm good."

"Ha! Rejected," Nick refills the shot glasses and I swear I can hear my liver protesting.

"I don't have a dad. My mam—" get the fuck down there, I'm not about to start crying right now. I cried when my mother died, and when Bobby died, my grandad was my father figure, the only one I needed. I never shed a tear again until Lottie came along. I shed a few tears when Ethan was born, she caught me by surprise on our wedding day, and when it came to Ellie's birth, I cried more than our newborn. With Matilda it was tears of sheer relief, her mother was a fucking antichrist in those last few weeks. That prick though, no. I didn't cry when he left and I'm certainly not going to cry now. "That's all that made me."

Nick lifts his head with great effort, "how did she do that?"

"What do you mean how did she do that? It's called a fucking turkey baster!" Jason stumbles back into the table, knocking over his glass. "Tiffy's going to kill me."

"Want to pass?" Nick asks, pushing a shot towards me.

"Not a chance, give it here!"

My eyes flit to the clock on the wall, 2: 30A.M, when did that happen? It was midnight ten minutes ago!

I don't know how I go from looking at the clock to the gallery on my phone, but I find myself staring at the beautiful bootylicious babe that I call my wife.

I didn't get to fight this one out of me. Jason refused to let me out of the house. He even stopped me from trying to escape through the window at one stage—he was right, of course, but I cursed him out regardless. Staring at my family photos right now, I realise that I don't want to fight anymore. I don't even want to be down in the kitchen or have another drink. "I'm going to bed."

Jason nods, kicks off his shoes and stumbles across the room, "me too!" he faceplants the couch cushion within seconds.

Nick settles himself on the blow-up bed with a pint of water beside him. I don't know who he's fooling, he'd need a reservoir to counteract the damage done tonight.

I trip on the third stair from the bottom, catch myself on the bannister, and then slowly stagger up the rest. I've no idea how I haven't woken the kids up yet.

Why is it always when you're trying to be quiet that you're much louder than intended?

I make it back to the bedroom in one piece—just about.

Attempting to pull my shirt overhead, I fall into the wardrobe, waking Lottie.

"Craig!" she's across the room before I manage to untangle myself.

"Who put that there?" I right myself and stretch out my back. If I wasn't drunk, I'm sure I would have popped a hip or blown out my back. That's gonna hurt in the morning. "You," I'm trying to go for charming right now, but I think I come across as the little drunk man from Tangled. "Are," I lean in to kiss her, Lottie must think I'm going to fall forwards because she lunges to keep me upright. Well, if I didn't have a bruised ego before, I certainly do now. "Stunning."

"Craig."

"You remembered my name," that's gotta be the tequila talking.

"How much—I don't want to know. Come on, let's get you to bed."

"That's exactly what I was thinking," I'd like to say that I'm more graceful taking my damn pants off, but sadly I end up on my back with my jeans around my ankles. At least I made it onto the bed. "Come to me, woman."

"You're pissed."

"And? I'm just re-enacting our first night together," I reach for her and pull her down to me. My tongue glides against hers.

Lottie pulls away, "I can't do anything, remember?"

We have towels!

"Lottie," I roll her onto her back, dropping my mouth to her breasts. I can feel the rising peaks of her nipples through the flimsy lace material on her nightshirt.

"Craig, you're drunk."

"Not drunk enough that I don't know what I'm doing."

Her back arches, gifting me with more than a mouthful to suckle.

"Craig," Lottie pushes me away. Her gaze burns into me, I don't know what she sees but whatever it is, it makes her relax beneath me and say, "you need this, don't you?"

"More than I need my next breath."

She holds onto me, guiding me to the mattress. She's

probably afraid that I'll fall off the bed otherwise. "Let me take care of you."

I kick free of my jeans and boxers, springing free. I grin up at her, if I was too drunk, I'd never be able to salute her like this.

I feel her tongue run from base to tip, flicking across the head. Her soft voice follows my breathy moan, "you like that, baby?"

"I need you to destroy me."

I feel her move, and then the bedside light comes on, dazzling me. "You can barely stand," she reasons.

"Want a bet?"

"Are you sure you can handle it?" concern and the tiniest hint of challenge spark behind those beautiful green eyes.

"Get on the bed," I get to my feet while Lottie moves to the edge of the mattress, hanging her head over the edge and waiting for me to come to her.

She runs her tongue up and down my cock before taking it into her mouth. Lottie reaches for my hips, pulling me closer and I get the hint, she's ready.

I thrust, feeling myself sliding straight down her throat. Lottie moans, and I lose all self-control. The sight of her on her back with my cock rammed down her throat, and my hands on her soft, perfect tits have me on the brink of explosion pretty damn quickly.

This blowjob is a fucking war crime in some countries. If the UN ever catches wind of what's happening in this bedroom, somebody's getting sanctioned.

"Fuck, yeah, just like that," I thrust harder. She takes everything I give her, and she takes it with pleasure.

I barely feel myself build to a climax, I must have blacked out from desire alone, is that possible?

With my wife if fucking is.

I've to reach for the headboard, to keep my legs from buckling. Lottie swallows every last drop, then rolls to her knees with a grin. Her cheeks are flushed, and her skin is glowing. I have teeth marks embedded in my knuckles from biting down on my fist, it looks like I broke the skin in places.

Lottie slides her hands over my shoulders and hauls me for a possessive kiss.

This is the only family I need. The people under this roof. My wife, kids, Jason, Nick... Josie, can't forget her. This is my family.

I pull away, elated, and pissed off, "I wanted to taste you."

"You'll have to wait a few more days."

"I hate waiting."

I know with some couples, they bitch and moan about going down on their other half, like it's some kind of chore. I don't know what their problem is. I love tongue-fucking Lottie. I love the way she tastes. I love hearing her moan, seeing her writhe beneath me, or better yet, on top of me. I do it for my own pleasure as well as hers.

My girl has a sex drive to match my own. We're in it for each other, it's not a case of getting ourselves off. It's more of a competition to see who can make the other come the hardest.

She got me good just now, I'm still seeing stars. I can't reciprocate right now, and I detest it.

Her lips brush mine again and I melt to her touch. I don't know if it's down to the alcohol or the orgasm but I'm feeling much better now.

I lower myself to the bed, pulling Lottie to me by the hips. "You're not to move for the night."

"Not even a little?" she giggles, reaching for the bedside lamp and turning it off.

I bring my hand down hard on her arse. She hisses then moans. "You like that?"

"Maybe."

I do it again and get the same reaction. My hand slams

down for a third time. Lottie turns, snagging my lower lip in her teeth, I growl. My grip on her hips tightening.

"As soon as we're all clear I want you to rattle this headboard. I want you to take your frustrations out on me, baby."

I can do it now if you'd let me. "How do you want it?"

"Deep, hard and fast."

I latch onto her neck, sucking hard. Lottie gasps, writhes, and moans as I mark her for the world to see.

"You arsehole."

"You love it."

"Shut up and kiss me."

Somewhere in between the groping and kisses, we fall asleep.

Blinking awake to the noise of the demon child running into the room, I groan. Her heavy footfall is amplified due to the hangover. "Daddy!"

"Mammy, help!" I moan, burying my face in Lottie's

neck, I attempt to hide from our toddler.

"Tilly," Lottie snorts, "Uncle Nick and Jason are downstairs. Go wake them up so they can turn on Micky Mouse."

"Ok!"

Ethan's next to pop his head in, "Dad?"

"I'm not here."

"Dad had a bit too much to drink last night, Ethan."

"Oh... do you need a bucket?"

That happened one time!

"No, buddy. I'm good. Just let me wake up first, yeah?"

"Ok," he turns for the stairs.

Ellie comes bounding into the room seconds later, "Daddy!"

"Do you lot not have a mother?" I grab the pillow and stuff my head under it.

"I'm an illusion," Lottie teases, pulling herself from me.

"Lottie, please!" *Get your tits out.* "I'm dying."

"You're old."

Screw you too, love.

"Daddy, are you still sick?"

"I've got the plague."

"Is that like man-flu?"

Lottie cackles, "that's exactly it, babe. You nailed it! The lesson here, Ellie, is when it comes to any sort of illness, a man is useless."

I pull my head from under the pillow scowling at the ensuite door, turning my head, I find my target. "Hey!"

"Mammy, what happened to your neck?"

Lottie stops pulling things from her drawer to look in the mirror, her head snaps to me, "Craig!"

"Daddy," Ellie looks horrified. "Did you do that?"

"My bad," I offer my wife a toothy smile before burying my head under the pillow again. "I must have thought mammy was a snack."

"How did you think that?"

"She just looked good enough to eat, I guess."

"Craig!"

I pull my head free of my squishy helmet, "what? You're the other white meat!"

Ellie's nose wrinkles, she turns to Lottie, frowning, "Daddy's being weird again."

"That's just the old age talking, sweetie."

"Still going with the pensioner jokes, huh?" I ask as Ellie turns to leave the room and sniff out her uncles.

"What are you going to do, spank me?" challenge flashes in her eyes and if it were not for the kids and this damn hangover, I'd have her over my knee right now.

“I’m starving here!” Matilda roars up the stairs, followed by Nick shouting, “yeah, come on, Lottie, we’re famished!”

“Jay’s cooking!” I call down to Jason’s dismay.

“I’m what now?”

“Tilly baby, tell Uncle Jay to throw on a fry up!” In 0.2 seconds, the dictator is barking out orders.

Lottie tosses on her oodie and follows the kids downstairs while I muster up the strength to get out of bed.

LOTTIE

I don't know what made me do it. Perhaps it is the mama bear instinct in me to protect my own. True, Craig is not my cub, but he is most definitely this bear's mate and I'm not about to send him out to have him hurt again.

I take a deep breath to calm the vortex raging inside me and then enter the restaurant. A blonde head springs up from the table nearest the bar, "Charlotte!" Jessica is up and out of her chair before I can take another step. "I'm so glad you called."

"It's good to see you again," she goes in for a hug, but I'm not really a hugger, not unless I know the person well. I dodge the incoming squeeze and offer my hand in place of my torso.

"I thought Craig would be joining us," the thing that hurt my husband whines. I turn to the owner of the gruff voice. His salt-and-pepper hair is neatly styled, his beard trimmed tightly against his square jaw. I'm already contemplating murder.

So, this is the arsehole who abandoned my husband all those years ago. Craig looks nothing like him.

A part of me wants to punch William's nose into the back of his skull, but I refrain.

I did agree to sit with them both when I contacted Jessica—William insisted he join us.

I take my seat across from him, he's as tense as a coiled spring.

Good.

Dickhead.

Jessica takes the seat beside her father and clears her throat, "how is he?"

"Good. He's doing good, it was a shock."

Jessica practically springs from her chair, "I never intended—"

"Shit happens, it can't be helped." I shrug, then turn my gaze to the man of the hour, "why are you here, William?" I knew he demanded to come but I want to know why. Why now?

"As I said," he rolls his shoulders back, trying to pass himself off as confident. "I thought my son would be here."

"So, he's your son now?" I scoff.

"I know what you must think of me."

"You have no idea," I tap my acrylic nails on the tabletop, I got stilettos today, especially for this occasion. It will make it easier to claw his eyes out.

There is a silence that I'm not about to fill, though I don't blame Jessica per se, she did go about it all wrong though, so I'll allow them both to stew.

"Craig and Lottie have three children, Daddy," Jessica blurts out, squirming in her seat. I don't know why. I didn't put the match there.

William's eyebrows shoot to his hairline, "three?"

"Yes," I confirm, "two more than you abandoned." I open the menu and hide behind it, laughing to myself; he hadn't expected that.

After a brief silence I hear a new voice, "are you ready to

order?" I peek over the menu to see our waitress pulling out a notepad and pen from her pocket.

Ooh food, yes. One of the reasons I haven't caused a scene yet. I'm starving.

"I'm so sorry," William turns on his charm and it's then that I catch the slightest glimpse of Craig in the man. "We were busy catching up on old times."

I'm half expecting his nose to double in length, Pinocchio style.

He hands the girl back the menu without looking at it. "We'll have the sharing platter. I saw one going by for another table, it looked amazing."

Our server clicks her pen and begins to scribble, "mixed meats or seafood?"

"Seafood."

"Actually," I slap my menu down on the table. "I can choose for myself. I'll take the barbecue wings to start with and then the grilled chicken burger, no red onion."

"Good choice," the waitress grins, "and to drink."

"Coke, please," William offers up a dapper smile.

"Fanta," I scowl at him briefly before passing our server the menu. She offers me a sly smirk as she stalks off.

"Well," William sighs. "That was embarrassing."

"Indeed, you must be used to making an arse out of yourself by now."

William's fist slams on the table, "just what is your problem with me?"

Ah, there he is. The prick incarnate.

"My problem," I lean in, matching his glare with one of my own. "Is that you abandoned your eight-year-old son shortly after his mother died. My problem is that you ensured to stay out of his life for thirty-two years and then you have the brass balls to show up out of the blue one day and expect to see him like you hadn't

Houdinied your way out of his life." My voice raises three octaves, and I'm drawing the eyes of other diners. I don't care. Let them watch. Let them record it and stick it on TikTok—expose me for being a psycho but I'll take this piece of shit down with me.

"You're lucky I promised to be on my best behaviour today," I jab a sharpened nail at him. "Otherwise, I would have bounced your head off the table by now."

William pushes himself back in his seat, his mouth ajar. He's speechless.

Jessica reaches for my hand, distracting me, "can you tell me a bit more about my brother, Charlotte?" This poor girl. I'll happily spit venom at the thing that sired her, but she has done nothing to earn my wrath.

"What do you want to know?" My shoulders relax, and I slowly push myself back in my seat.

"How long have you known him?"

"Thirteen years."

"Wow, and what is he like, usually? I've only caught glimpses."

"Craig is—"

"Your drinks," our server places our drinks on the table and I'm debating asking her for something stronger.

"Thank you," we all say in unison.

"Perfect," I admit. "My husband is a good man. He is a devoted father." I take a sip of Fanta, allowing my words to sink in. "He's a hard worker, highly intelligent. He does have a temper but having to fend for himself from a young age, who wouldn't?"

"He seems very," Jessica takes a sip from her drink, debating the right choice of wording before she continues, "closed off."

"He doesn't trust a lot of people. Craig has always kept people at arm's length. Only those lucky enough to wriggle their way closer to him get to see what he is."

"You really love him."

"I do. He is my husband and best friend rolled into one."

I'm sensing William wants to ask me something, but he seems a bit unnerved.

"So," Jessica perks up, flipping her long platinum blonde hair behind her shoulder. "How old are the kids?"

"Eight, six and three," I smirk. It all makes sense why she was acting so strange. She was asking about Craig and the kids to try and get to know her brother and her nieces and nephew. "Though Tilly is more like a hormonal teenager than a toddler."

"She's gorgeous."

"She has to be to make up for that attitude," I'm soon laughing with Jessica, almost forgetting the elephant at the table until he finally finds his voice, asking "all girls?"

"No," and the smile is gone. How dare he ruin my happy buzz. "Two girls and a boy. Ethan is our eldest."

Jessica gasps, "you were pregnant with him when," she stops herself. Her eyes double in size.

"When Michael came to our house and tried to stab Craig," I nod.

William gulps half his glass, "he's blessed to have walked away from that."

"He's blessed that Bobby put him into martial arts from the age of nine. Craig is a black belt in Taekwondo, a champion boxer, and has won numerous MMA fights."

Sometimes I have to remind myself that this is the man I married and not just another fictional character living rent-free in my head. My husband is a force of nature. It's easy to forget that when I'm busy staring at his arse or begging him to fuck me.

"Michael," I continue, "came to our house with a weapon, trying to get the upper hand on a man he knew he couldn't take. He failed to see that Craig is a weapon all on his own."

Ooh, the first chance I get, I'm so getting those handcuffs

out. Locating my phone in my handbag, I type out a quick suggestive text to Craig.

"So, it's Ethan, Matilda and..." Jessica pulls me from the lurid text on my screen.

"Eleanor, we call her Ellie."

"Eleanor," William echoes. He seems shocked for some strange reason. We called Ellie after Craig's mother.

"Daddy's girl through and through, they both are" I admit.

Our waitress is back with our food, "is there anything else I can get you?"

"No, thank you," I reach for a chicken wing, spinning it in my fingers while I glance at Jessica. "Why now?"

She chews on her bottom lip and shoots an awkward glance at her father. "Once I found out I had another brother, I... I had to find him."

"Understandably," I nod, practically suck the chicken from the bone and then glare at William. "You never told her?"

"No."

I bite into another wing, feeling my features harden at his admission. I tear into three more wings, giving my mouth something to do than take a chunk out of William, I'm two seconds away from skewering the bastard. Turning my gaze back to Jessica, I ask, "how did you find out?"

"My friends were going on about some hot hero carpenter that was all over the news," she glances anxiously at her father before continuing. "Dad found me looking him up," her eyes flit to me, "just out of curiosity to see what all of the fuss was about."

"I thought someone told her," William admits. His guilty expression is enough for me to put together what happened next.

"Lose your shit, huh," I say more than ask as I toss a bone back into the bowl and reach for another wing.

"He had to explain in the end," Jessica sighs, then glares at

William. “He told me to stay away. I tried, I really did but then my friend Darcy hired a company to help her renovate her new house and Craig showed up. She didn’t know he is my brother, she just bragged about the “hot carpenter” from the news working on her house.” Jessica pokes at the food on her plate, “when mum agreed to sell me the old family house, I got the idea to call the company about doing the kitchen.”

I can understand that it was an easier way to look into this man and meet him.

“I never thought daddy would show up with the work being done.”

“I see,” poor Jessica, next to Craig, she really got the shit end of the stick.

“You can think what you want of me,” William begins.

“Don’t worry, I was doing that without your permission.”

“Don’t judge without being in my position,” he contends.

It’s something that has me laughing, albeit cruelly. “I’m a mother of three. If, God forbid, anything happened to Craig, I would never abandon my children.”

“You don’t know what you’re talking about!”

Forget his eyes, I’m clawing out his tongue.

“My wife died, slowly. She withered away in front of us. I was heartbroken. Craig looks just like her…”

Thank God for that.

“Every time I looked at him, I saw Eleanor. I had to leave.”

“Dickhead.”

“Excuse me?” he has the audacity to look affronted.

“Dickhead. Coward. Wanker. Scrotum licker—”

“I don’t have to put up with this shit!” He slams his hands on the table and moves to stand.

“By all means, run away, it’s what you do best.”

His face is turning crimson. He wants to call me out, but he has absolutely nothing to go on, other than me being rude. Sue me.

"My father died when I was twelve," I sit back, cold and calculating. This is a side of myself that I don't show very often. One that surfaced after Michael tried to steal away the love of my life. Or perhaps she was always there, and I needed one more trauma for her to blink her callous eyes open and step in for the sweet bumbling Disney fan. "Similar circumstance," I continue. If he wants me to feel sorry for him, he's sadly mistaken. "We were in the room when he died. My brother is every bit my father. He even has his name." I pause, allowing that information to sink in before I pop that overinflated ego of his. "My mother never ran. Not once. She never abandoned us because she felt sorry for herself. Justify it as much as you want in your own head, William. At the end of the day, you chose to walk, and you chose to stay away. You were a shit father."

"Hey!" Jessica hisses.

"Hello," my eyes flit to meet hers. "You may have come from the same sac, but you and Craig have two very different fathers."

She gulps, unsure of what to say to that.

"You look like a daddy's girl. Be thankful he got his shit together by the time you came along, but my husband was the price paid for the man you know now."

"I made a mistake," William all but growls at me.

"A mistake is getting drunk and having sex without a condom. A mistake is missing your turn-off on the motorway. A mistake is any insignificant detail in daily life. This, on the other hand, is no mistake. You had years to reach out and you never did so spare me the pity party."

"I do love him, you know."

"You've got a funny fucking way of showing it."

"Charlotte," Jessica starts, calmly. "Do you think there is any chance for a relationship with us?"

I sigh, pinching the bridge of my nose. I need to remind myself that Jessica is not the problem here, just the catalyst. "For you, if you genuinely want to have a relationship with him, I can't see him shutting you out. It might be a slow process," I lower my hand and look at her big doe eyes. "It's a lot to take in."

"I understand," she smiles weakly, but there is a glimmer of hope in her eyes now.

I turn back to the whiney man-baby, "don't expect to be welcomed back with open arms, William. Curse me out, call me whatever name you want. I couldn't care less what a slimy, good-for-nothing cockroach like yourself has to say about me. If you want back in with Craig... grovel."

I lean back in the chair, admiring the play of light on my new claws. I allow my fingers to dance in the stream of sunlight, catching the sun in my eternity ring and sending tiny rainbows onto the table. Craig is mine. I'll go to bat for him every time. If that results in covering up a body... I'm sure AJ would help... for a price.

"Get on your hands and knees and repent. Crawl over hot coals and when your skin is scorched, blistered and bleeding profusely maybe he will forgive you. *Maybe.* If by some miracle my husband does forgive you and allow you into our lives—" I contemplate swallowing the ball of venom building in the back of my throat. Instead, I sharpen my tongue. "If you ever so much as pass on a cold to him, I swear to Christ, I will bury you."

Willaim scoffs, "resorting to empty threats now?"

"Empty," my head falls back on a cackle. "My brother is a detective. I have a degree in forensic psychology, criminology and crime scene investigation. You'd be surprised what I can do with some kitty litter and a shovel."

William gulps audibly.

CRAIG

I hear the front door opening and Lottie's heels tapping on the floor as she comes into the kitchen. "Hey, handsome."

"Hey, baby."

"I'm the baby!" Tilly protests.

"Of course, how stupid of me," I roll my eyes to the heavens. This one just doesn't come with an off switch.

"Have they had dinner?" Lottie asks, strutting her way to the counter and plopping a box down.

"All done."

"And you?" she spins, quirking an eyebrow at me.

"Tilly spoon-fed me, I'm good," I lean to the side to catch a glimpse of what she's hiding. "What you got there?"

"I want to Kelly Lou's on the way home—"

"CAKE!" Tilly yells, she's practically scaling the counters to get to the box.

"Ethan, Ellie!" Lottie calls.

"Cake!" Matilda roars.

It's like a stampede coming downstairs.

Ethan is the first in the door, "cake?"

"What kind?" Ellie shoves past him.

Lottie pulls out a variety box of muffins and, like the savages my kids are, they pounce.

Lottie's heels clip-clop on the tiles as she moves for me, grinning, "I managed to save this for you."

Red velvet. My second favourite thing to eat. "Thanks, babe." I clock the colourful daggers on her hands and ask, "new claws?"

"Yep!" she squeaks, then skips across the tiles. "I went to the salon. I know how much you like it when I get my nails done," she winks and saunters towards the presses putting extra emphasis on her hips.

I do love it when she gets her nails done, specifically when we get a window for sex, and she scrapes them along my back and chest.

Damn, I'm starting to tent just thinking about it.

"You're awfully perky today, who did you kill?" I ask, watching her fish out two glasses.

"No one!"

"Baby—"

"I'm the baby!" Tilly roars around a mouthful of muffin.

"Sorry!"

"I promise," Lottie smiles, "I never raised a hand or weapon to anyone."

"Hungry?"

"No, I had a big lunch."

"Oh?"

"I feasted on the souls of the damned," she snorts.

"Ah, that explains it."

The kids scurry into the sitting room, and I'm left staring at my boobalicious wife. Getting to my feet, I approach her, "so," I stretch out the word for all it's worth. "Last night was fun."

"I'm surprised you remember it," she pours herself a glass of milk, watching me as if she's expecting me to swoop in on her.

"Can't forget a blow like that."

"How romantic."

"I do try," I slide behind her, bringing my mouth to her ear. "Besides, you were anything but ladylike last night."

"I didn't hear you complain," she straightens, possibly debating if she should slap me or not.

"You never will," I squeeze her tightly and snag the whorl of her ear between my teeth. "That was hotter than hell," she lets out a breathy moan as I nip at her neck. "You're my little minx."

"And what does that make you?" she looks up at me, grinning.

"Your bitch for the most part."

"Can't argue there."

"Hey, if the collar fits," pulling up a seat, I take a bite from my muffin. Happy to stay here with Lottie while the kids are quiet.

Her eyes twinkle, and she steps toward me slowly. Then she straddles me, running the tip of her tongue over the seam of my lips.

I lean in to kiss her, but she pulls away, grinning. "You fucking tease."

"Careful now, or I might have to spank you."

"I'll put you over my knee a hell of a lot faster than you can put me over yours," I'd love nothing more than to redden that peachy arse.

"I quite enjoy that," she leans in, kissing me again. "I'm glad you're feeling better."

"How can I not? Between your magical mouth last night and Tilly not drop-kicking me in the balls for two days, it's been quite pleasant." Then I say the words I know will make her uneasy. "I'm going back to work tomorrow.

She stiffens, the lazy smile disappearing from her face quicker than a blink, "you sure?"

"Yeah," I sigh. I'm not really but I can't hide at home forever. "Office only. I'm not ready to..." I try for a casual smile, but I know it's tighter than my belt after Christmas.

"Craig," Lottie tilts my chin up so I have to look her in the eye. "You don't need to justify yourself to me. Take all the time you need."

"I need to get on with things," I admit. "Sorting out the paperwork will be the distraction I need to keep my mind off everything. Jason and I have been falling behind on it lately because neither of us can be arsed, two birds one stone."

"You know I love you."

I know. I can see it in her eyes as she looks at me right now, "I love you too."

"I was thinking—"

"Sex?"

"Still bleeding."

"Bollocks," there goes my plan.

"Jessica," Lottie pauses, allowing the name to sink in. Gauging my reaction before she continues, "what's the plan with her?"

"I—" I was not expecting to have this conversation so quickly. "I don't know."

"She did try to reach out. I think she genuinely wants to get to know you."

"Why?"

Lottie shakes her head, smirking. "Well, you are her big brother."

"He—"

"Has nothing to do with it. He doesn't exist," Lottie grumbles, "Jessica?"

I don't know. I honestly haven't a clue what I should do. How do you go from being an only child for forty years to suddenly having younger siblings? It's weird. It's complicated. I'm getting a headache just thinking about it. "What do you think I should do?"

"I think it would be nice for you two to get to know each other. William be damned. He does not need to be in our lives. Jessica shouldn't be punished for his actions."

Why must she be so rational? "She has a brother you know."

"Well," Lottie grins again, "so do you."

I open my mouth to argue but she beats me to it, "if you never want to see that prick again, I'll stand by you, but if your siblings want to reach out, don't you think you can at least try?"

"And say what?" the question comes out more aggressive than I mean it to. I'm at a loss, how do I open that can of worms? Hi, I'm the kid your dad never wanted, sorry my existence is an inconvenience to you.

"You'll figure it out."

"How would I even go about it?" I beg. She's the smart one. I can't be left to my own devices here. I'll crack and end up locked up.

"Josie is doing that barbecue soon; you could invite Jessica."

"I don't know, Lottie."

"Think about it?"

"Ok," I tilt my head back, staring at the ceiling. "For you."

"I. Love. You" every word is punctuated by a kiss.

"Drop. Your. Pants."

Lottie giggles, pushing herself from my lap, "nice try."

CRAIG

It's rare when I end up in the office, it happens about twice a month. If that. The perks of running this place mean Jay and I do very little work. We spend most of our time at home, only going on site when we are short-staffed, we don't even need to work the phones anymore, that's Amy's job.

"Mr Barnes," she practically bounds off her seat when she sees me enter.

"Amy," I offer her a curt nod in response and head for my office. Well, Jay and I share despite there being ample space for two. We just end up in the same room anyway.

Jay is more of a people person out of us both, he is on a first-name basis with Amy. She tends to refer to me as Mr Barnes or Sir when I'm around.

At the end of the day, she's an employee, the formality makes it easier to keep things professional here.

I step into the office and sigh at the decorating job Lottie and Tiffy did here. I think Tiffy wanted somewhere to act out her Fifty Shades fantasy. She's down here with Jason a hell of a lot more than Lottie's here with me.

There is a pile of contracts on the desk, and I'm really not arsed in dealing with them, but it's better to work here than to go back to Jessica's. I did my part anyway. I pulled out everything. Jason had Stephen install the new floors upstairs, and I'll probably only be called to help put in the new kitchen when the guys are done rewiring and tiling the place.

A hesitant knock sounds from the door. I glance up to see Amy slowly edging her way into the room. "Can I get you anything, sir?"

"No, Amy. I'm good thanks," I look about the room and ask, "when was the last time Jason was here?"

"Two days ago," I could be mistaking but I'm almost certain that there is a hue of pink in her cheeks.

"Alone?"

"With his wife," she admits. Oh yeah, that pink is turning crimson. Poor girl.

"Ah," instinctively I push away from the desk.

"I already cleaned up after they left," her brown eyes are locked on the floor as if the mere sight of the desk brings back memories she would rather forget.

"Remind me to sort out a pay rise for you, yeah."

She stifles a laugh, nods, and then turns for the door. As soon as I hear the click, I turn Spotify on full blast and get started with the paperwork.

The next thing I know, I'm glancing at the clock to see it's 12:30. Those three hours flew by. Nothing on my phone from Lottie or Jay so I ignore the other messages.

Digging through the drawers, I find a packet of cigarettes and a lighter stuffed in the back of the second last drawer. A box of condoms is shoved in the top—obviously Jason's.

Cracking open the window, I light up. I've cut right back since having kids, usually only having the odd cigarette on a night out, but after the week I've had, I think I deserve one.

I spot something moving out of the corner of my eye and see Amy's wavy brown head poking into the room. She must have knocked, the music is still blasting so I didn't hear her. "Alexa, stop."

"Sorry, sir. There is someone here to see you," she says sheepishly.

"Who?"

"A young woman. Blonde hair, thin, tried to say she's your sister," Amy says in a tone that says *does it look like I was born yesterday?*

I'm going to have to fill her in at some point.

Urgh, I hate being put on the spot. I knew this was coming but I had hoped I could escape this conversation a bit longer. "Yeah, ok. Send her in."

Pulling the window shut, I circle the desk. My arse just hits the seat when the sound of heels clip, clop on my wooden floor. "Jessica."

"How are you?" her hands are behind her back. She looks anxious.

"Good thanks. What are you doing here?"

She glances around, worrying her bottom lip, "can we talk?" She offers up a familiar white box with and pink ribbon sealing it shut. "Lottie said you're a fan of Kelly Lou's. I thought you might be hungry."

That devious little— "I didn't realise you two were in contact." I don't want to do this but I've no choice now. Not that I'm face-to-face with her. I take Jessica's measure. There aren't many similarities between us. She's shorter, fairer skinned, different jawline—she's blessed there. Her delicate features would be ruined by the Desperate Dan jaw.

I look at the chair opposite me and she takes the hint. "I didn't mean for him to be there," she starts before she's even sitting down.

"It's fine."

"It's not. I still don't know what to make of it all," she admits. "Finding out about you, about what he did—"

"Shit happens."

"It shouldn't have happened."

I sit back in my chair, running my hands over my face and through my hair. What am I supposed to say to that? What's done is done. The man is scum, no use dwelling on it.

Jessica pops the lid on the box open and pushes it towards me, "you must be hungry."

Damn.

She got the afternoon tea. Sandwiches. Cream cakes. Cookies. Scones... goodbye abs, I just found you again.

"I don't want to talk about him," I confess, eyeballing a particularly mouth-watering mini red velvet muffin.

"That's fine. I understand, but if it's ok with you, I would like to get to know my brother."

Well shit. She brought my weakness right at lunchtime.

She's obviously been speaking with my wife who is going to have an exceptionally cherry-red arse after this. The little minx must approve of Jessica, or she wouldn't have told her how to soften me up.

I guess I can't really blame Jessica for her father's actions.

I reach for the red velvet mini muffin and a few of the little cream cakes that I never get at home because Lottie and the kids get there first. Biting down, savouring the sweet flavours, I wish I had a bottle of whisky in here to take the sting out of this conversation.

I swallow the cake and my pride, "what do you want to know?"

LOTTIE

I don't know how Craig is going to take it today. I know his feelings for *he who should not be named* but Jessica seems genuinely interested in wanting to get to know Craig. To get to know her brother. Is that such a crime? I can imagine this whole thing has been hard on her too. I mean, if I just discovered that I had a brother out there that I knew nothing about—first, I'd be pissed, necks would be snapped, jaws would be broken. I'm talking total bitch fit.

I would want to know who he is, where he is. I'd want a chance to know this person and make up my mind to decide if I wanted them in my life. I feel sorry for Jessica, having the rug pulled out from under her like that, I can imagine she felt a sense of betrayal too—obviously nothing compared to Craig's but still, the sperm donor has a lot of explaining to do. To her, at least. I doubt Craig will give him the time of day and I'm not listening to his piss poor excuses.

I hear the front door open and brace myself for hurricane husband.

Matilda must have gone to investigate; I hear her greet Craig as warmly as ever.

"Hey, baby," his gruff voice comes from the hall. It's happy, albeit forced. I know him well enough by now to know the level of pissed-off laced in even his 'happy words.'

"Where's mammy?"

Oh shit.

Matilda, bless her little cotton socks, outright lies for me and says she doesn't know. She must sense daddy is out for blood.

"Lottie?" his footsteps scrape and pad down the hallway in a casual stride. "Charlotte?"

Double shit! He never calls me that. I'm screwed.

Sorry, Tilly, you're on your own. Mamma has a plane to catch.

I bolt into the kitchen, hearing him gaining on me. "Charlotte."

I can't hear you.

He skids into the kitchen, blocking my way to the backdoor. I turn, slide, and run back for the stairs taking two at a time. That lanky bastard is quick to follow.

Craig catches me in a dive, sending us both tumbling through the threshold of the door to our bedroom.

His primal breathing is loud and husky. I shrink into the floorboards beneath me as he looks me in the eye and growls, "Charlotte." He covers my body with his, pinning my hands to the floor.

"Oh, you're home early," I grin sheepishly, and he narrows his eyes in response.

"You've been a very naughty girl."

"You're sexy when you're angry," I wiggle under him, for comfort more than anything else, I'm almost certain that I've a tiny action figure poking into my back.

"I'm not angry," his eyes flash, dark and menacing.

I gulp, "disappointed?"

"No."

"Horny?"

"A little," I follow his gaze to my breasts and back again. He inhales deeply, getting his bearings, "you've been speaking to Jessica. Explain yourself."

"No."

"What?"

Craig and I share similar traits, our dark sense of humour, our high libidos, and one other trait he seems to be forgetting right now, we tend to hold grudges. "No," I say obstinately. "You have kept things from me in the past *for my own good.*"

I'm referring to Michael's harassment and the phone calls Craig never told me about.

"So," he looks between us again, the tip of his tongue darts out, wetting his lips, "this is payback?"

"This is you practically mounting me."

The corners of his mouth kick up, "you should have told me."

"You should have kissed me. Instead, I got rugby tackled."

He has the gall to look abashed, "you like it rough."

"Yeah, I do!"

Craig snorts, rising to his full height. He reaches out, helping me to my feet. "So?" I prod. He obviously spoke with her. I want to know how it went.

"Jessica will be at Josie's barbecue," he concedes.

"Good."

"Daddy!" Tilly roars from the hallway.

"Yes, baby?"

"Mickey's gone!"

I smirk at him, "you best go down and hit continue or she'll scream the house down."

We go downstairs and Craig sets up another round of Mickey Mouse for Tilly. I was hoping she would nap for me, I had her at the park all morning and she refused to sleep when we got home, so now I've grouchy pants on my hands. Tiffy took Ethan for a day out and a sleepover tonight because Jamie was doing her last nerve in, and she needed a distraction for him.

Ellie is gone off with Abbie and Nick to the zoo, so at least I only have one demon to worry about.

I hear Craig approaching, I make it my business to bend over to pick an invisible something up from the floor, hoping my face down, arse up pose is enough to distract him from the lecture I'm about to get.

His hands grip my hips as he presses himself against me, I

turn ever-so-slightly to look back at him and ask, "may I help you?"

Craig slides his hands down my back, grips my shoulders then yanks me up, "I'm not done with you yet."

"I hope not."

"Charlotte."

Ooh. The way he says my name like that. His darkened gaze meeting mine makes me tingle all over. I know he's trying to be serious here, but I'd gladly allow him to throw me up against the wall and have his way with me. "Yes, Daddy?"

He spins me, walking me backwards until my arse hits the counter. "Did you," he starts with a growl, "threaten to murder Jessica's father?"

"No."

"No," he echoes, giving me a look that says he doesn't believe a word of it.

"I promised to do it."

His lips kick out in a gorgeous, panty dropping grin. Craig leans in, kissing me tenderly at first, then the predator in him takes control.

Tilly thunders into the room, "no. No kissies!" She stomps to us, hands slapped on her hips. "I only get the kissies!"

Craig pulls back and we both glance at the mega beast scowling at us, with her Mickey Mouse teddy shoved under her arm.

"You go clean," she shoves me by the legs towards the sink, then turns for Craig, pushing him towards the sitting room.

"Tilly," Craig warns.

"Nap time!"

"It's too late for a nap," I argue.

"NAP TIME!"

The sitting room door crashes shut as she locks herself and Craig away. I can hear Craig attempting to lecture her but we both know that's falling on deaf ears.

Craig manages to escape about ten minutes later. I hear the kettle boiling while I'm working in my office on my latest book —well, on one of the five projects I have going at the moment. It doesn't matter what I do, the voices in my head never stop. The joys of being a writer, you're constantly haunted by fictional people telling you their life stories

"No kissies!" I hear from the kitchen, pushing back from the desk, I catch sight of the back of my husband's head.

"I'm making coffee."

"No."

"Don't start."

"You sneaking off for kissies!"

"I'm getting a bloody drink!" Craig snaps.

"I the only one that gets kissies."

I hear Craig sigh; I see a hand rising to his face. I can only assume from this angle that he's pinching the bridge of his nose. "You'll go on a time-out if you keep it up," he warns.

"Make me!"

Ooh shit, kid. You've pushed it.

"Matilda!" Craig snarls.

"No."

"Matilda. Hannah. Barnes."

I didn't even do anything and I'm about to jump out the window to avoid his wrath. I have to admit it, Tilly's got some brass balls.

"You naughty, Daddy!"

"I'm counting to three."

"Stinky head."

"One."

"No!"

"TWO!"

"NO!" Tilly roars.

"THREE!"

"But I'm your girl, Daddy."

And... he's caved.

I see his shoulders shake ever-so-slightly, "go inside and behave."

I hear her feet padding away quickly. She's most likely laughing like the evil genius she is, patting herself on the back for a job well done.

"So Jessica is coming to the auld barbecue?" I get up and slowly approach him.

"Yeah," Craig pours himself a cup of coffee, letting out a little laugh as he adds, "she's actually a little frightened of you."

"Oh yay! I love that. I'm small but feisty," I punch air, then boop him on the nose. I can be cute too!

"You're not that small."

"I'm five-six and a half, don't forget the half!"

Craig chuckles lowly, taking a mouthful of some much-needed caffeine. "It's that feisty attitude that made me fall for you," he leans in, placing a chaste kiss on my cheek before turning to fetch the milk from the fridge. Clearly black coffee isn't going to cut it today.

I hop up on the counter, watching him, "I thought it was my oral skills?"

"That too," he winks, adds his milk, and stirs. "You'd hide a body for me?" he turns to pop the milk back in the fridge and I snort. Clearly the kitty litter thing came up when he was speaking to Jessica.

"Without batting an eyelid," I shuffle closer to him, wrapping my legs around his waist. "Just like you would do it for me, Batman."

I hear a door opening and brace myself for the almighty roar that follows, "NO KISSIES!"

LOTTIE

"I don't know what you're so embarrassed over, you have a great arse," Craig chuckles, pulling up the handbrake and then killing the engine.

"I didn't need the entire world to know that though!"

The holy mortifying shame of it.

I had to run to the shops before we went to Josie's, only for me to realise my leggings were see-through under the fluorescent lights. Nothing screams shame like your toddler announcing to the world, "Mammy, I can see your bum!"

Of course Craig found this fucking hilarious when I got home red-faced and ready to live the rest of my life incognito.

The kids are first out of the car. They spring into Josie's, she's expecting us, so the door is naturally unlocked. It's safer. Better to allow the house to be easily accessible than having one of the kids put a window in trying to get in.

Mam and Nick are already here. I clock a pint in Nick's hand almost instantly. Craig snorts, "starting early?"

"Meh," Nick shrugs, his tired eyes looking about ready to drop and stay shut.

"He did the night feeds last night," Abbie stalks out of the kitchen with a can of 7up. "You'd swear that he's traumatised for life now."

"Oh yeah, they can stay up on the Xbox all night, but God forbid they give the child a bottle," I empathise entirely. Craig will still have games nights with the boys or occasionally stay up reading until the early hours of the morning, yet I've never heard half as much complaint out of him the next morning as I did with the kids' night feeds.

Mam waltzes out from the kitchen with a cocktail in hand, another Evans on the gargle, "Craig!"

Oh sure, ignore me.

Craig turns to Mam and beams, "there's my favourite girl."

I see the wine glass before I spot Josie, "hello, darlings!" The kids flock to her like she's Mary Poppins, that is until they find out about the bouncy castle out back.

Matilda leads the charge, "out of my way!" she grabs James by the hand, and he goes willingly. "Bouncy!"

"Tilly be careful!" Ethan begs. He and Jamie make a run for their younger siblings and almost take Jay out in the process.

"Jamie, calm the f—" Jay stops, clocking his wife standing behind him.

Tiffy steps forward, poking her head out the window at the herd of animals making a beeline for the bouncy castle. "Calm down!"

"What she said!" Jay shouts.

I set my sights on Abbie. "Where is my little butternut squash?"

"Asleep in the buggy in the kitchen."

George steps into the room, chuckling. "Not for long with that noise."

Craig grimaces, giving Nick an apologetic grin before turning to Josie. "Shouldn't have taken out the bouncy castle."

"Nonsense," Josie titters. "When is Jessica getting here?"

Craig shrugs, "I guess she'll get here when she gets here."

Mam places her hand on his arm, "are you ok with everything, love?"

"I'm fine, Kim, thanks."

Ellie loiters by the window, "Daddy?"

"Yes, princess?"

"May I have a drink, please?"

Craig grins smugly, announcing, "she's the only good one!" he steps for the kitchen, gesturing for Ellie to follow him.

I follow because I'm parched. Embarrassment takes it out of a girl. Peeking over Craig's shoulder, I'm not surprised to find that Josie has stockpiled the fridge for the grandkids. Jason's two aren't technically Josie's but try telling her that. She is nana to the two boys just as much as she is to our kids.

Hearing wheels crunching on the gravel outside, I poke my head into the sitting room and spot Jessica's car slowing to a stop. "Here she is."

It's a stampede.

A flock of vultures, and for once it's not the kids. Every adult is cramming into the front room to catch a glimpse of the mysterious sister.

I push past the lot of them to get to the door, "Hi, Jessica," I go for a smile that I hope is more friendly than it is psychotic.

"Hi," she beams, tugging at the ends of her sleeves. She must be nervous. The crowd behind me can't be making it easy on her.

Mam knocks me into the wall as she shoves forwards, able to save her cocktail but not her daughter apparently. "Hi. I'm Kim, Lottie's mom."

"Abbie, Nick's wife," Abbie has to wedge herself in there, but she gets the arm across for a handshake, nonetheless. Her words have a bit of bite to them, *message received, no need to threaten the new girl!*

Josephine practically bulldozes her way through the lot of

them. For a woman in her eighties, she has not slowed down one bit. "I'm Josie!"

Jessica looks taken aback, she blinks several times before composing herself and offering up a glamorous, albeit genuine smile, "It's so nice to meet you all," she turns her bright eyes to Josie. "Thank you for having me."

"The pleasure is all ours, dear."

CRAIG

I glance over at Nick, who is quite clearly ogling Jessica.

"Wanna pick your jaw up off the floor?"

"Ha!" Jay barks, slapping Nick on the back, "it was Craig and Lottie first, now you're drooling over his sister." Abbie shoots daggers in Jason's direction, something he notices instantly. Jay makes a point of looking over his shoulder for the invisible culprit, "who said that?"

His saviour comes bounding into the room, he must have escaped Tilly. No idea how he got away unscathed. Tilly watches James like a hawk. "Dada!"

Jessica watches the toddler shoving Jason by the legs towards the kitchen, "he's so cute!"

"Thanks," Jay beams, all the while been manhandled by his three year old. "He takes after me." Tiffy makes a point of elbowing Jason in the ribs as he passes her, then turns to greet Jessica. She's the only one bar George who hasn't jumped at her yet. "I'm Tiffany."

Oh, someone has her poker face on.

I nudge my way between them, sparing Jessica another stare-down from a possessive wife. "Come on, I'll—"

"Daddy!" I cover my crotch on instinct before turning to look for Satan. Tilly spots Jessica, stops in her tracks then screams, "stranger danger!"

She's gone.

"You've met Tilly already," thankfully Jessica finds the little demon amusing, she giggles softly, "I have."

Josie is on my arse in seconds, "Craig, get the girl a drink!"

"Yeah, ok."

"Now!"

"Keep your knickers on!" now I know where Tilly gets it from. I don't know what Jessica drinks, so I pull out a selection of bottles and bring them inside in time to hear her speaking with Lottie.

"I read your book in one sitting," Jessica gifts Lottie a smile that's as bright as her platinum blonde hair.

Nick groans, inserting himself into the conversation, "are you traumatised too?"

"Nick!" Lottie thumps him in the arm.

"You didn't have to put your sex life in there! The least you could have done was given a guy a warning," Nick grumbles, his cheeks glow with a pink tint.

Lottie turns her back on him, "ask my arse."

Jessica tries and fails to hide a laugh. She looks at me, and her brow furrows. "I just find the way you described Craig's... conquests... before you odd."

"The models you mean?" Nick interjects once again and it's clear by Jessica's expression that she thought it was a fabrication meant for entertainment purposes, or to tick a certain box. After all, that's what big publishing houses look for. Box tickers. If you don't tick enough, no matter how good your story, you get rejected, the thing they don't realise is people are sick of box tickers books. That's why the indie market has grown dramatically. People want something new, they want offensive, they want entertainment, they want dark romance and monster porn. Everyone has a kink, and the indies give the people what they want. Sure, some books aren't as polished as they would be from a large publishing house, but a lot of these people cannot afford the editors, formatters, et cetera, needed to give it that polished look. It costs hundreds if not thousands for these people, it all adds up, and that's before marketing. Yet, I never see anyone rip into a traditionally published author for a typo or two in their work, and they have teams of people behind them.

"Yeah," Jessica blushes.

Tiffy snorts, she steps up beside Lottie and says, "you're wondering how Craig went from runway to Lottie."

"Oh no! I didn't mean—"

Lottie beams, offering Jessica an olive branch, "it's fine. I get asked that all the time."

"Get what all the time?" I can't help but frown as I wait for her to elaborate.

"Asked how you dated a specific type for years then ended up with this fat bottom gal," she gestures to herself, and adds in a twirl and booty shake for good measure.

Remembering the bottles in my hands I turn to Jessica and ask, "what's your poison?" She takes a west coast cooler as expected.

"Care to take the lead on this one, Batman?" Lottie nudges me playfully.

"It's simple," I slide my arm around my beautiful wife, pulling her against me. "I wanted Lottie, I couldn't have Lottie, so I made sure that anyone I brought back looked as far away from Lottie as possible."

Jay grins like an imp, adding, "yeah after the Jenny incident."

"Thanks for that."

"Oh my God!" Nick almost chokes on his beer.

Lottie turns to look at me, "what am I missing?"

Nick composes himself, just about, "you never said it was —" he cringes and storms off to safety, knowing Jason is going to fill in the blanks with or without my consent.

"He was seeing this girl, Jenny. Red hair and curvy. He brought her to your barbecue if I remember right." I love how quick off the mark he is to sell me out.

"Oh, that Jenny!" Lottie's jaw is ajar, her eyes flick from one side of the room to the next as she pinpoints the culprit.

It was one of the first times I ever saw Lottie, the second time I got a chance to speak to her one to one. Nick invited Jason and me over. Jay had already met Tiffy, and they were in the early stages of dating. Lottie was still with Michael.

"Long story short," I'd rather embarrass myself right now than have Jason do it for me. "We were together one night and I —" I thought I'd never have to tell this. I can feel the blood rush to my face.

"What did you do?" Jessica presses, eyebrows raised into her perfectly styled hair.

Jason sees me struggling to find the words, and like the bastard he is, he decides to go ahead and blurt it out, "he called out Lottie's name halfway through."

All the women in the room gasp and turn to me wide-eyed. Including my nan. Great. Just what I needed her to hear.

Lottie stifles a laugh, "you never told me that."

"You never asked."

"Craig Barnes!" Josie growls, "I hope you apologised to that poor girl. She must have been mortified."

"Nothing like what I'm feeling right now, I'm sure."

I'm collared into cooking for everyone. Penance for my crimes as Josie called it.

After everyone lets up interrogating Jessica, Lottie introduces her to the kids.

"Presents!"

"Matilda!" Lottie growls, safe to say Tilly is officially over the stranger danger thing and is now demanding payment.

"Kissmas and birthday."

"Matilda," I warn, glaring at her over the barbecue set.

"Now!"

"Matilda!"

She's gone running into the bouncy castle, laughing her little arse off.

Ellie doesn't take the news as well, "but... my nana Ellie is in heaven."

"Yes, princess. She is," I purposefully avoid eye contact with Jessica as I say it. We haven't discussed my mam yet. Not because I don't want to. It's just... my mother is a precious topic to me. I didn't want to tarnish her memory by even mentioning her in the same sentence as the asshat.

"How is she your sister?" Ellie presses.

Jessica hunkers down to eye level, "your daddy and I have the same—"

"Stork!"

"Stork?" Ethan echoes, looking at me like I'm off my head.

"Yep, sort of like the Grinch, big mix-up," that's my story and I'm sticking to it.

"There is no stork," Jamie contends, *the little shithead.*

"Jamie!" Tiffany yells, clicking her fingers and pointing at her side. Jamie knows better than to defy his mother.

"How are babies made then?" Ethan looks at me, demanding answers.

Jamie grins over his shoulder and shouts, "sex."

Sweet loving hell.

Ethan looks more confused than ever, "what's sex?"

Tiffy thankfully comes to my rescue, "a special hug, now move along or I'll murder you both."

JESSICA

It's incredible being here and seeing everyone. It's good to know that despite everything, my brother had a loving environment to grow up in. His nan is a hoot. The kids are hilarious. I feel better already.

The way he looks at Lottie is something you can't fake. He adores her.

Lottie still unnerves me a bit. She seems lovely but she did threaten to murder my father, seeing how devoted she is to Craig, I no longer think that it was an empty threat. I think she is capable of hurting someone to protect her family.

I've been giving my father the cold shoulder. I'm not in the wrong for wanting to get to know my own brother. He should have never kept Craig from us.

I catch Craig dancing with Josie to The Beautiful South, Perfect Ten. He spins her and laughs with her as they serenade each other. It's the most adorable thing ever. No one could be that devoted to a grandparent and be a bad person. Behind that rough exterior, it's clear to see that Craig is a sweetheart.

My phone rings and I step to the side of the bouncy castle to answer it.

"Hi, Daddy," I say lowly into the phone. I could have ignored him again, but I can't avoid him forever.

"Hi, pumpkin. Where are you? I came to see you today and Danny said you went out for the day."

"Yes," I glance back at Craig and Josie, chewing my bottom lip. "I won't be back until later tonight."

"Out with friends?"

"No. I'm with Craig."

I hear him inhale sharply, "Jessica—"

"I have every right to get to know my brother."

"It's complicated, Pumpkin."

"For you, yes. Not for me," I know I must come across as snotty right now, but I don't care. I'm a grown woman, I can make my own decisions. If I want to be part of Craig's life, our father cannot stop me.

"Jessica, look—"

"I have to go, Daddy. I'll call you later."

"But—"

"Bye!"

Craig's approaching with another drink for me, "everything ok?"

"Yeah, it's fine," shoving my phone back into my pocket, I then reach for the drink he's offering me. "Do you need help with the food?"

"No, I'm good. Josie might need a hand with the snacks for the kids though."

"I'm on it!"

CRAIG

Lottie moans, clutching her head and shielding her face from the light as if she's going to go up in flame. "I can't do life right now."

"Being a bit dramatic now?" adjusting Lottie in my arms, I carry her upstairs.

She started complaining of a headache shortly after the grub was served up. Soon after she ate, she began complaining about seeing spots and we were on high alert for a migraine. Lottie had some tablets in her bag, just in case. She took them, but now she's basically out of it.

Jessica ushers the kids into the house and closes the door, "can I help at all?"

"Nah, she's good. Aren't you, baby?"

"Why are you talking so loud?" she whines, burying her face in my chest.

"See?" I gift Jessica a grin before hauling arse up to our bedroom. I made good time considering I'm carrying my own personal Moaning Myrtle up the stairs.

Yanking back the covers, I put Lottie on the bed, she groans and rolls into my pillow.

"We need to get you out of those clothes," I say before she gets too comfortable.

"I can't, I'm dead."

"Come on," I strip her down and Lottie opts for one of my T-shirts instead of her pyjamas. She wriggles into it with a pout. I can see her left eye is already swollen. Lottie grunts, leans forward and falls against my chest. "Don't leave me."

"I'm here, baby," wrapping my arms around her, I pull her closer.

"Rub my back and tell me I'm pretty."

"You're gorgeous."

"Liar. I look like the elephant man."

"Still beautiful," pressing my lips to her crown, I hear her sigh then she reclines against the pillows. Her eyes already heavy from the tablets. "Try to sleep it off, baby."

"Don't leave me, "she whines again.

"Daddy!" Tilly calls.

"Kill it!"

I can't help but laugh. Lottie would walk through hell for her kids but right now, with a migraine, Matilda is at the top of the list of people who need to be away from Lottie right now, considering how loud she can be.

I pull the duvet cover over her and tuck her in, then pull the curtains closed before leaving Lottie to rest.

The two eldest are fine. They've parked themselves in front of the TV. Matilda, on the other hand, is scruffy. I don't know how she did it to herself considering she was on the bouncy castle for the best part of the day, and it's dry out, she still managed to cover herself in mud.

"Come on, Satan, bath time."

The child is running around the house in her nappy looking like some sort of stunted tribal warrior while I run her bath.

"Done!" she charges into the room, ready to free herself of her nappy.

"Not yet."

"Done."

"The water is too hot, go play in your room for a minute."

"Hurry up!"

"Yes, boss."

Jessica snorts, handing me two towels. I'm assuming Ellie got them for her. Ethan wouldn't bother his arse unless they were blocking the Xbox.

Jessica leans against the doorjamb. "Not at all shy about saying what she wants, is she?"

"Tilly? She doesn't care... unless your name is Mickey Mouse."

Ethan pops his head in, looking sheepish, "is Tilly going for a bath?"

"Yep."

He charges down the hallway just as Tilly comes bounding out of her room to check on her bath, "release the Kraken!"

She steps up beside me, "done?"

"Done."

"Release the Kraken?" Jessica presses.

"Oh, you'll see."

Not even five minutes later, Tilly has the bathroom flooded and us drowned.

Jessica was not expecting half of her makeup to be washed off but that's what happens with a toddler. Nothing is safe.

"Oh my gosh!" Jessica laughs, ringing out the ends of her crop top.

"Ollie the ocopus, splash, *splash! Die!!"* Tilly takes the purple octopus, slamming it down on the unsuspecting bath toys floating on the surface. "Nom nom nom."

"Look," Jessica laughs, squatting down to play with Tilly. "That one's getting away."

"Not for long. Nom nom," Tilly whirls on me when she spots me coming with the shampoo. "Freeze, or you're next!"

"You need to have your hair washed."

"You need to have YOUR hair washed."

"Tilly."

"Never," the water from the bath splashes out, if I wasn't drenched before I most certainly am now.

"That's it," I growl.

Tilly drops Ollie the octopus. "Uh-oh."

I reach in, securing her in place with one arm while I quickly wash her hair with the other.

"Stranger danger! HELP! Off! Off!" she tries to fight but

I'm not about to let up. "Stinky daddy, stop! I bite you!"

"Try it and see what happens."

She freezes. Then scoffs and folds her arms, allowing me to rinse her off.

"All done."

"Bout time!"

Jessica is getting great amusement out of this.

"Ready to come out?" I hold up the towel, ready for her highness to move her moody butt.

"You gots the powder?"

"In your room."

"You gots jammys?" she presses.

Why does she never ask Lottie these things?

"In your room."

"Chocci?"

"No chocolate this close to bedtime."

"Chocci!"

"No," I reach in and pull the little gremlin from the bath and carry her into her room.

After I towel her off, she struts across to her bed and falls belly down, "powder my butt!"

As soon as Matilda is ready for bed, I bring down pillows and a duvet for Jessica. She had a few drinks at Josie's so there was no way I was letting her drive home. I'll bring her to collect her car tomorrow.

"Has Lottie always suffered from migraines?" Jessica asks when I've a spare second to sit down.

"For as long as I've known her, yeah. She gets them more since she got signed. Countless hours looking at screens doesn't help."

"A friend of mine gets Botox to help with hers."

I throw my head back and laugh, "I'm not even suggesting that. I'll be clubbed over the head."

I leave Jessica around half ten to go to bed, I'm shattered. Lottie is practically a corpse in the bed. I had to shake her to make she was still alive, she told me to piss off and went back to sleep.

I wake up, dazed, and confused. Mainly because I am spooning Lottie's pillow and have with a raging hard-on. It takes me a minute to tune into the sounds of the house, I can hear Lottie downstairs talking to Jessica. I best get dressed and join them, jeans will do, any excuse to wear a belt right now.

"Morning!" Lottie chirps as she pours me a mug of coffee.

"Morning, baby," I tap away at my phone, boosting the water. I'm in desperate need of a shower right now, I'm still half asleep. Turning to Jessica, I ask, "sleep ok?"

"Like the dead," she smirks.

"How's the head?" I nudge Lottie, she's in the way of my caffeine fix.

"Much better now, and a good thing too. I've got a deadline."

"Ooh," Jessica perks up. "Another thriller?"

"Not exactly."

I throw her under the bus, "she writes erotica under a pen name. Does well for herself too, don't you, baby."

"I do ok."

"Thousands of people are getting off to my wife's books. I'm strangely proud."

"It doesn't bother you?" Jessica asks before practically inhaling her caramel latte. Lottie broke out the good stuff for her.

"Why would it bother me? It's not like she's doing porn."

"True," Jessica bobs her head from side to side, "you're very supportive."

"Have to be, I don't want any sex ban," Lottie turns and slaps me across the arm for that one.

I keep forgetting that Jessica is my sister and not just a friend. It's going to take some getting used to. I've gone forty years being an only child, now I have siblings. One

I've yet to meet.

Jessica looks between me and Lottie, worrying her lower lip. "I was thinking... if you wouldn't mind, I'd like to take the kids out someday. Get to know my nieces and nephew better."

Hmm.

I'm not sure how to answer that.

Jessica is their aunt but she's still a stranger.

"Erm," I clear my throat. "I don't know if they'd stay with you just yet." It's the kindest answer I can give right now.

"One or both of us can come along though," Lottie adds. "That way we can be sure they'll behave."

And keep William at arm's length. I'm not having him move in on my kids when I'm not around. That arsehole has not right to them, he isn't going to meet them. Not if I have a say.

"That sounds lovely," Jessica is all sunshine and rainbows. She has to get that from her mother. "What about Dublin Zoo?"

"Sounds great. Craig?" Lottie turns to me, awaiting an answer.

"Yeah, that's fine."

"You're sure?" Jessica presses.

"Yeah, the zoo is good. The kids love it."

"Great, well how about Thursday?"

"Should be fine, I don't think I've anything on," Lottie is mirroring Jessica's big happy head right now and it's freaking me out. My wife is not a morning person.

Lottie makes breakfast for us before I drop Jessica back off at Josie's to collect her car. I stay talking to my nan for about an hour before heading home.

This whole thing is still very strange to me. Having a sister, getting to know her. She wants to be involved and I appreciate that. At the same time, I cannot help but think that her father will use her to worm his way back in.

I put that thought to the back of my head.

There is no way that I'm allowing William a chance to come near my family. He missed his chance to come back and make amends.

CRAIG

Lottie stuffed me with breakfast this morning and then dragged my arse out the door to go visit Kaylee. The two met online a few years ago on Instagram. The Bookstagram community is fierce and, for the most part, loyal unless someone sees you as competition then things have been known to get ugly.

Kaylee, like Lottie at the time, kept receiving rejection after rejection for her work so she decided to go the indie route instead. It worked out well for her, her debut novel gathered a small amount of interest at first, and then as supportive as the online book community is, Kaylee's work went viral. She met her now husband after she signed with Netflix, and he was cast as the male protagonist. Her ex-husband was an absolute arsehole at the time, neglected her and from what I've been told, he was a shite father to their autistic son. Kaylee did everything for Alex, and still does, but now she has Dean who has taken Alex on as his own.

Soon after Kaylee's success, Lottie got signed and now the two are each other's ride or die when it comes to social media. Some readers can be a bit nasty. Keyboard warriors. Everyone's all good to thrash someone from behind a screen.

Dean bounds into the room, pointing at Kaylee, “hey, what’s that?”

She glances down at her blouse, “what?”

“Boobies!” Dean squeezes Kaylee’s tits, laughs and then runs as her hand flies.

Did I mention Dean is like eight years Kaylee’s junior?

Kaylee whirls around to look at Lottie, “does he act like this?”

He, meaning me.

“Craig’s worse,” Lottie smirks. There is no point in me protesting, she’s right.

“So, it’s finally happening?” Kaylee picks up her mug of coffee and blows on the contents. “You got the green light for your own show.”

“It looks like it,” Lottie nods, she’s downplaying her excitement right now. She’s ecstatic. Her first book, our book, is being made into a TV show. “How are you feeling about playing Craig?” she asks, turning to Dean.

“Great!” his eyes lock on mine, “I’m going to be your new shadow.”

“I’m really not that interesting.”

“Not true. I read the book. Getting into the MMA ring should be interesting.”

Kaylee almost chokes on her coffee, “you... fight?”

Dean gives me his best puppy dog-eyed expression, “I’m gonna get my ass handed to me, aren’t I?”

Kaylee answers for me, “yep.”

“I’ll go easy on you,” I reassure him. I did promise to show him the ropes, a form of method acting if you will. I’m not as fit as I was ten years ago. I have to go easy on him, for my own sake. Bad back and all that jazz. It comes with the years of being a chippy.

“So,” Dean plops himself down in the nearest seat to me,

and strands of his light-brown hair fall in front of his eyes. "Your dad's back then?"

"Dean!" Kaylee barks.

"It's fine," I insist, she looks like she's about to bounce his head off the kitchen table for that one. "He is—if you can call him that."

"I imagine that hit a bit of a sore spot," Dean offers me an empathetic smile.

If anyone gets where I'm coming from about the "daddy issues" it's him. It's my understanding that he doesn't know his dad at all. The man got himself locked up before Dean was born and Dean never wanted anything to do with him.

I heard the scumbag came seeking him out after he made a name for himself as an actor. He's no Hollywood A-lister but he's definitely a known talent. His old man showed up looking for a handout and when he didn't get it, he went to the papers causing a lot of shite.

Placing my cup down on the table, I mirror his grin and say, "he didn't make as colourful an entrance as yours did."

Dean lets out a gruff laugh, "no, I imagine that one is hard to top," he reaches for Kaylee's hand and gives a squeeze. "Then again, I had Kaylee and Stephen. The prick wasn't ready for Stephen chasing him out of the garden dressed as the fairy godmother from Shrek."

"I saw that video!" Lottie cackles.

We all saw that video. Kaylee uploaded it. It went viral and, in all fairness, it was fucking hilarious. More so for us, because we've met Stephen, Kaylee's best friend. Never piss off a drag queen.

"Are you going to let him back in, Craig?" I'm met with Dean's big puppy-dog eyes once again.

"He can shove it. Why should I allow him back? He's been out of my life since I was eight. He had plenty of time to come back and he never did."

"Yeah, I can't say I blame you," Dean mutters. "So, changing the subject. When it came to that fight with Michael, where you scared?"

"No."

"Really?" his eyebrows shoot to his hairline. "Never?"

It's Lottie's turn to grip my hand and squeeze, "he was as cool as a cucumber throughout everything. I never saw him freak out. I think I did enough of that for both of us."

"The only time I was afraid was in the split second he pulled the knife out. Then Lottie flashed before my eyes and I was livid," I admit. "She could have been in the house. We were blessed that she was at her baby shower at the time," I turn to look at her beautiful sparkling eyes. "My only concern was for her and Ethan."

"Even after you were arrested?" Dean leans closer as if to check for a tell that I'm bullshitting him.

Lottie laughs maniacally, "he was in the holding cell playing cards with Nick's partner."

"Seriously?" Kaylee looks somewhat impressed.

"Well, it wasn't very comfortable. My arse was killing me after I was released."

Dean chuckles, "you're unreal."

Lottie sighs, "Tilly has the same approach when it comes to authority. We're fucked when she's older."

"Most people start a college fund for their kids, we're setting up a bail fund," I add.

Lottie looks around the peaceful house, asking, "no Millie today?"

"My mam has her at the moment," Dean takes a mouthful of coffee and then adds, "Alex is with Paul."

"How's he getting on in school?"

"Great!" Kaylee beams. "He loves the centre and has made a few friends there. He's come so far socially."

Lottie beams back at her, "that's great news."

"Yeah, we're so proud," Kaylee leans into Dean. "The pups have helped settle him too."

Dean frowns, "too bad we can't keep them all."

"Pups?" Lottie perks up immediately and I know in that instant that we're bringing at least one home.

"Yeah, Peach had puppies. Want to see?"

She's gone with a fucking rocket up her arse. I hear Lottie's squeals of delight before I even see the room the puppies are sleeping in.

Sure enough, there are five sets of eyes staring up at my wife as I enter behind her.

"Oh my God!" Lottie sings. "They're so cute and fat. Craig, look!" she leans in for a closer look. "Ooh look at that grey marble one!"

"No can do," Dean snickers. "Stephen's already laid claim to that one."

"Alex has a special bond with the dark brown one in the back," Kaylee adds.

"The rest you are welcome to claim," Dean hops up on the table by the window.

Yes, this is all very endearing but from what I know,

British Bulldogs come with a hefty price tag, "how much?" Kaylee turns to me and grins, "for you guys, nothing. We just want them to go to good homes," she hunkers down next to Lottie, adding, "if you were a stranger, I'd crack the price right up. No one is going to pay thousands for a puppy just to neglect them."

Dean snorts, "she practically runs background checks on people as it is."

"I want the puppies looked after!"

"I'm not arguing," he holds his hands up in surrender.

"So that leaves three puppies looking for homes?" I

reiterate, all the while staring down at the back of Lottie's happy head.

"Yep," Dean offers me a toothy grin.

Lottie spins to me, "we have three kids."

"You can't be serious."

She's deadly serious.

Not a hope in hell. I love you, but you can get fucked.

"What?" Lottie's brow furrows as if she's reading my thoughts. "It's them or a fluffy pussy," she grins, wickedly.

"Do I even want to know?" Dean asks.

"No," I step up beside Lottie, attempting to be the voice of reason. "Three puppies are a lot of work, Lottie."

"I know," she sulks for a split second before insisting, "Nick would love one."

"That leaves two." She gives me her best Puss-in-boots impression and I throw my eyes to the heavens. I'm not winning this. I know I'm not. "Looks like we're taking the puppies."

"Love you!"

"You better."

"I does!" Oh no, she's talking baby talk. I'm screwed. No going back now. "Who's a good boy? Who's a good fatty? You're coming home with me, yes you are, yes you are."

"We'll have to train them. House train them. Put up with the separation anxiety from their mother for a few nights."

I want a blowjob and some kinky fuckery for this!

Dean slides from the table, looks at Lottie and says, "I should warn you; they snore like truckers."

Make that two blowjobs.

"They also need regular vet checks," Kaylee adds. "Unfortunately, they are a breed that can come with a hefty vet bill."

Anal.

"They're also prone to flatulence," Dean shoves his hands in his pockets, offering me a sheepish smirk.

Bondage.

"We don't mind," Lottie bounces to her feet, a blue-eyed bitch already in her arms. "Do we, honey?"

"Not at all."

I'm so spanking her tonight.

LOTTIE

The kids are over the moon when we get home. We rang Nick first, and as expected, he jumped at the opportunity to get a puppy.

After dropping off Nick's pup we came home and got attacked by the kids for their fur babies.

We kept the two boys to stop any nasty surprises when they're old enough to start breeding. Tilly is not happy that she couldn't have the name Minnie for one because they are boys. Now we have a Mickey (no surprise there) and Ethan and Ellie are debating on a name for the other puppy.

Ethan is the quickest off the mark with suggestions, "Cannon!"

"No," Ellie protests. "What about Rover?"

"Chomper!"

"No, he's not a dinosaur. Cuddles?"

"No chance. I'm not calling him cuddles," Ethan contends. "What about Thor?"

"Yes!" Ellie beams in agreement.

That was easy.

Great, so now we have Mickey and Thor.

Craig pulls off the grumpy dad look so well. The kids seem to think that he's not pushed about the pups, but I've caught him playing with them when he thinks that nobody is watching.

He's just acting up so he can "guilt" me into kinky sex later. He thinks I don't know what he's playing at. I'll let him think he's an enigma by allowing him to think he's catching me off guard.

If I know him as well as I think I do, I've a feeling that I'm getting blindfolded and handcuffed as soon as the opportunity presents itself.

Not that I mind, I like the fact that we have kept the spark going between us.

Craig's nose scrunches in offense, "who farted?"

Ethan's the first to insist it wasn't him. Ellie shakes her head dismissively, refusing to budge from Thor. Tilly giggles her little arse off, "Mickey did it!"

"What the hell was Kaylee feeding them?" Craig groans.

The puppies are a welcomed distraction from the tension of William's return.

"They're not much worse than you," I admit.

Ooh, the ice glare. I'm shaking in my bra right now.

"Hey, Dad?" Ethan's on Craig in a heartbeat.

"Yeah?"

"What did Santa say to his reindeer?"

"What?"

"Let's all pull together, and we'll have a white Christmas."

Ellie's brow furrows, "I don't get it."

"Me neither," Ethan admits, but he's still staring at Craig to gauge if his joke was funny or not.

I'm frozen on the spot. I glance at Craig whose eyes are wide and his jaw is tight. I'm not sure if he's on the brink of laughing or yelling.

His eyes flit to me and I shrug in response, I've no idea where Ethan got that one from, I'm sure as hell not going to be the one to explain why it's inappropriate.

Craig shakes out his shoulders, and insists, "he's yours."

"I didn't make him myself; you know!"

"No, you had sex," Ethan beams, still not certain of what he just said, thanks be to God.

"That's a special hug, right?" Ellie asks.

"Unbelievable," Craig barks, storming into the kitchen.

"Batman?" I follow him in, he's opening and shutting presses without ever looking into them.

"Nope."

"Craig," I reach for his arm, and he freezes. He braces himself against the countertop and hangs his head, "I'm tired, Lottie."

He has been out a lot with Jason and Nick, though he doesn't get into what they're up to together. I imagine it's setting up their new venture in private security.

"Well go to bed then."

"Not that kind of tired," he pinches the bridge of his nose, breathing deeply for a moment before he turns to face me.

"Talk to me."

"It's just," his fists ball at his sides. I notice his jaw tic as he says, "since *his* return, I just feel... off."

"Baby," standing on my tiptoes, I reach up, pulling Craig's head to my shoulder. His body starts to relax in my hold. "It's a lot to take in. It's a lot to deal with. I'd be worried if it didn't affect you."

"I don't want to be like this," he mumbles into my shoulder, his arms snaking around me, squeezing me tightly. "I want to just snap out of it."

"What do you need?"

"I don't know," he admits.

"Do you need a break from me and the kids?"

"No!" he pulls back, affronted. "God no. I don't want that. I don't want that at all. I just feel," he pauses as if contemplating his next choice of words. I allow him all the time he needs to figure it out. "Numb? Anxious, irritable, tired—all the damn time. It doesn't matter how much I sleep; I can't seem to wake up."

"Maybe you should take some time off. You've been working so hard. You could be burning out."

"Maybe," his jaw tics again, he looks everywhere but at me and admits, "I feel like I'm failing you."

"You will never fail me. Never," I take his hands in mine, lacing our fingers together. "You could be depressed."

He freezes, and something flashes in his eyes at the word. It takes him a moment to speak, "I don't feel it."

"Depression is more than feeling sad, baby. Take it from someone who has battled it on several occasions. Counselling might help."

"But—"

"No buts. You need to put yourself first."

"Counselling though," he visibly cringes at the thought. "What sort of superhero would I be if I let this thing kick my arse?"

"Even heroes have the right to bleed,*" yes I just quoted a song lyric but I love that line and it's a perfect fit for this conversation.* Sliding my arms around his neck, I make him look at me. "Besides, it's not kicking your arse because you're strong enough to admit there is an issue."

His eyes soften. "I'll try it but I'm not sure how good it will do."

"I'm by your side one hundred percent of the way," I kiss the tip of his nose, and his lips pull into a boyish grin. "I'm glad you spoke to me about this, I'm proud of you."

"I love you."

"I love you too."

Matilda comes bounding into the kitchen, "Daddy, Mickey done a wee wee!"

His eyes go wide, and I can't help but laugh, "I'll sort that."

"Thank you!"

LOTTIE

"Where are we going?" Matilda demands, holding my hand and half digging her heels into the ground in protest.

"To get something nice for daddy," I gave Ellie and Ethan fifty euros each to spend on Craig while they're out with Nick today, and I'm bringing Tilly with me to the shops while she picks out his gift.

I was never in a position to spoil him at the start of our relationship, but now since my books are hitting the best sellers list, I can afford to splurge every now and then. Right now, I think he could do with a pick-me-up.

Craig always tries to do right by us. Sure, he has guys on the roster to do a lot of the jobs but Craig goes out of his way to look after my mom, Josie, and everyone close to us, so he's never really done working.

When he's not working, he's training with the guys or Ethan, bringing the girls to dance and self-defence classes. He goes to all the kids' events and busts his arse to make time for them when all he wants to do is fall into bed and be left alone after a long day.

He does it all without complaint.

Now my man needs me, and I'll be damned if I let him fight this alone.

Tilly and I bump into Nick and the kids in the shopping centre. Ethan is very proud of his purchase but refuses to show me what he's bought his father, instead he opts for asking me if we can go to Kelly Lou's because, "dad likes the cakes there."

"Good thinking, SpongeBob."

After an afternoon of the kids arguing over who got Craig the better gift, we finally get home in time before Craig gets in. I had Jason take him out for the day. God only knows what they got up to, knowing them—actually, I'd rather not know.

Tilly couldn't decide on anything but sweets for Craig, so when we got in, she finger-painted him a batman picture.

I put out the box from the bakery and Ethan sets new batman pyjamas, a Lynx Africa set and a mug down next to the box of cakes. I glance at the mug and laugh.

Ellie makes room for a bottle of Jean Paul Gaultier, Le Male. I have a feeling Nick flipped her the extra for it, either that or she got it on sale. It's Craig's favourite fragrance, he'll love it.

I place down a fresh bottle of JD honey, just in time to get run at by a flustered Ellie who has quickly backtracked on her way to the sitting room, "mammy!"

Judging from her reaction, I'm guessing Craig is home. "Everybody by the table," I gesture for them to move out of the doorway while we wait to hear Craig open the front door.

The door creaks open. There is a pregnant pause, and then Craig finally calls out, "anyone home?"

"In here!" I bring my finger to my lips, hushing the kids giggles momentarily.

His soft footfall gets closer. When he pushes the ajar door open, the kids practically devour him while screaming "SURPRISE," at the top of their lungs.

The puppies are terrified.

"What's all this?" Craig steps back, beaming and visibly confused. He scans the table with wide eyes.

Ethan is the first to speak, "look, dad, cake!"

Craig lets out a shaky laugh, "I can see that."

"Red velvet, your favourite," Ethan shoves the box at Craig, giving a smug grin to Ellie who sticks out her tongue in response.

"Thanks, buddy."

Ethan, of course, is not about to give up the spotlight that easily, "and look," he drags Craig to the table, pointing at the mug and surrounding gifts. Craig reads the mug and chuckles, outstretching his arms for Ethan to run into. "Love you, dad."

"Love you too, buddy."

Matilda looks like she's two seconds away from kneecapping her brother, "WELL, I DID THIS." She shoves her still-damp painting forward, striking Ethan in the face and leaving a black smudge on his cheek.

"I love it," Craig beams.

"Coz I did it?" Tilly presses.

"That's right, baby."

Matilda gives the room a look which basically says, "damn straight!" Then she turns for the sweets that she demanded I pick up, practically throws the bag at Craig, waits for him to open it, takes a handful and runs out of the room to watch Mickey Mouse Clubhouse.

Ellie steps up to Craig, "I got you this, daddy," she plucks up the bottle of Le Male. Craig's eyes shine with unshed tears. This is all the kids, sure, I gave them the money for their gifts, but they know their father like the backs of their tiny hands.

"Thank you, princess."

She jumps at him, latching onto his legs and squeezing tightly. "Mam got you something too."

"Did she now?" Craig cocks an eyebrow in my direction. He's all boyish smiles and warm fuzzies right now.

I nod to the bottle of JD on the table, "you looked like you were running a little low."

Craig hugs the kids, kisses them on the head and then steps to me, engulfing me in his arms, "you didn't have to."

"No," I admit. "But we wanted to."

CRAIG

I cannot believe that Lottie did all that.

I've said it before and I'll say it again, she's incredible. I've really felt like crap lately, despite the little heart-to-heart with Jay, and Nick today at the office, I still felt... wrong.

Coming home today has really boosted my mood.

It's not even the gifts, nice and all as they are. It's my family. My wife. Our kids. We drive each other nuts at times but it's days like this that make me stop and appreciate just how lucky I am.

We get the kids ready for bed and considering they were dragged all over town today, the three of them went to bed with no resistance.

I let the puppies outside for the final time tonight and put down the training mats before locking up and going to bed.

Pushing the door open to my bedroom, I freeze.

Lottie is not done with surprises, and I cannot believe what I'm seeing.

Green.

A tiny yet tight bright green dress that does nothing for my blood pressure and everything for those tits. She's wearing a bright red wig, and she's wrapped in an artificial Ivy climber.

Ivy.

"Poison Ivy!" only one of my top ten fantasies, along with Catwoman

Pure raw desire snakes through my system as I look at her.

Lottie gives me such a sexy little grin that I almost explode at the mere sight of her. "Come join me, my garden needs tending."

"Yes, ma'am," one by one, pieces of my clothing fly onto the floor. I dive onto the bed, capturing Lottie's wrists and pinning them above her head. She looks at me through lowered lashes as I use her vines to bind her wrists together.

"You're going to have trouble undressing me now," she sniggers.

"This outfit is not coming off," pushing the material of her dress up, I grab hold of her panties and tear them off her.

Lottie radiates sexual tension and it's fuelling me.

Reaching for the nightstand, I pull out an eye mask and secure it over her eyes.

LOTTIE

His chilled fingertips trace the inner halves of my legs. I can't see a thing and it's driving me wild. I love when he does this. I can feel his gaze burning into my body. I know I'm already wet and it's confirmed when Craig runs a finger through my folds, humming with approval. "Always so eager," he murmurs, goosebumps rising all over my skin. He pulls away and I whimper. "Patience, baby."

I can hear the nightstand opening again, the sound of him searching for something.

The sound of the click of a button and vibrations follow instantly.

Craig presses the bullet against my clit, and I cry out wantonly.

"Shh, can't have you waking up the kids, baby. You're going to have to be quiet," his low, husky voice sends delicious shivers through me.

I know he gets off on hearing me moan, hearing my screams, but he's right. We can't risk waking the kids.

Craig presses the bullet against me, rubbing it in slow circles against my clit. The combination of his words and the intense vibrations right on my sensitive pearl push me alarmingly quickly to climax.

My hips rock fervently against the toy, I'm close, so goddamn close. Craig can tell by the way I bite my lip to stop myself from calling out. My legs tremble and I writhe, not being able to keep still no matter how much I try to force my treacherous body to behave.

I hear a click and the vibrations stop, "Craig," I pout, I was so close.

I crane my neck, turning every which way, trying to figure out where he is.

"I decide when you cum, Lottie," I feel the mattress sink under his weight. His movements are slow and calculated as he takes his place between my parted legs. "You're going to have to be very quiet, think you can do that?" His lips come crashing down on mine in a bruising kiss.

"Yes."

He starts lapping up my juices. His tongue traces my folds delicately, almost treasuring them. He dips his tongue slowly and deliberately between my lips, deep inside my pussy. I moan quietly, enjoying the sensation of Craig's tongue. He begins a steady pace, dipping in and out and making sure the upper half of his tongue brushes the tip of my clit every time he retreats, then dives back in. I feel his thumb begin to rub at my clit as he devours me.

"Baby," my bound hands fall to his head, clawing at his hair. It takes everything in me not to cry out.

Craig pulls away, I feel him crawling up the bed. He removes my blindfold, and I'm momentarily dazzled by the light.

I blink to clear my vision and see his lidded, darkened gaze staring back at me. "You want to cum, baby?"

"Yes!"

"Ask me nicely."

"Please, baby. Please make me cum," I muffle a cry as I feel that delicious stretch of my man filling me.

Craig fucks me at an unforgiving pace, one hand rests on my throat keeping me pinned to the mattress, the other on my hip.

He groans. The muffled noises he emits only fuel the fire.

Every time he spears my G spot with acute accuracy, I bite down harder on my lip, almost drawing blood.

My muscles contract as I'm propelled into elation. My chest heaves as I convulse with raw ecstasy, drenching Craig's still-pumping cock with my juices. It's easily the most intense orgasm he has ever given me. Craig continues to move in a frenzy, his growls turning to a hoarse moan, "Lottie, fuck! Lottie—"

His bites down so hard as he releases that I'm expecting him to crack his molars, bliss spreads over his features.

Craig kisses me fiercely, still panting, breathing sporadic, "marry me," he chuckles, pulling out and rolling onto his back, taking me with him.

"Did that already."

"Do it again."

I push myself up on his chest and ask, "do what again, marriage or sex?"

He lets out a satisfied grunt. I feel his hold tighten on me, "feel better, Batman?"

"Much," he rubs at his eyes, grinning from ear to ear. "Oh my God, Poison Ivy." He pulls at my binds, freeing me.

"Not bad if I do say so myself."

"Fucking amazing," he moves to kiss me but is stopped in his tracks by the sound of a cry.

"I'll check on her," sliding from the bed, I pull on my robe and hurry from the room.

Tilly's still fast asleep, she's wrapped in her covers like a little caterpillar. I use the main bathroom to clean up before returning to Craig.

"Is she ok?"

"Grand, she's still asleep. Must be a bad dream," changing out of my outfit now that I'm finally allowed to take it off, Craig watches me like a hawk as I trade the tiny green dress for my comfy, fluffy pjs.

Climbing into his outstretched arms, I rest my head on his chest, "I love you," sliding my hands down his body, I manage to force them under him and squeeze that delectable tush. "And your butt."

"I'd never have guessed," he chuckles lowly.

"I love your arse like you love my boobs," I grin up at him. His eyes are lidded, and his words come out slightly slurred, he's exhausted, "that much?"

"And more."

LOTTIE

Craig has gone to his first counselling session today, and I'm bored off my head, so I take the kids to see Nick and Abbie.

Ellie loves being a big cousin and is swinging out of Abbie so she can be close to Maddison.

I spot Nick at the kitchen table, hunched over a file with a mountain of paperwork spread across the wooden surface.

"What flew up your arse and died today?" I plop down in the seat across from him and, being the nosey bitch I am, I scan the photos and sheets of paper in front of him.

"Nothing," he mumbles, taking a mouthful of what I can only assume is cold coffee.

"Uh-huh," I lean closer. One particular mugshot catches my attention. "Hey, I know her! She's the one that hacked up her boyfriend Lizzy Borden style, right?"

"Allegedly," Nick takes another mouthful of cold coffee, rubbing at his temples the same way dad used to do when he couldn't figure something out.

"You don't think that she did it?"

"I'm not so sure," he admits. Lifts his mug to take a drink then thinks better of it. Getting to his feet, Nick tosses the remaining coffee into the sink, rinses out his cup and opts to make a fresh batch. "Remember Joe?"

"Hot Joe from the Garda College?"

He glares at me. *What like I'm lying? He can arrest me any day.*

"He's looking into this case and," Nick grabs another cup from the press, he's clearly being a good host for once and not having me fend for myself. "Well, the thing is," he rubs at his head again. "Some things just aren't adding up."

"Like?"

"Like the timeline for example. Joe went to check out the drive she would have had to do, technically speaking she would have had enough time to get there, kill Tommy and get back, but—"

Ah, I see where this is going, "the clean-up?"

"Yeah," he fills the two mugs, adds sugar and milk, and then makes his way back to me. "There wasn't enough time."

Technically this is a closed case so Nick can share the details, I point to the crime scene photos in front of Nick, "let me see that."

Yikes.

"What is it?" Nick presses.

I grimace, thankful that I didn't have breakfast before looking at this mess, "an axe?"

"Apparently so."

"A knife I could believe but..." I look at Éabha Ryan's picture again. She's still a baby in her mugshot. Early twenties at the latest. If I remember right, she was twenty-two when she was convicted.

She's not exactly a bodybuilder. This much destruction required a lot of strength and stamina, there is no way you could do this much damage in such a short space of time without both.

The blood spray indicates that Tommy was struck with

force, the kind brought on by a man. One can argue that the assailant was taller OR that Tommy was already on the floor when his murderer start swinging.

"Quick job?" I ask stupidly. Of course, it was a quick job, the evidence of that is staring me in the face but I'm still trying to process the level of gore winking me in the face.

"Yeah," Nick nods, his eyes distant and glazed as if he's been staring at this file all night.

"And messy," I say more to myself than Nick. Holy hell, the killer would have to of come out of there resembling Carrie. "No trace of blood, hair, bone?"

"Not so much as an eyelash was found on her," Nick admits.

"No cut or abrasions indicating a struggle?"

"None," Nick groans. "You're thinking what I'm thinking, right?"

"I'm thinking even if she acted fast, Tommy would have fought for his life. You saw the state Craig was left in despite him getting the upper hand on Michael."

"I know."

"How long did she have to clean up?"

"Going by Joe's timeline, fifteen minutes at best."

"That's fifteen minutes for both her and the car?"

Nick nods in response.

"No bleach in the car," I mutter, reading the report out loud. "Was she wet or freshly showered when she was arrested?"

"Nope, dry as a bone."

I toss the file down, this is bullshit. How did she even get convicted? There is sweet fuck all to go on. I knew the case smelled fishy when I heard it on the news but this... it's bollocks. "There is no way in hell, I don't care how good you are— there is no way you walk away from a mess like that without having something on you."

Nick concurs and then adds, "she could have dumped the clothes."

"And went home in the nip?"

"Could have had a gym bag handy."

"Yeah, but that doesn't explain why she does not even have a bruise to her name in this mug shot. No trace of blood in her hair or under her nails? No footprints!"

"Maybe she was smart enough to step over the blood spatter?"

"I imagine that axe got stuck in places," I scoff. "I've helped Craig break down some old furniture and even then, I had to kick off some pieces to dislodge the axe. Where are those footprints? What was her motive?"

"She was his partner; it was assumed that it was a domestic dispute gone wrong."

"For this much rage? That want to be some dispute."

Nick groans, covers his mouth and looks about ready to cry, "they got the wrong person for this, didn't they."

"By the look of it, yes," I hold up the crime scene photos. "How did she even get convicted?"

"Eyewitnesses," Nick drinks half of his mug of coffee in one desperate gulp, "three of them."

"This happened at night, right?" My focus is on the files again, I flip page after page until I get to the eyewitness statements.

"Between ten-thirty and eleven."

"It says here that this witness is a known crackhead, how reliable." I look through all three statements, each one is less dependable than the last. "How long has this poor girl served?"

"Five years."

"Fuckin hell, Nick!"

"I didn't put her there!"

This is... disgusting. It's disgusting. I'm ranting to Tiffy about this later on because someone needs to work on getting this girl out. "Joe obviously thinks that she's innocent or he wouldn't have asked for your help."

"It's proving her innocence that's the problem. If they slapped her away on circumstantial evidence, we would need something solid to bring to the table."

Again, Tiffy comes to mind. Her father is a high-ranking judge. We could have more leeway with Charles than anyone else. Then I get another thought that makes my stomach churn, "if someone is setting her up to take the fall then Joe will not get close enough to prove her innocent, unless—"

Nick nods, "I can get her out into protective custody. But I need a reason. I can't just sign anyone out."

"What's that you got there?" I point to an unopened file on the edge of the table.

"One of Tommy's friends bit the big one, much like Tommy, it was... vicious."

"And Éabha knew this guy?" Nick nods in response, finally, we're getting somewhere. "Use that. Say she has information on him, and you need to transfer her or get her temporarily released into your custody."

"If she is being set up," Nick glances out the window into the back garden to see the kids playing in the back garden. "This is going to be dangerous. Someone in power has obvious pull here."

"You're worried for Joe."

"If he digs and gets on the wrong end of this—"

"I get it, I do," reaching for my cup I take my first mouthful of warm frothy coffee.

"How's Craig?" Nick asks, he looks like he could use a distraction right about now.

"He's good, well, as good as he can be... he's trying."

"Yeah, he seemed a little off the other day."

"He won't see the doctor, but he agreed to see a counsellor and talk to someone about everything that's going on.

Sometimes it helps to talk to a stranger rather than those closest to you."

"He's lucky to have you."

"Wow," I almost choke. "Can I have that in writing?"

A teasing smile tugs at the corner of his lips. Nick scrubs his face in his hands and begins to tidy up the paperwork.

"Nick?"

"Yeah?"

"Just be careful. I know Joe is a friend and I understand wanting to help, but you have Abbie and Maddie to think of. If this is what we think it is, tread carefully." I will not cry. I will *not* cry, I'm a very tired woman with a severe case of writer's block. That is all. Nick is fine. Craig is fine. Everything will be ok.

"I will."

I reach for his hand, "promise me."

Nick looks me over, his tired eyes softening as he gifts me a smile that reminds me of dad, "Lottie, I'll be careful. I swear it."

My phone buzzes, I look down and see Craig's name flash on my screen. "Hey, handsome."

"Hey, baby!"

"You sound perky, I take it that everything went well?"

"Yeah," I hear the car unlock and Craig opening the door to climb in. "I feel a lot better after talking about it, surprisingly."

"That's good to hear!"

The engine starts up, followed by Craig asking, "are you home?"

"No, we're at Nick's."

"I'll drop over if you're going to be there a while?"

"Sure thing. I've yet to give Maddie a cuddle."

"Is Ellie hijacking her again?" he chuckles, his voice is a bit more muffled now, I must be on Bluetooth.

"Wouldn't you know it," I roll my eyes to the heavens.

"Ok, I'll be there in about half an hour."

"Ok, see you then. Love you."

"Love you too, my little Ivy goddess!"

I snort, hang up the phone and catch Nick eyeing me suspiciously. "Craig?"

"Yep."

"I'm ordering out. There is no way that I'm cooking for this mob."

I laugh and watch him leave the room to make the call for food. Downing my coffee, I take the cup to the sink and rinse it out before going out to Abbie for some girl time.

CRAIG

Falling back against the cushions, I'm still seeing stars. My legs are all tingly. There is no way that I'm walking for at least ten minutes after that.

I've no idea what I did to deserve that welcome home but I want to do it again.

My wife can suck like a Dyson.

"There is something I want to speak to you about," Lottie kneels beside me, pushing her chest out and worrying her lip.

Oh no!

She lured me into a false sense of security with oral and now I can't fucking move!

Shit, what did I break?

Whom did I offend now?

I gulp, "what about?"

"I was speaking to Abbie today," she starts.

We're on babysitting duty, aren't we? Four kids in one house, bollocks.

I only got this blow because two of ours are outside playing while Satan has a nap.

"Yeah?"

"You know she and Nick had a lot of trouble conceiving. Maddie is a miracle baby."

"I remember."

Do they want one of ours? I'll give them Satan... part-time. Life wouldn't be the same without her Bulldogs charging my bollocks at least once a week.

"Abbie wants another," Lottie continues.

"They need money for IVF?"

"Not exactly."

"Adoption?"

"Is an option."

I push myself onto my forearms and demand, "what aren't you telling me?"

"Abbie wants another baby," Lottie repeats. "And I offered to be her surrogate."

Wow, I did not see that coming. "Huh?"

"Craig?"

"You want to have another baby?"

"Not for us, three is enough."

"Thank God for that," I fall back against the cushions once again.

"It would be Abbie and Nick's baby. I'll just be the oven."

I think it over. I'm not surprised Lottie jumped at the chance to help, she's impulsive like that. "I think it's an amazing thing that you want to do for them—"

"But?" Lottie presses.

"Are you sure that's what you really want to do?" I sit up again, pulling her onto my lap. "I mean, think about it. Nausea, heartburn, birth... plus," it's my turn to chew the hell out of my lower lip. "Baby, you suffered from postpartum depression and anxiety after having our three. I just want to make sure that you know what you're signing up for."

Lottie smiles, putting her silver lining spin on it that she always does, "I know, but it will be worth it."

"If that's what you want to do then I'm behind you 100%."

"You're sure?"

"Absolutely."

Only Lottie could be so selfless. I've no idea where I got her from. I witnessed all three births and I can safely say I would not be signing up to go through that for someone else.

She's on me, her lips fusing with mine. I pull her closer, deepening the kiss.

"I awake!" Tilly calls from her room.

"I can't move."

Lottie wiggles off my lap, "fix yourself before she charges in here." She smirks and steps from the room.

The effort. I assume tucking myself back in is the equivalent of Lottie putting on a bra. I couldn't be arsed.

But needs must.

I hear Tilly sing from her bedroom, "M.I.C.K.E.Y M.O.U.S.E."

Stupid fucking mouse. At least she can spell that if nothing else.

"Daddy!" she sprints into the hallway.

"Yes, Satan?"

"Where's my sippy?"

"Ask your mother."

"I asking you."

Cheeky little—

"Craig," Lottie calls.

"Yeah?"

"Nick is on the phone!"

I hurry downstairs and grab my phone off Lottie while she sorts Satan out with a drink. "Hello?"

"I need a favour."

Like what? You're already getting my wife pregnant! "What's up?"

"Remember Joe?"

"Hot Joe from your wedding?"

Nick chuckles lowly "that name stuck, huh?"

"Well, they're not wrong. I mean, he's not exactly my type but if I decided to swing that way, I wouldn't kick him out of bed for farting."

"Big spoon or little spoon?"

"Switch. I'll take it both ways," I snort, watching Lottie look at me like I've finally lost my reason.

"You can stop now," Nick is still laughing.

"Sometimes a guy just wants a cuddle."

"Right now I need you to fight."

"Fight?" I echo. Lottie stops dead in her tracks; she's making a beeline for me so I do the only thing I can think of. I run away.

"Well... teach someone else how to fight," Nick mumbles. He's obviously trying to keep Abbie from overhearing this conversation.

"This is about the girl."

"There's been a big drug bust. A lot of people are pissed off. Joe says she's very jittery. PTSD most likely from all the shite she's been put through."

"You want me to show her how to defend herself."

"Yeah."

"Why not Jason?"

"He's helping me with something else."

"Which would be?"

"Classified."

"Oh, don't go pulling rank on me now!"

"I can't talk about it."

Which means it's most likely illegal. "Fine. Keep your secrets."

"Don't act pissy."

"Who's being pissy?"

"You're annoyed because I'm not telling you."

"Nope, I'm just thinking of how I'm going to violate your sister later," I turn around to spot Lottie staring at me from the adjoining room. "I'm thinking double penetration—hello?"

Who's being pissy now? I'm not the one who hung up the phone.

Lottie's folding clothes and getting ready to bring them upstairs.

"I might be leaving soon," I mumble.

"Where are you going?"

"Erm, self-defence classes."

"Nick asked you to help Éabha?" her hands slam down on her hips. My unzipped, oversized hoodie hits the top of her thighs. She looks sexy as hell right now, just my hoodie, and a sports bra and a pair of sinfully tight shorts. Her eyebrow raises, daring me to argue with her.

"Yeah."

"Be careful!"

"I will be."

Her eyes narrow as her gaze travels over the hard contours of my face. "Craig, I'm serious!"

"Lottie, baby, calm down. I'll be fine."

Her jaw clamps tight, and she practically growls out, "ring me when you get there."

"I will."

Her chin tips back as she peers up at me over her lashes, "and when you're leaving."

"I will!"

"Check your mirrors!"

"Babe! No one knows where she is, ok. Calm down," Nick just transferred her out of prison to a safehouse, if anyone looks into it, it looks like Éabha's been moved to another prison. Lottie walks to the bookshelf in our room and starts packing books into a bag. "What are you doing?"

"She likes to read. I'd say she will run out of material soon. Give her these."

"Hey," I grab her shoulders and make her look at me. "I love you."

"I love you too," her lower lip wobbles. It breaks my heart to see her this anxious.

"It's ok, doll. Everything will be ok," my arms circle around her waist, pulling her against me. My lips fuse with hers in a gentle caress. When I pull back, she offers me a woeful smile. Looking over my shoulder, I call out, "come on, Satan!"

"You're bringing Tilly!" Lottie is pulled from her anxiety and instead, looks about ready to throttle me.

"Yeah, if anyone starts, she'll knock the bollocks off them."

CRAIG

Dean is on the warpath when Jason and Tiffy arrive. "No! Where do you get off in telling me my son needs a specialist school? Where is your qualification to make that assessment? Oh, you're just saying. Well, I'm just saying Alex is well able to stay in your school. We've been told you wouldn't even know he's there half the time. He's not the only child to disrupt a class! You know what? I'll take this up with the board of education! Because you're discriminating against my son because he's different! Oh yes, you fucking are! I hope you have full pockets because when I take this to court, you'll be paying out the nose!" Dean hangs up and then scrolls through the phone. "Shit, did you see this?" He points the phone at me.

A video of a black Honda Civic tearing rubber all over the city centre last night.

"Gangland thing most likely," Dean mumbles as I watch the car dart from one lane to another. "I'd drive that fast too if someone was trying to fill my ass full of led."

The car skids around corners and masterfully dodges incoming traffic. *No wonder Joe was as white as a sheet when they got back last night.*

Tiffy bounds into the room and turns on the TV so we're all watching the Civic tear arse towards oncoming traffic. "Did you guys see that bloody lunatic?"

I'd love to point out that that lunatic she is referring to is her husband, but Tiffy doesn't know he helped us last night. She knows about his past but I'm pretty sure she thinks the street racing he was referring to is more Grease Lightning when in reality it was more Fast and Furious.

I've been in the car with Jay when he used to race. It's fucking terrifying. I'd lose my lunch quicker in the car with him than on the waltzers at Funderland.

"I'll give it to the driver, nerves of steel. I wouldn't be able to do that shit, I'd total the car," Dean admits.

"Apparently the car was found burnt out near the N7," Tiffy adds.

Someone's going to claim big on their insurance.

Jay... commandeered another car, so it couldn't be traced back to him should anyone go searching. The owner would have reported it stolen and cashed in when it was found in flames.

Jay steps into the room with James in his arms, "what are we talking about?"

"Apparently some lunatic robbed a car and turned the city centre into his own private racecourse," I smirk up at the TV.

Tiffy turns on me, eyebrow quirked, "How do you know it was a he? It could have been a woman?"

Jay snorts.

"What? You don't think a woman could drive like that?" Tiffy presses.

"I never debated it. So, I take it they never caught the guy," Jason feigns ignorance as he kisses Tiffy on the cheek.

They wouldn't, would they?

Jay was never fucking caught.

Ever.

Try as they might, Jay always outran them.

"Nope," I smirk. "Got away Scot free."

Jay grins smugly and offers an oat bar to James who happily takes it and darts into the sitting room.

Tiffy is still ranting, "dragged up little toe rags."

"Hey!"

"You had the sense to give that shit up!"

I snort into my mug of coffee; Jay gives me the death stare. I could seriously hang him by the bollocks right now.

Kind of tempted.

"Where's Jamie?" I ask.

"With my dad," Tiffy declares.

"Ah."

"What are you doing here?" Jason asks, turning to Dean.

"Tailing him, method acting and all that jazz."

"And emptying out my presses while he's at it," I add.

"Lottie?" Tiffy asks.

"On her back with her legs in the air."

"I'm sorry?"

"At the clinic getting checked out for the surrogacy thing," Dean clarifies.

"Just use a turkey baster, same result," Jason adds.

"You're lucky you're pretty."

"You're lucky I love brats."

My phone flashes and Jessica's name pops up, "hey."

"Hey! The guy here is finished, well mostly. Do you mind coming by and fitting those last parts for me now?"

"Is *he* there?"

"No. I promise you that."

"Ok then, yeah. I'll swing by with Jay and fit that for you."

"Thanks, bro!"

That still takes some getting used to.

I arrive at Jessica's with Jay and Dean. Safe to say, Jessica is only too happy to have Dean land on her doorstep. She turns all fan girl on him and is practically swooning.

Dean doesn't seem to mind though, I guess he's used to the attention now. He happily poses for pictures and signs some shit for her while I finish fitting the cabinets.

"There we go."

"Oh my gosh! I love it! Thank you!" She squeezes the life out of me before taking pictures to post on her Instagram. From what she has told me she has been gaining quite a few followers lately. I'm only recently following her, so I had no idea about the jump in number.

She's starting to get sponsors and is now officially an influencer.

"Hashtag, best brother ever!" Jessica squeals. "Quick smile!"

"Wait what?" Too fucking late. I'm dazzled by the flash.

Dean all but cackles, "hashtag deer in the headlights!"

"Hashtag screw you too!"

"Hashtag dinner first?"

"Hashtag you're buying."

"Touché."

"I love it, Craig. I really do! It's so much better and you were right about the island the little blast of colour really makes a difference!"

"Meh, it's part of the job."

"Well, this is part of mine!" Jessica swipes onto TikTok.

"What are you doing?"

"Spamming the shit out of your company!" She clicks live and starts talking into her phone. Within seconds hundreds of people are watching us. This shit is intimidating. "So, as you guys know I've been doing some remodelling and I had to share the result!" She points the camera around the room to her newly renovated kitchen. "I want you all to meet the men behind the transformation," she points the camera at Jay, and he goes on unfazed. "And *this—* "

Bollocks.

I drop behind the island.

"Craig!" Jessica growls. "Get up here and say hello!" She turns to the camera and smiles with a roll of her eyes. "Honestly, he's such a goofball."

I peek my head up to see if she's moved on and I'm greeted by my own face, "eh... hi!"

"He's super talented, guys. I mean look at this!" she points the camera around the room again. "So beautiful, I'll definitely have to learn to cook now! And look!" she points the camera at Dean who runs up beside her, putting his arm around her waist.

Jessica turns into a tomato as she squeaks, "they even brought eye candy!"

"Hello, from Candyland," Dean offers the few thousand people watching a megawatt smile.

"If any of you guys are looking for work done in your home, look up *Nailed it!* You might get a visit from Dean Kearney." As soon as Jessica ends her thing on TikTok, Jay's phone starts hopping.

"Amy? Slow down. Wait, what? How many? Fuck me sideways," he glances at me. "Eh, yeah. I'll talk to him. Ok! Ok! Yeah, bye!" he hangs up and shoves the phone into his pocket. "Holy shit balls, batman!"

"We got a few new clients?" I ask.

"A few? We got ten calls and she's looking at least another twenty emails."

"That fast?"

"You're welcome," Jessica beams.

Jay chuckles lowly, "I'd kiss you, but I've already done enough to potentially piss my wife off."

Dean taps Jessica on the shoulder, she turns, and he plants a closed-mouth kiss on her lips. I'm almost certain that I see her knees buckling.

"One short stream did that," Jay laughs again.

"Sex sells, I guess," I shrug."

"In that case..."

"Jason, what the hell!" he grapples me, pulling the ever-loving shit out of me until he finally pulls away and takes my shirt with him. "You ripped my shirt!"

"Oh well," he shrugs, fumbles with his phone, and says, "say cheese!"

"What the—"

Spots.

I'm seeing fucking spots.

"And post," Jay's thumbs tap away at his screen.

"Wait!" Chris demands. "You can do better than that. Quick, drag him out back."

"What? Why?" *Where is the nearest exit?*

Before I know it, I'm being thrown clothes and a hammer and told to stand in the garage.

"Hold the hammer down by your crotch," Dean demands.

"Why?"

"It's symbolic," Jay snorts.

"Wait!" Jessica tosses me a towel. "Put that over your shoulder.

So much for saving me, she's setting up a ring light.

"Good, now tie this around your waist," Dean's on me in seconds.

"What the hell?"

"Ooh we have a good one," Jay muses. I didn't even know he was taking pictures yet.

"One what?"

"Shut your mouth, you're ruining it!" Another flash goes off and I'm feeling oddly violated. "Got it!" Jason announces.

"Why the hell am I the one being made to do this?"

"You're working out again, I'm still suffering from dad bod."

"Someone's been watching his carb intake," Dean pouts, most likely imagining the diet he's going to be made go on before shooting.

"Not really."

"How are you staying in such good shape?"

"Gym, work—"

"And a lot of sex!" Jay adds.

"That too!"

"Eww," Jessica cringes. "I didn't need to know that."

"Try walking in on them," Jay shudders.

"I'd rather not."

"Posted!" Dean declares.

I gulp, "to your account?"

"Yep!"

By the time we get home, Jason and I have a waiting list of over two hundred clients. We'll definitely need to hire more staff.

I get home to see Abbie's car parked in our garden, *oh good, Lottie's home.*

I find the girls in the kitchen; Lottie has the mixer going. She's started anxiety baking again, "how did it go?" I glance in the bowl and then over at my wife who's rummaging through the presses looking for God knows what.

"Great, everything looks good to go," Lottie's on her tiptoes trying to reach the chocolate chips. I reach above her and grab the packet which she takes with a warm smile.

"So when is the baby planting thing happening?" I look to Abbie and then back to Lottie, unsure whom I should address about this whole thing.

Abbie is tapping out a text at the kitchen table, most likely updating Nick on everything that happened. She doesn't look up from her screen as she says, "Pretty soon. They have my eggs, they just need Nick in tomorrow and once the egg is fertilised..." she trails off, finally glancing at Lottie with watery eyes.

"That soon?" I turn to my wife.

"Yep," she worries her lower lip as she pours the chocolate chips into the mixture.

Abbie smirks and nods at me, "did you tell him yet?"

"Tell me what?"

Lottie lets out a noise somewhere between a whimper and a squeal. "To ensure there are no hiccups and that the baby is Nick and Abbie's," her eyes dart to Abbie and then back to me. "I can't have sex for a bit."

I can feel my eyes narrow, "how long are we talking about here?" Cracking open a can of Fanta on the kitchen island, I take a mouthful.

She spins for the mixing bowl, refusing to look at me. This cannot be good. "Two weeks before and two weeks after implantation."

And I'm choking.

She really should have waited for me to swallow before dropping that information. "A month? A MONTH? No sex for a month! Four weeks!"

"Pretty much," Lottie squeaks.

"A month!"

Abbie is silently chuckling in her seat, "glad to see you're taking it so well."

"A MONTH!"

For most couples, it does not seem like a long time to go without. However, Lottie and I made a deal after having the kids that we would not go more than two weeks without being intimate with each other. We would prefer to have a more frequent sex life but with the kids, work and life, two weeks is more realistic.

The only exception is immediately after childbirth for obvious reasons. Other than three times in almost nine years we have never gone more than two weeks without keeping the spark going—even if it was quiet vanilla quickies.

"So," I shove my way in front of the blender, she's going to have to look at me for this. "You'll be getting implanted sometime in the next three weeks?"

"Give or take, yeah," those big, beautiful eyes look into mine. There is a faint tinge of blush on her cheeks.

"Abbie, congratulations, you're taking my kids."

That makes her head spring up from her phone, "what?"

"You heard."

"Craig," Lottie groans, it's her way of telling me to behave myself.

"Nope, it's a fair deal. She gets you pregnant, she takes the kids for a night or two."

"Two nights?"

"I have got a month to make up for, Abs," I look her dead in the eye. "Keep complaining and I'll make it three."

"I'd have to talk to Nick—"

"No need," I pull out my phone and find his name in my recent calls.

"What are you doing?" Lottie presses.

Nick answers and I reply to my wife with a devious grin, "Hey, guess what? You're babysitting for the long weekend."

"What? Why?"

"Because I'm going to ride your sister like I'm entering the rodeo. Nick?" My gaze flits to Lottie who is cackling her arse off. "The bastard hung up!"

Abbie groans and rubs at her temples, "can't imagine why."

I see Ellie approaching from the hallway, "Abbie?"

"Yeah, sweetie?"

“Can I take Maddie for a walk when she wakes up?”

“Sure, sweetie. We can take her to the park.”

Lottie’s phone rings. I know who it is before she even mutters, “oh good, my husband got me in trouble again.” She glares at me as she answers, “yes?”

I can hear Nick demanding an explanation.

“Craig found out he has to go without for a month. He’s not happy.”

Some more mumbling on Nick’s side, I don’t catch it all, but I do hear the words *so I’m taking the kids.*

“Yeah. It’s good practise for you,” she retorts.

I step up beside her to eavesdrop just in time to hear Nick say, “I’m going to pretend you’re going away for the weekend and not entering a rodeo.”

Lottie snorts, “what makes you think that there are no rodeos when we go away?”

“For fuck’s sake, Lottie!” Nick barks.

I grin, pulling her closer, “that’s my girl!”

CRAIG

After a wildly inappropriate afternoon—and by that, I mean Jason quizzing Éabha every five seconds about her hook-up with hot Joe from the wedding, we finally got home.

Protect and serve indeed.

We all have families to look after, Joe is the only one of us unattached—also the only one of us pining for a convict but whatever floats your boat. We obviously don't believe Éabha is guilty of murder, hence why we are sticking our necks on the line trying to keep her alive until we can prove it. Joe just stuck that bit extra in.

Lottie was not there when I arrived. She left me a note to say she will meet me at 7:00 PM for dinner at Dandelions, another one of AJ's restaurants. I can't complain about the food, we tend to go here for anniversaries and date nights, it's definitely not the sort of place you'd get a chicken tender basket or fries.

Nick's got my three for the next two nights So there is no need to rush my time with my queen. I jump in the shower and quickly change before heading out to meet my date.

She is already sitting at a table when I arrive at the

restaurant, wearing something exceptionally sexy from what I can see.

We engage in role-play every now and then to keep things fresh. The last time I was her handyman coming by to fix the house while her husband was at work (not too farfetched considering what I do for a living.)

Tonight, she is my mistress and holy hell, can I pick them!

"Sorry I'm late," I lower myself into the seat across from her and I'm momentarily dazzled by those gorgeous eyes. "Had trouble shaking the Mrs."

"Is that so? What did you tell her in the end?" she runs her finger around the rim of her glass and offers me a sultry smile.

I'm the luckiest bastard alive.

"Working late," reaching out, I grab her hand. Bringing her fingertips to my lips I kiss each one individually. Her wedding ring is missing, she left it at home beside mine.

The waitress comes over to take our order, I sit back allowing Lottie to choose whatever she wants and then add my order to the mix.

"Excellent choice, and to drink?"

Lacing our fingers together, I lean back and grin up at the waitress. "You know, it's actually sort of a special occasion tonight. How about we take a bottle of your Napa Valley Cabernet Sauvignon."

Lottie's eyes go wide.

Did I just order a €120 bottle of wine?

Yep.

Do I regret it?

My eyes flit to the goddess sitting across from me and fall into her cleavage for a split second before they jump back to her eyes.

She's worth every cent.

"An excellent choice!" our waitress smiles warmly, takes our menus, and leaves us.

"Wow, what are we celebrating?" Lottie asks, so shocked by my impulsive order that she almost drops character.

"You."

The meal goes in like the most expensive first date in history—Four bottles of wine alone.

We're all over each other in the taxi home. I'm sure the driver is delighted to have us. I toss him €50 despite it only being €15 to drive us home. He can keep the change, I'm feeling generous. If I don't get Lottie in that house in the next five seconds, then I'm mounting her in the street.

We stumble to the door, lips locked hands roaming freely over each other's bodies. Pushing her against the door I kiss her neck, dragging my teeth across any exposed skin. Lottie exhales sharply.

I eventually locate my keys in my pocket though my throbbing cock didn't make that an easy task, I manage to open the door without breaking away from her, and we fall into the house.

Her mouth moves against mine with barely restrained passion. I want to see her lose control.

Pressing her against the wall, I grind my hips against hers. Lottie rakes her fingers through my hair while I fumble with her dress. "Urgh, fucking—" I grab the fabric with both hands and pull, hearing a ripping sound.

"You ruined my dress!"

"I'll buy you another one."

"You better!"

"Shut up and screw me before my wife gets home," we tumble onto the stairs, Lottie rips off my shirt and tosses it aside —I'm assuming that's revenge for her dress.

Clothes are flying everywhere as we slowly make our way upstairs. Lottie is the first one fully naked. The cool air causes her nipples to pebble. They look like they're craving the warmth of my mouth. Something I am all too happy to provide.

Rolling Lottie onto her back, I drop my mouth to her breast and give a good hard suckle.

Lottie moans and my cock jumps at the sound.

Slowly retreating a few steps until I'm hovering just above her entrance, I nudge her thighs apart and dip down to taste her.

"Craig!"

Using my fingers to part her folds, I gift her with long, slow licks. My tongue drags across her aching bud, causing her to cry out.

"How do I taste?"

"So fucking sweet," I continue to devour her, sucking her clit while I pump her with two fingers until she's trembling, crying out as she comes undone.

"You're so good at that," she attempts to stand on shaking legs, I pick her up, her legs locking around my waist while I carry her to the bedroom. "Show me what you want," she demands, planting a hungry kiss on my lips before she slides down my body.

"Open your mouth."

She does so obediently.

LOTTIE

Craig pushes down his boxers and that beautiful, thick cock springs out.

I lean in, my lips are pink and swollen. My hot breath

caresses the head of his cock. I flick my tongue over the slit. Craig gasps. His sculpted body melts to my touch.

I flick my tongue again; Craig grabs a fistful of my hair, tilting his hips forward. I take his full length into my mouth.

"Ooh fuck," his head tips back on a moan.

I pump him with my mouth, adding a hand to heighten his pleasure.

"Good girl. Fuck. Just like that," he begins to thrust, wrapping my hair around his fist. "Stop—stop!"

"Change your mind?" I look up to meet his lustful gaze.

"Not a chance."

"Go home to your wife before you do something you can't take back."

He pulls me to him; his tongue delves into my mouth. When he pulls away, I'm left breathless. "I showed you what I want, now you show me what you want." He smacks me hard on the arse.

I spin for the bed, slowly crawling towards the pillows.

Craig's gaze burns into me the entire time. "Go home, Craig. Is this pussy worth destroying your life for?"

I hear him growl as he follows me onto the bed.

Feeling the bed dip behind me, I look over my shoulder to see Craig braced on the mattress.

He kisses and nips his way from my arse, up to my shoulder where he bites down. Flipping me onto my back, he covers my body with his, and Craig's lips come crashing down on mine.

I feel him rub himself between my folds. He breaks the kiss, and without warning, plunges inside.

He moves in long deliberate, powerful strokes. I grasp his shoulders for purchase. It's rare when we take things slow. I forgot how erotic it can be.

A feral sound leaves his throat as he crushes his lips against mine.

He draws back and presses in again, deeper, more intimate.

I grip his arse, encouraging him, "you feel so good, baby—so good."

He drops his lips to my neck, and I bask in the delicious stretch of him, filling me with every thrust.

"Get behind me," I beg.

He pulls away, eyes hooded with near-mindless desire. I get on all fours, gasping as his hand slaps my rear, once, twice, three times before he positions himself at my entrance.

"Take me."

"With pleasure," he buries himself in me and I cry out. Pulling me against him, his powerful arms hold me steady while he pleasures me.

I turn my head to him, and he captures my mouth in a hot, messy kiss.

"You feel so fucking good," he growls against my throat.

Dropping to all fours, I slide my hand between my legs until I find what I'm looking for.

"Holy shit, Lottie!"

My fingers wrap around the base of his shaft, pumping him while he fucks me. His moans are driving me insane. He thrusts deeper and I feel his cock twitch, his body tenses.

He calls my name as if seeking salvation. I feel him pull out, and his hot seed spills over my back.

"Was I worth it?" I ask, turning to him and grinning victoriously.

"Always," his head is tilted back, his mouth ajar. Lifting his head, his gaze locks on mine, "you didn't finish." Craig grabs my legs, his chest still heaving. He pulls me down the bed towards him. "I've still got a job to do."

I watch as his head of tousled brown hair nestles between my legs.

Craig laps at my juices, moaning as he sucks my clit between his lips.

My hips buck of their own accord, "right there!"

I soon feel a familiar knot forming in my stomach, my legs begin to tremble uncontrollably.

Craig continues to tend to my over-sensitive flesh, bringing me through my orgasm.

He crawls up the bed, kissing me tenderly and then reaches for our wedding rings on the nightstand. He slides mine on first, kissing the tips of my fingers before it's secure and then pushes his ring back in place.

"You're home," I grin up at him. "How was your day?"

His grey eyes sparkle back at me. He gives me a boyish grin and says, "un-fucking-believable."

LOTTIE

"YES!" Tossing my leg up on the table, presenting it to he-who-must-not-be-named at this hour of the morning, I grin victoriously. "Look at that!"

Craig glances at my leg, his tired eyes drifting up to meet mine, "you got a tan."

"I got a tan on these milk bottles! Fucking get in!" Pulling my leg from the table, I thrust my way across the room doing my best bad Ace Ventura impression.

"How much caffeine have you had?" Craig asks, trying to keep a straight face.

"None! Don't need it. The ginger got a fucking tan. Quick, call Oprah! I was a pasty pastry, now I'm a crispy biski."

"What the hell did I marry?"

"A ginger nut."

"I can see that."

"Then why did you ask, my little noodle?" I spin for the fridge. "Quick get the lotion, I'm turning our bed into a slip-and-slide."

Craig buries his face in his hands, "sweet mother of all things unholy."

"Ding dong!" Josie calls from the hallway.

Craig's head springs up, "ah, there she is now."

"JoJo!"

"What poor soul are you here to harvest?" Craig asks, blatantly ignoring me.

I turn to him and growl, "yours if you don't shut up."

Josie places her handbag on the kitchen island, sighing as she looks at her grandson, "we need to talk."

"Nope," he's up. "Not here. It's an illusion."

"Craig," Josie moves in.

"Nothing good ever comes from that sentence," he protests.

"It's about your father."

Craig looks about ready to flee. I lunge at the door, kicking it shut, he's not going to get away that easily. If Josie feels this is important enough to bring up, I'm backing her all the way. "Sit down."

"Move," his hackles are raised, he looks about ready to start throwing things... me included.

"Down boy."

"MOVE," Craig attempts to side-step me, but I catch him and pull him back. He shakes free and I jump on his back like an overweight spider monkey suffering from a bad case of anchor arse.

I'm being slowly dragged down by the weight of my baby-making booty.

"Lottie!"

"No surrender!" *Oh crap.* Not only is my arse weighing me down, but my pants are also following the direction to the floor. I'm almost certain it's a bit early for a full moon. "Don't mind me, Josie!"

"Let go!" Craig snarls.

"Sit. Da. Fook. Down," he tries again to shake me off. He's already pissed off so if he's going to start growling like an animal, I might as well poke the bear. "Tickle, tickle."

"Lottie!"

"What's the story with Billy no balls anyway?" I ask Josie, as I cling to Craig's neck with my jiggly bits on show.

Poor Josie.

I imagine with the cellulite and stretch marks it's like looking at a sizeable chunk of cottage cheese.

"He came to see me," she admits.

Craig stops in his tracks. I lean over his shoulder, turning my ear in her direction to listen closer. "And?"

"He had no right!"

"I know, son," Josie sighs again and then pulls up a seat.

"What did you do?" Craig presses.

"I hit him in the head with my handbag."

"I hope there was a fucking brick in it."

Josie chuckles lowly, "when George calmed me down, I gave the bastard a chance to be heard."

"You're getting soft in your old age," Craig chides.

"He wants to get to know you again."

"Well, he missed his fucking chance."

"Do you need a tummy rub?" I slide my hands down his chest to his tense abdominal muscles.

"LOTTIE!"

"We know you hate the prick, but do you have to lose your shit every time he's mentioned?" I'm talking directly into his ear as the swine refuses to look at me.

"She has a point, Craig. You have a lot of rage towards him. I cannot blame you for it, but this kind of aggression is not healthy," Josie reasons.

"I had a father; he's buried with my mam."

"I know how much you loved Bobby. He was your grandfather, and, in many ways, he took on the role of your father when William left," Josie shrugs out of her bright red cardigan. "Don't you think that you should at least hear him out?"

"No."

"That's fair. I just think—" Josie takes a moment to compose herself. "Sweetie, I never had a good relationship with my mother. When she died, we were on bad terms. That ate away at me for years, and it still does. I could have fixed it if I just swallowed my pride."

My hold on Craig loosens, "are you saying he's sick?"

"Not at all," she offers me a kind smile.

"Too bad."

"Craig!"

"Just think about it, son. The least that can happen from speaking to him is that you get some closure."

"Or," I add. "You could just get yourself arrested again. Your call, babe." He begins to relax under my weight. I'm certain that at least 75% of my arse is on show by now.

"I have nothing to say to him."

"That's fine," I reassure him.

"I don't want to see him."

"Also fine."

His shoulders relax as he says, "you can get down now."

"That's not what you said last night."

"Lottie!" his cheeks flush.

Josie sniggers as she gets to her feet, "I'll pop the kettle on." It takes her a moment to find her bearings before asking, "where are my grandbabies?"

"At Nick's so Craig could violate me for the night."

"Lottie!"

"Ask my arse," I turn to Josie as I yank my bottoms up to my boobs. "Speaking of which, sorry about the view there, Josie."

"No problem at all, love. You've got a very nice tush."

"Aww thank you." I need to start doing squats but it's hard to find the motivation for that. I'd happily squat for a chocolate bar, but I'd forget to come back up.

"Lottie?" Craig nudges me.

"Huh?"

"Josie was asking about the surrogacy thing."

Damn, I need to stop thinking about chocolate. "Oh right, sorry! Zoned out."

"That's ok, dear. How did you tell the kids?"

"At first, they were a little confused. They thought they'd be getting a little brother or sister. We sat them down and explained that sometimes mammies can't carry the babies until they're ready to be born because they get too tired or feel too unwell, so they get someone they trust to mind their baby for them."

"That's a lovely way of putting it."

"It was," I agree. "Until Ethan began asking questions about sex, in which case lovely flew out the window and the whisky flew from the shelf and into Craig's hand."

Josie snorts, "how did that conversation go?"

"It didn't," Craig grunts.

"He ran. I laughed. Tilly caught up and headbutted Craig in the nuts."

"I'm pretty sure that I'm sterile now. No need to get the snip."

Josie pours herself a mug of tea, adds two heaping teaspoons of sugar, and then asks, "business is going well?"

"Booming thanks to Jessica and Dean. Jason and I had to hire another ten guys this week alone. With the contracts pouring in, we might have to hire another twenty."

"Try fifty," I contend. I've got a peek at their business emails. Flooded is an understatement.

"That's amazing," Josie outstretches her arms and Craig steps forward to hug his nan. "I'm so proud of you."

"Thanks, Josie."

She kisses him on the cheek, her eyes shining with pride as she takes him in. "So," she takes her phone and slides a picture of the robbed car from the news the other night across the island to me. "Our Jason is up to his old tricks again."

Craig's eyes widen, "how did you know?"

"You just told me," She smiles mischievously.

I can't keep the bark of laughter in, "you're good!"

"Only Jason is capable of rallying through streets that busy and get away with it. I knew as soon as I saw the video that it was him," Josie takes a sip of her tea, leans back with her arms folded, holds Craig's gaze and demands, "what have you boys gotten yourselves into now?"

LOTTIE

The doorbell sounds and that can only mean one thing. I march to the door, psyching myself up for this *war of the arseholes.* My arsehole always wins so I'm feeling pretty confident.

Swinging the door open, William's eyes widen, and he clears his throat. Clearly, he's uncomfortable seeing me after I threatened to bury him the last time I saw him. "Craig?"

"No, it's Lottie but I can understand your confusion seeing that you've only seen him once in thirty-something years."

The puppies run for the door. I retaliate by slamming it in William's face then realise he is supposed to come in, much to my disappointment.

Once the puppies are a safe distance away from the door, I crack it open and yank him inside by the collar, then slam the door again.

I lead him down the hallway towards my office, "you will not start shite in my house. You will not upset him. You will not speak unless spoken to."

"You cannot be serious."

"Bitch, I will end you!"

"Charlotte," Craig's low rumbling growl comes down the hall. He's been listening. Most likely establishing an alibi should William piss him off.

"Right this way," I turn for the office. William begins to follow at my heels, "dickhead."

Entering my office, I find my husband sitting behind my desk like the Godfather or some maniacal evil genius, all he's missing is the cat.

I click my fingers and point to the empty chair opposite Craig, "you sit!"

William hesitantly takes a step forward, "Craig, I—"

"What did I say about waiting your damn turn!"

"Lottie," Craig's grey gaze flits to me. He nods to the door, and I squish my lips to the side, my nose crinkling in displeasure. Most likely from William's cheap aftershave.

"Fine, but I'm right outside," I tell him, then turn to the sperm donor and add, "waiting."

Stalking back to the kitchen, I find Tiffy sniggering at me. "What?"

"You're worse than Craig."

"And what?"

"It's fucking hilarious."

I offer her a warm smile, then slide into the seat next to her, remembering our conversation before the doorbell sounded, "so, what did the nurse say?"

Tiffy sighs, I know this is a sore issue right now. "James has some red flags for autism. He's been referred to the early intervention team."

"That's good though, no?"

"It can be a four-year wait," she frowns and picks at her freshly manicured nails.

Early intervention my hole. Four years? How's that early intervention?

"Can you go private?"

"Yeah, it's not cheap though. It's almost two thousand euros for a diagnostic assessment alone."

"That's a fucking crime right there!"

"I know. We have that option luckily but those poor families who can't afford it financially… my heart goes out to them."

"It's a disgrace," everything's a bloody money racket in this country. "I can give you Kaylee's number. Her son is autistic, she knows the ins and outs of it. I get that all kids are different, and the spectrum is vast but I'm sure she can help in some way shape or form."

Tiffy nods in response and I search my phone for Kaylee's number. Shooting her a quick text to be certain it's ok before I hand it out. "How's Jay handling it?"

"He's still in denial. He says there is nothing wrong with James."

"There is nothing wrong with James," I insist.

"You know what I mean. Autistic or not, he is still our little man, he just needs a bit of extra help in certain areas."

"I WAS EIGHT!" Craig's voice travels down the hallway, shaking the walls in the process.

"Be right back," I'm off my seat and charging down the hallway before Tiffy can blink.

Swinging the office door open, I spot Craig behind the desk, grinding his teeth until sparks fly.

I lock eyes with William and scowl, "what did I tell you?"

"I—"

I turn to meet Craig's furious gaze and ask, "do you want me to shank him? I'll do it!"

"No," he exhales loudly and runs his hands over his face, his jaw still clenched. "It's fine."

I don't move. I'm fixed to the floor, staring at the pair of them.

"Scuse me and my beautiful body," Jay brushes by me,

tapping a hand on my back as a form of reassurance. He has arrived and almost certainly has a shovel and a bag of quicklime in the boot of his car "just in case."

Ethan must have heard him come in because he's in the hallway in a heartbeat, "Jason!"

"Hey, buddy!"

William turns to Ethan, taking his measure.

Craig looks about ready to combust.

"Come on, Ethan, we better go," I nudge him gently away from the door but his feet slam into the ground as he asks, "who's he?"

"No one," Craig barks.

In all fairness, William does look hurt by that one. I almost feel sorry for him, then I look at Craig and any sympathy I have flies out the window.

"Hey, Craig," Jamie is bounding up the hallway. Jason intercepts him, "not now, Jamie."

"But—" he leans to the side to peek in the room, "I need help with my spinning sidekick."

"I'll help you later, bud, ok?" Craig calls.

"Yeah, ok," he falls in line with Ethan as they disappear down the hall, whispering. Possibly wondering what the hell is going on.

Ellie comes out of nowhere, "Daddy!"

"Not now, Ellie," she doesn't listen to me, why would she? I'm only her mother. Instead, she presses into the room and is perching herself on Craig's lap before anyone can say any different.

"Daddy, I heard shouting."

"I'm sorry, princess," his eyes soften and the venom in his voice dissipates. "I need to have a word with," Craig glances at William, his face gives nothing away. "Mr Dempsey," he turns back to Ellie and asks, "can you give us a minute?"

"Ok," she kisses him on the cheek and takes off.

"Mr Dempsey?" William echoes.

"That is your name."

"That's right, you," he swallows. "You changed your name after..."

Don't even go there, pal. I've seen enough crocodile tears in my time to spot them a mile off. "Do you need anything to drink?" My question is directed at my husband.

"No," he offers me a tight smile.

"No, thank you," William replies.

Jason, of course, has other ideas, "three whisky sours, doll face." He winks at me as I leave the room.

I return a few minutes later with the drinks only to find Satan climbing onto her father's lap looking cattier than an actual feline. "Who you?"

"I'm—"

"What you want?" Why you here?"

"I—"

"Why did daddy yell at you?" she turns to Craig, eyes narrowed, "is he a naughty boy?"

"Yes," Craig nods. "Very naughty."

"Ooh," she turns to me wide-eyed. "Mama call Nicky! He'll awest him!"

William tries to get a word in again, he has no idea who he's up against, "I don't think—"

"NO!" Matilda barks, her grey eyes blazing with the worst kind of fury there is. Toddler wrath. "You naughty boy. My daddy will beat you up!"

"I—"

"He spank your bum."

"I don't think—"

"Jay will sit on you!"

Jason almost chokes on his drink, "I will not!"

Matilda holds her finger to her mouth, "he naughty."

"I'm not naughty," William insists. "I'm your grandfather!"

"I no have one," Tilly crosses her arms over her chest. "I have a Georgie."

"Georgie?"

"Georgie!" Tilly rolls her eyes like it is the most obvious statement in the world. "Josie's boy toy."

"Excuse me?"

"Did you fart?"

"What?" William's neck reddens. *Never try to argue with a toddler, mate. They have an answer for everything.* This is great craic. I should have recorded this.

Tilly points an accusing finger at him and declares, "he stinky man!"

"Tilly," I'm really trying hard not to laugh right now. "Come on now."

"Daddy?"

"Yeah?" Craig looks like the perfect blend of amused and homicidal right now.

"He's not my Georgie?"

"No, baby. He's not Georgie."

"Or grandad Bobby?"

"No, baby."

"Why is he lying?"

"He—" Craig stops himself, debating how to go about this.

William doesn't wait, afraid of being told he's no one again, "I'm your daddy's daddy."

"No, daddy has no daddy," Tilly looks like she's seconds away from jumping across the table and bitch slapping her grandfather.

"It's... true, Tilly," it looks painful for Craig to admit it.

Tilly turns to him, looking like a confused puppy, "he's your daddy?"

"Yes."

"He's my Bobby?"

"No, baby."

"He's my grandad?"

"Yes, baby."

Tilly pulls her confused gaze from her father and instead, looks at William as if willing his spirit to leave his body. "Presents."

"What?"

"Presents, where are they?"

"I... I—"

"You don't have pressies?" fuck me she's up on the desk. She's gonna clothesline him. "Daddy, did you hear that? No pressies for Tilly!" *That's bloody sacrilege right there.* "I gots no burthday or Kissmas pressies from him! He's a naughty grandad. I don't like him. He smells funny."

"Enough, Tilly," I grab hold of her before she decides to try out for the WWE and place her on the floor.

She charges from the room with smoke flying from her ears, *"Tiffy call Nicky! I've been robbed!"*

I turn to look at Craig whose face is buried in his hands and his shoulders are shaking. Jason is leaning against the wall, wiping stray tears from his eyes as he fights to compose himself.

"I'll be right outside if you need me."

"I know," Craig's words are strangled by his silent laughter. "Thanks, baby."

Turning to William on my way out the door, I say, "if you start, I'll send Tilly back in here. Watch yourself."

William blinks at me in shock. I'm not sure if it's down to seeing his grandchildren for the first time, my threat of sending Matilda back in here, or him losing an argument to a toddler threatening to call the gardaí on him that's baffled him. At least I know he will play nice now after all of that.

CRAIG

It's a lovely sunny day. The kids are back in school, and I've pulled up to the safe house to check in on Jay since his separation from Tiffy. I can't see it lasting long. It's a rough patch. They'll work through it.

I'm putting it down to the stress of Jay trying to keep bullets out of his arse as well as Joe's and Éabha's and Tiffy being frustrated as hell with trying to get James assessed for Autism and having a husband who still refuses to accept it.

I can't blame Jay; he's grieving the life he thought his son would have. If James is autistic, life becomes so much more challenging for everyone involved. I can't imagine that Jay will do too well with the people who still look at neurodivergent kids like they have the plague. Autism isn't contagious but being a cunt seems to be. If some dickhead says anything about James, I'll either need bail money or I'll be twiddling my thumbs in the cell next to Jay—it wouldn't be the first time.

I find him bent over a car, doing God only knows what under the bonnet. Damo and Ivor's Big Box Little Box is on full blast, and Éabha is shuffling in the corner like a squirrel having a fit. "Hey, squirt."

"Hey, hot stuff!"

Someone's extra perky this morning. Must have gotten a good dicken from Joe before he left for work this morning.

Jay peeks up from the hood of the car, "Hola, senorita!"

"Whose car is that?"

My question makes him frown. Worse, it makes him move from behind the car faster than I could have anticipated. His whole body language takes on a more threatening vibe. Those amber eyes shine with violence as he steps up to me and grunts lowly so only I can hear, "AJ's."

Fuck me, he's involved now?

Things must have gone belly-up somewhere if they've asked Aiden Quinn for help.

"Does Nick know?"

Jason smiles wickedly, "we're on a don't ask, don't tell sort of level right now." He takes the rag stuffed in his back pocket and wipes the grease from his hands. He reads the concern painting its way across my features, "someone was killed," he continues speaking lowly so as not to alarm Éabha. I can't help but look at her, she's still shuffling outside, looking through a pile of papers that Joe must have given her.

"I heard," I admit. "Nick told me."

"If we don't find a way to clear her name," his fingers curl around the rag. He doesn't need to continue with that sentence. I can see it in his eyes. If Jason thinks Éabha will be the next one to meet a gruesome fate, then Joe sure as hell thinks so too. He's been massively on edge lately, and this explains it.

I look at Éabha again. She's got her whole life ahead of her. Twenty-eight, petite, she's got the girl next door look about her but there is an underlying wildness to her beauty. Something untamed. It's that ferocity that's kept her alive for so long. She's a fighter. She needs to keep fighting.

I'm not about to leave her behind and one look at Jason

tells me he feels the same. We're all too invested in this case. In her.

Jay follows my gaze to Éabha, an amused expression on his face. "What you thinking, Batman?"

"I'm thinking we need to start somewhere," I can almost feel a wave of violence wash over me. I wanted to start this venture for Lottie. For people like Lottie, then I get dragged into this mess. If we can clear Éabha's name, we won't only hit the ground running. We'll be set for life and save her in the process. "That little rascal is a fucking goldmine should we play our cards right."

"You want her to be our first case?"

"We're already working it and for free. Why not use this opportunity to set ourselves up? If we can do this—"

"Hey, I've already been dodging bullets, why not benefit from it?" Jay chuckles. "Shit," his phone vibrates, his alarm going off. "I've to collect James from school."

"I'll come with you and collect Satan while I'm there," I shoot Lottie a text to say she can stay home and continue working while I do the first of the school runs.

When we get to the school, both Jason and I are hauled into the principal's office. It turns out that some of the older kids were teasing James, and Tilly marched her little arse across to the big kids yard and told them to stop. They didn't, so she pushed the main one taunting James on his arse.

One of the bully's friends saw it and tried to start on Tilly which is when Ethan noticed, intervened, and kicked two litres of shite out of the kid.

I'd like to say that we behave like grownups, but we are not in the office alone. One of the fathers is there and tries to have a go at us. Jason and I flip and abandon all pretence of acting like grownups. I'm pretty sure Jason breaks his nose before giving him a lecture about his child who is roughly seven-years-old picking on two toddlers.

Long story short, our kids ran into bullies, kicked their arses and we brought them for ice cream on the way home.

Don't get me wrong, my kids are no angels but I'm hardly going to give out to Matilda for standing up for a friend who cannot defend himself; and I'm not about to dish out a bollocking to Ethan for protecting his sister.

His principal tried to suspend him but thought the better of it when we brought up their no-bullying policy. Instead, Ethan was told to go to a teacher in future—advice I may have told him to forget immediately.

Josie is in the kitchen when we get in. She slips the kids a fiver each thinking I don't see her sleight of hand. I'm not even going to argue with her, she'd give it to them anyway.

"So, you sorted things out with himself?"

"Define sorting things out?" I smirk.

"William is allowed to visit the kids, and to be involved in their lives for now but if he pulls a single disappearing act all bets are off," Lottie explains.

It's the best I could do. He's not my father, he will never be my father. I can't forgive and forget but if he's serious about wanting to know the kids... I could deny him that, but I'll allow it for now. Begrudgingly.

"I'm glad you could be the better man, son," Josie gets up and locks me in a bear hug. "I'm so proud of you."

"Thanks, nan." I only did it for her to begin with.

Lottie scoops her hair over her shoulder and begins to braid it, "how did you get to be so forgiving, Josie?"

"When you get to be my age, you learn that anger does nothing but get you into the grave faster," she gives me a warm Josie smile. The kind that only she can give. The kind that reminds me I'm home. "William made a massive mistake in his life. I believe he knows this and is trying to make amends." She turns to me, reaching up, she rests her palm on my cheek. "He missed out on you, he wants to be there for your children the way he never was for you, Craig."

"And if he pulls another stunt?" Lottie growls, twisting a bobbin around the ends of her hair to keep her braid intact.

Josie's eyes spark dangerously, "grab a shovel and start digging."

Lottie cackles. "This is why I love you, Josie."

Kim comes in from the back garden armed with a pitcher of God knows what, "sangria anyone?"

"Mom, it's 2:30 in the afternoon!" Lottie protests.

"Your point?"

"Only the small glasses," Lottie begins searching the presses with her mom for the appropriately sized drinking glasses for this time of the day.

I hear shuffling and the sound of heels coming into the house. That can only be one person, "Craig!" Jessica beams, using her foot to kick the door shut behind her. How she does that and keeps her balance in those heels is beyond me.

"Jessica!" Ellie is bounding down the stairs in a heartbeat. She must have heard the heels.

"Hi, sweetie!"

Matilda practically bowls me over, "you got sweets?"

"Sure thing!"

The kids adore Jessica. They're delighted to have another aunt to spoil them and spoil them she does!

I think she's making up for the years missed or the fact that she is a new aunty to three terrors. Either way, she goes above and beyond for them.

Tilly points an accusatory finger at Lottie, "Mammy's having a baby."

"Congratulations!" Jessica spins to Lottie.

"My cousin!"

Jessica's face drops. Yeah, I can imagine that's a shock to

hear without further explanation. "Lottie is being a surrogate for her brother," I add.

The wave of relief that rushes over Jessica's features is comical, "Oh, wow, Lottie, that's incredible."

"Well, I'm not pregnant yet. I go in on Monday."

Jason stretches as he enters the room, "and they go in with the turkey baster," he kisses Lottie's cheek before he rummages through my fridge.

I hear the front door opening and spot William carrying in a handful of bags. Tilly clocks him straight away and moves in. "Wait right there, mister!" she's all pouty face and diva-level sass right now. "You gots sweets?"

"Yeah," he looks rattled. Good.

"What kind?" Tilly waits with her arms folded, looking unimpressed with the assortment of jellies and lollies being presented. "What else you got?"

"Matilda!" I choke on a laugh. Little miss sassy pants indeed. I love this little nightmare.

"They the yucky sweets, daddy!"

William drops the snubbed bag and opens another. Tilly reaches in and pulls out some chocolates and fizzy cola bottles. "Better."

James comes bounding into the room, he's after stripping himself out of his pants again and is running around like Tommy Pickles with just a t-shirt and nappy on, "Tee Tee!"

Tilly demands the packet of cola bottles be opened immediately and hands the bag to James. "This is my friend," she announces.

William looks between the toddlers and grins, "I see, hello..."

"He don't talk good."

"Oh, ok."

"He's not weird!"

"I didn't say—"

"His name is James," she continues talking over William.

"Hello, James."

"He don't talk good, dummy!" Tilly rolls her eyes to the heavens, takes James by the hand, and leads him into the sitting room.

James seems more interested in playing by himself right now, but Tilly doesn't mind. She sits on the couch having a munch, waiting for him to approach her. She acts like his mother half the time.

Tiffy doesn't have to worry about James being picked on with Matilda around. If today is anything to go by, she'll sooner flatten whoever picks on him than let them get away with it.

My three-year-old is taking on bigger kids and winning. No surprise there. I'm keeping her around for when I'm old, if anyone pisses me off, they'll have to deal with her.

Jessica peeks into the sitting room to see the pair watching TV, Tilly even allows the Cookie Monster Roadshow to play for James. He's the only one allowed to turn off the mouse and not get his head kicked in. "She's so good with him."

"I know," Lottie beams. "Probably because she can hand him back at the end of the day. As long as she stays the baby, we stay safe."

"So no more babies?"

"Nah, we're good with three," I admit. "I'm booked for the old snip snip on Monday. It works out well, I can't touch Lottie for two weeks anyway."

Jason laughs, biting into half a baguette. I didn't even see him make the damn roll. "And nothing's going to make him stick to that more than a sore bollocks."

"Thanks for that."

"Any time, man."

"What about you, Jason?" Jessica asks, she doesn't know about the separation. I glance at Jay who has his mouth full and then to Tiffy who adopts a breezy demeanour. "Any more kids?"

Tiffy's poker face is working overtime right now, "we're going to see how James gets on first with his assessments. If he is autistic, it gives us a 50/50 chance of having another with autism and they could be worse."

Jay manages to swallow the mammoth size bite he chewed off. He seems relieved by Tiffy's answer. If there was no hope of them getting back together Tiffy would have told Jessica about the temporary split. "Plus, we don't know how James will cope with the change. I mean; besides Tilly, he doesn't like any other kids his age. They're too noisy and he hates it when they cry."

"It's mad how something that should be so black and white can turn into a real debate when you have a child with additional needs," Jessica sounds fascinated. She has mentioned an interest in child psychology, maybe she'll pursue it one day. "I mean, usually it's a yes or no answer with having kids or adding on to the family. I don't think most people appreciate how hard a choice like that can be when you know there is a possibility of having another with additional needs. Plus, as you said, Jason, you have to think of James."

"Meh, it is what it is," he reaches for a can of coke and cracks it open with a hiss. "I just think James is a little behind with his words. I mean, whatever happened to they'll talk when they're ready?" He takes two large gulps before continuing. "Now they want milestones to hit every few weeks, and what? If you don't hit them, you're either a shit parent or there is something wrong with your kid? It's bullshit!"

Matilda thunders out into the hallway, "you naughty boy!"

"Sorry, chicken!"

CRAIG

So, the treatment worked. my wife has a womb like Wonder Woman. First time and she's preggers. Her titties are huge, and that arse has some more oomph behind it. She's also a raging nymphomaniac. I'm happy.

Satan went into school once we got the news that Lottie was pregnant and decided to tell her teacher that, "mammy is pregnant with Uncle Nicky's baby."

I could have explained the situation immediately, but it was more fun watching her squirm when I confirmed that that is the case.

What was even funnier was when Ms Coffey found out that I don't have a brother (well, not one that I've met yet) and that Nick is, in fact, Lottie's older brother.

Jason was practically rolling around the yard laughing at that reaction, and we were both waiting for Tusla to wind up at the door later that day.

Lottie took the fun out of it and explained the surrogacy thing when she collected Matilda later that day. Now I'm a prick for not correcting the teacher in the first place. Ah well, I got an uninterrupted blowjob before that, so I still see it as a massive win.

William has been surprisingly good with the kids. Ellie has taken to him more than the others. Matilda still has a chip on her shoulder about the lack of presents and demands that she gets three years' worth on her birthday, or he will no longer be welcome in the house.

I love that kid.

I've healed up great from the old snip snip too. If Lottie gets pregnant after this the ginger has some explaining to do.

The business is in full swing. Since Jessica's stunt we have tripled our profit and continue to grow and expand. Jason is taking a little too much pleasure in being Co-CEO.

Lottie is at that stage of pregnancy where she is not showing, but she's tired as hell all the time. She could sleep for twelve hours, wake up, have breakfast, and go back for a nap.

I heard one of the new guys remark on her, not knowing she is my wife. He tried to be a smart arse saying, "she's good-looking for a fat chick."

Safe to say that arsehat went over the fucking wall.

Fat chick?

Fucking prick.

My wife is not fat. My wife is a fucking goddess. Big, beautiful green eyes, long full lashes. Tits that would make a porn star jealous, most women have to pay for titties like hers!

She's a modern-day Monroe, and that prick called her fat! The only fat thing I saw was the fat lip he had when he stood back up.

Jay strolls into the office with his hands shoved in his pockets, "so, you skewered Glen."

"The prick deserved it."

"Fair enough," Jay sucks on his teeth. "He passed a remark on Lottie?"

"Called her fat," I grumble as I rummage through the desk looking for a particular contract.

Jay pauses, glances outside then turns to face me, "and he's still breathing?"

"I was feeling generous."

Jay's lips squish to the side as he lowers himself into the seat opposite me, "she's not even fat though."

"I know! And if she was, she would still be fucking gorgeous. I should go back out there and strangle him for good measure."

"Fired him?"

Ah, there's the little bastard now. I pull out Glen's contract and slam it on my desk. "Not yet. I'm debating it."

"I can't believe he said that. I'd motorboat the shit out of Lottie."

"Oi!"

"It's a compliment," Jay has the gall to look affronted.

"She's my wife."

"With a rack that won't quit and an arse I'd play bongo's on."

I narrow my eyes at him, "you get one more of those."

"I wouldn't just eat my dinner off that arse, that arse is the dinner."

"And you're done."

"Worth it."

Dean staggers into the room armed with three large Costa coffees, "what are we talking about?"

Jason looks over his shoulder and grins, "Lottie's tits."

"Those kissable squishables?"

"Hey!" *not him too!*

"Compliment," Dean slides a coffee to me and then blows on the contents of his own takeaway cup.

"I don't comment on your wives' racks."

Dean smacks his lips together, "that's coz your wife wins that one."

"Ba dum dum tss!" Jay air squeezes a pair of imaginary tits and I kick him under the table. "Wank bank material!"

"I'm going to fucking—"

"Nestle in that cleavage for winter," Jason goads.

"Death by snu-snu!" Dean chimes in.

I best text Josie. Today is the day that I'm done for multiple murders.

"You pair need help," I growl as I pop the lid off my Costa cup.

Jason grins wickedly, "I'll help myself to your sister."

"What!"

"Glen, shut your face, you're already in trouble!" Jay yells, earning a confused retort back from his scapegoat. That prick will say anything to get a rise out of me.

Dean finds a spot on the windowsill to perch himself on, "so what's all this about you expanding the business?"

"We have been," how do I say this without putting my foot in it? "Doing some private security work for a friend."

"Got us thinking about branching out," Jay adds.

"Private security?" Dean echoes, "like bodyguards?"

Bodyguards, getaway drivers, private detectives. Whatever floats your boat. "Something like that."

"Wouldn't you need a license?"

"Already finished the courses," I grin back at him.

"What about your records?"

"Expunged."

"Who would you hire? I mean, you can't really go to your guys on the construction roster."

Meaning half the guys are ex-cons, like us.

It doesn't bother us, most on our roster have the typical background, a troubled teen that acted out or someone who got hooked on substances young and got clean.

Jay and I give guys like that a job because they're looking for a fresh start and most places won't look at you with a record.

What we don't hire are sex offenders and woman beaters, those scumbags can take a long walk off a short plank.

"We know a guy," I say after some contemplation. "Nick's friend Joe for example. He's a garda and is sort of looking for a change of pace. Ex-military, gardaí, and security guards, they'll all come in handy for what we plan. Three of us can start the ball rolling while we look to fill the roster."

"You guys and Joe?" Dean presses.

"Us and Nick. The pay will be better, hours will be better and he doesn't have to worry about being assaulted by stepping out of the house in his uniform."

"Wow, you guys are really doing well for yourselves, aren't you."

"It's all thanks to his willy," Jay gets to his feet, comes around the desk and rummages for his pack of cigarettes.

"What?"

"If he didn't give in and finally sleep with Lottie, we

wouldn't be here. It's amazing what one decision can do for a person," Jay pops a cigarette between his lips and lights up.

He's not wrong. If Lottie and I never happened, the Michael thing never would have happened which means that the court case never would have happened. I'd never have known about Jessica because she wouldn't have known about me and never would have hunted me down. Jay and I wouldn't have had Jessica and Dean to boost the business and we never would have had the money to branch out further.

My penis did us proud.

LOTTIE

I collect Tilly from school today, she walks, and I waddle. I'm not even waddling because of the pregnancy, I'm far from being heavily pregnant. I'm waddling because when Craig dropped the kids at school this morning, he came back and pounced on me before his keys could hit the table behind the front door.

He always loved me being pregnant because he could go without condoms. Now, since the vasectomy, he can happily go without being sheathed from here on out. Something he is taking full advantage of.

He grabbed me in the kitchen and I've no idea when it happened, but we ended up on the landing by the end. I'm assuming we were aiming for the bed and remembered there were no kids in the house, so every surface was up for grabs.

It's nice having those few hours of freedom again. As much as we love the kids, we love the few hours alone to just be adults. To be with each other, not just for the sex, the novelty of that will wear off after a while.

I'm definitely not complaining about the sex either. It's still thoroughly enjoyable, but what I really love is having the time to just be with Craig. To snuggle up on the couch and watch bad TV or after having a rough night, being able to curl up next to him in bed and have a nap or read. Even tasks like bringing the puppies on a walk are more enjoyable.

So many of my readers still ask me how we are able to work together after so long. I tell them that it's not about the sex. Being friends for years before we ever kissed or made love, before we ever conceived the possibility of us being together, gave us time to really get to know each other and to form a bond.

If I were only after Craig for his looks and sex, we would be another figure in the divorce line. Passion fades away over time. Looks fade. People age. People change.

"That's for daddy," Tilly points to the red velvet muffins in the bakery, she has already picked out a sticky toffee muffin for Ethan and a raspberry and white chocolate one for Ellie. "That's for mammy," she points to a mint chocolate muffin and waits for the girl behind the counter to pick it up and add it to the box with the other cakes.

"And what do you want, sweetie?"

"That one!" she points to a large box marked as the Mega Cookie.

Oh, joy.

So much sugar.

I'm screwed.

Mega Cookie indeed, it's the size of a small pizza. Tilly refuses to wait, she begins breaking off pieces and devouring them on the way home.

By the time we get in the front door, her hands and face are covered in melted chocolate chip, and she still has three-quarters of it left.

"Woah," Craig takes a step back, "cookie monster."

"Hi, stinky!"

"Good day in school?"

"Yep," she toddles inside and goes straight for the puppies.

Craig runs at her with a wet wipe and takes the remaining segments of cookie into the kitchen and away from the dogs.

He snakes his arms around me, his head peeking over my shoulder, "how are you feeling?" his lips find my cheek under my mass of curls.

"A little tired, but good."

"Yeah? This morning was—"

"Good?"

"Amazing."

I turn in his hold, resting my head against his chest. Reaching up, I play with the hair on the back of his neck.

"When is the big day again?" he asks.

"Next week. Abbie is over the moon." It will be weird having Abbie with me and not Craig for the doctor's appointments and the labour. He was my rock through all three pregnancies, and he never missed a single appointment.

Of course, this is Abbie's baby, and I'm only allowed one person in the room with me for scans and the delivery, it's only right that she is with me through everything.

"Cravings?" Craig mumbles against my crown.

"Not yet."

"Heartburn?"

"A little."

"Nausea?"

"Meh..." I stifle a yawn. "Just tired."

"Do you want to head to bed for a while? I'll keep an eye on Matilda down here while you get some rest."

"She's due her nap soon, I'll take her up with me."

Tilly demands that Craig comes up and reads her a story because, "daddy does it better," so we are all huddled in the one bed, Tilly in the middle.

CRAIG

I finish reading Stickman and look over at Tilly, she is already fast asleep. Lottie is curled on her side, snoring lightly.

Tilly is just as beautiful as her mother, and just as feisty too.

She has the same spray of freckles on her cheeks and going

across the bridge of her nose. The same cheeky smile and pouty face when she's sulking.

She has my eyes and Lottie's bright strawberry-blonde hair.

My two selfless girls.

Lottie. The love of my life, putting her body through the trauma of pregnancy and birth because of her love for Nick and Abbie.

Matilda. My little terror. She already knows who she is at three years old, she stands up for James and refuses to be pushed around. If she keeps that spark going, I'll never have to worry about her.

The two not sleeping in bed right now, Ethan. My only son. Mammy's boy to his very core, and he is as impulsive as his mother. Unfortunately, he has my mouth and that tends to get him into trouble. He's so smart, he has to get that from Lottie because he sure as hell doesn't get it from me.

Ellie. My little princess. She's as bad as her mother. I'm going to come home to a zoo in the house one of these days. She is the first to help someone in need and has brought home numerous strays over the years. She also made sure that we got them vet care and rehomed them.

I honestly don't know where I got my kids from but those big hearts of theirs come from Lottie.

I pull the blanket over my girls to keep them warm while they rest. Kiss them both on the head before going downstairs and prepping dinner before I have to collect the other pair from school.

I know what I have to do. I have to win. For them.

I have to beat this monkey on my back, and I have to win this game of Russian roulette with Éabha. Lottie taught me how to love, but one thing I've known how to do long before Lottie is fight.

CRAIG

I spot the mop of blonde hair before she comes into view, "hello gorgeous." Kim struts into the room arms out wide. As soon as she gets her claws on me, she squeezes the life out of me like a python.

"There's my girl."

"Someone's been working out."

"Not that much."

"Not you, me! Look at this tush!" Kim spins, unapologetically trying to get me to comment on her arse.

"Mam!"

"Squats," Kim beams, "the trick is to come back up."

"That's what he said," Lottie snorts.

"And back down again," I add.

"Behave," Kim warns.

"Never!"

"Where are my grandbabies?"

"Ethan is out with Jamie. Ellie and Tilly are gone for a Disney sleepover at Jessica's," I stifle a yawn and stretch. It's nice that the girls have taken to her so well and are now comfortable enough to stay with her. Ellie took little convincing, she just saw a pretty, big sister type and was all over her. Tilly took some bribing.

"How is Jessica?"

"Doing good, thanks."

"And Voldemort?" Kim refers to William as Voldemort ever since Lottie referred to him as you know who.

"Meh. He comes and goes. The kids are starting to take to him."

There is a brief pause as Kim assesses me, "and you?"

"I guess... meh. That's all I can say on the matter. Just meh."

"As good of terms as any."

Lottie turns to her mother and asks, "how did the date go?"

"Dreadful! Being a single gal nowadays is scary."

"Too many creeps?" I ask.

"Yes! Did you know anal is basic nowadays?"

"Mam!" Lottie looks nauseated.

"One guy wanted to lick it!"

"Oh. My. God," Lottie turns her head into my chest, hoping to hide from her mother's admission.

"That's what she said," I snort.

Lottie slaps me across the chest and storms out of the room.

Kim sighs, then gives me the side-eye, "you wouldn't be into that sort of thing?"

"Who me?" I ask.

"Yes, you!"

"Lick Lottie? Like a lollipop."

"Craig!" Lottie roars.

"Well, at least you're honest. Charlotte, Mammy needs a strong drink."

"I need a fucking sedative," Lottie retorts.

"Wine?" I ask.

"Please!"

"Red, right?"

"Good man yourself!"

"You know Nick is working with Joe again?" Lottie comes back into the room after getting her bearings.

"Joe?" Kim asks. "Hot Joe?"

"I love the way that is how everyone describes him," I chuckle."

"Hey, I've seen that tush!"

"I thought you liked mine?" I feign outrage.

"You're taken."

"I'm sorry, baby," Lottie rubs her belly. "Your family is fucking dysfunctional."

"Every family is, we just admit it."

"Damn straight!"

"I think it's a wonderful thing you're doing for Nick, Lottie."

"Thanks, Mam."

"Daddy would be so proud of you. I know I am."

Poor Kim. After all this time you can still see the love she holds for Big Nick. I can't imagine how painful that was to lose him and go on this long without him.

She always refers to him as Daddy when speaking to Nick and Lottie. Still refers to him as her husband. Still celebrates his birthday and their wedding anniversary. She keeps his memory alive which is wonderful to see. I've heard so many stories about the man, I'm just sorry I never met him.

"So," Kim clears her throat. "Hot Joe, huh? Is he single?"

"Ma!"

"Oh please, if Madonna can do it so can I!"

"Preach!" I pass her a glass of wine, chuckling at her reasoning.

"Knock knock!" Dean calls from the hallway.

"Ooh, look at this delectable piece of man cake!"

"Ma!" Lottie snaps.

"And hello to you too!"

"Drink?" I ask, turning for the kitchen.

"Please!"

"It's Dean, right?" Kim steps up beside him.

"I'll be whomever you want me to be," he winks at Kim.

"Want me to tell your wife that?" Lottie snorts.

"All the good ones are married," Kim sighs. "So, you're the man playing my boy in this Netflix thing."

"That's right!"

"Turn around, show me the tush." Lottie facepalms herself, grumbling under her breath. Dean happily obliges, spinning slowly and hiking up his shirt. "Nice tush."

"Thank you, I do my bum busters every day."

"I like him!"

Dean chuckles and turns to me, "ready to kick this delectable tush?"

"Yeah, just let me grab my gym bag and we'll go."

"I'm ready to be humbled yet again when you send my ass crashing to the mat."

"You're getting better though."

"You have to remember Craig has like twenty-eight years of experience, can't expect to be the best overnight," Lottie adds.

She's hesitant trying to add up how long I've been fighting. She's right though. Twenty-eight years. Great. Now I feel like a fossil.

I don't fight anymore anyway, not really. I spar with the other guys and mainly stick to teaching self-defence classes when they need a stand-in.

To this day, Lottie was the hardest person for me to train. Not because she was a bad student, far from it. It was because it was close contact and any time I was trying to show her how to get free of holds, I was popping awkward boners left, right and centre.

Not so awkward with just us two in a room, but in the gym

full of guys, especially guys I work with like Jason and Dylan, it makes the situation all the more awkward.

Finishing up in the ring, beads of sweat trickle down my chest and the nape of my neck. Dean is huffing and puffing from the corner of the ring.

"Craig?" I know that voice. How do I know that voice?

I spin towards the familiar sound, and it takes me a little more than two seconds to register who it is.

An ex-girlfriend, "Claire? Hi!"

"Hi, how are you?" she hasn't changed a bit. Her body is the same as I remember, tanned, toned, tiny waist. Soft wisps of her blonde hair fall on her face.

"I'm good thanks, you?"

"Great," she takes a swig from her water bottle, "just back from a shoot."

Of course she is.

Wow, it's been about twelve years since I last saw her, and she hasn't aged a day.

"You're still modelling?" I ask, noticing a particularly shiny forehead under all that hair. *Ah, that explains it.*

Botox.

"Yeah, not as much as I used to. I've done a few acting gigs too. Travelled, you know, the usual."

The usual indeed.

We were together for about six months before we broke up. At that time, I was constantly at parties, and mingling with beautifully shallow people of the world. I went to a few of her shoots which I won't complain about, it was an experience. One I refuse to let my daughters have after seeing what goes on behind the scenes.

"Great, I'm glad things are going well for you."

"Thanks." She takes another swig from her bottle, and I

realise her lips are bigger than they were before. "So how have you been?"

"Good. Great. Fantastic actually," it's not a lie, things are going amazing, I just wish my stupid brain would accept it. "Business is booming, the kids are all finally in school, so we have the few hours of freedom back."

"You have kids now?" she asks with wide eyes.

"Three."

"Wow, the regular family man," she smirks.

Why is that so surprising?

"Who's the lucky woman?" Claire asks before I get a word in. "Anyone I know?"

"Yeah, you know her. Remember Nick my old roommate? It's his sister Lottie."

I watch her try to put a face to the name. For a split second, she looks like she has been hit in the face with a frying pan. Then she cracks the largest, fake smile I've ever seen. "Wow. Ginger Lottie? The... curvy girl?"

Don't even go there with me.

I'm not one for slapping women, but I'm not against grabbing Tilly and having her kick this bitch in the flaps.

"Yeah, *Lottie,*" I try and hold back the growl but some of it escapes regardless of my efforts. "What's the matter?"

"Huh?"

"Your face gave you away. What was that look?" come on, say it to my face. I dare you. I don't care how much filler you pump into those distorted fish lips, I'll fucking end you.

She laughs nervously, "always so forward."

"Yeah, some things never change." Amazing how someone can have such a big head with nothing but air between her ears.

"Apparently not," she mutters, turning to look for an excuse to run off.

"So," I force a smirk that I highly doubt comes across as friendly. "What's your problem?"

"No problem," she says quickly. "I'm just surprised."

"What's so surprising?"

"I never pegged her as your type," she looks everywhere but me.

"Don't like redheads?"

"No, nothing like that. She's a lovely girl."

"Yeah, she is."

"A little... young, don't you think?"

I scoff. "She's four years my junior. I'm hardly a cradle snatcher."

"I guess I never pictured you together."

"If you have trouble with the mental image, I can show you a picture."

She glares at me. "A bit defensive today?"

"Not in the slightest."

She exhales, slapping that fake smile on her plastic face as she attempts to change the subject, "you look good."

"I know."

"So," she worries her lip and looks at the ground, "business is doing well?"

"Yep."

She peeks over my shoulder at the moaning body struggling to get up from the mat, "Oh, hi! You're Dean Kearney, right?"

"That's me," Dean pants as he fights to catch his breath.

"I'm a huge fan!"

Of course you are.

"Thank you!"

I'm being blatantly ignored right now. I couldn't care less. Claire is a beautiful girl, even better before she started pumping chemicals into her face, but she's the epitome of shallow. She never saw Lottie as "competition" because she has a bit of meat on her. Claire is convinced that because she is a model and has a great body that that's enough to get her by in life, which it has done, so far.

Claire couldn't understand why I ended things. She asked if there was someone else and I told her outright that there was. Although I never mentioned who. Even then, while I was trying to move on and date other women while Lottie was still with Michael, I was fucking crazy about her.

Claire, beautiful and all as she is, couldn't measure up. No matter what way I looked at it, she wasn't Lottie. So she had to go. They all had to go.

Cheeky bitch and her insinuations though. I've never understood that double standard. If someone like Claire was to date an average or chubby guy, he'd be high-fived and known as a lucky bastard. Switch the tables around and the girl gets insulted, with people constantly wondering what the guy sees in her just because she has a bit of meat on her bones.

I turn to Dean who is taking a selfie with Claire and wipe down my neck with the towel before signalling to the doors to let him know I'm hitting the showers.

"It was good to see you again, Craig," Claire calls as I pass the mats.

"I wish I could say the same."

When I get home, I find Lottie and Ethan sitting down, watching the Avengers and munching on popcorn and minstrels.

"That's mam to dad," Ethan laughs as the Hulk smashes Loki into the ground.

"You're not wrong there, buddy," I chuckle, reaching over Lottie for a handful of popcorn.

"Good workout?" Lottie asks.

"Meh. Better being home," I glance around, "where's Kim?"

"Got a taxi home about an hour ago."

"Ah, right."

Lottie looks up at me, her brow furrows, “are you ok?”

“Yeah, fine.”

“Sure?”

“Positive,” leaning over, I place a gentle kiss on her lips. Ethan makes his disgust known. I toss the handful of popcorn at him in response.

“Dad!”

CRAIG

"Hey, look! I'm Madonna!" I turn around to find Lottie holding a pair of empty ice cream cone nipples.

This is why I love the woman. She's nuts.

"Look at how precious our little lamb is!" Abbie is cooing over the sonogram pictures. "Look, Maddie, you're going to be a big sister." Maddie is too busy stuffing her toes in her mouth to give a damn. She's too young to understand, at ten months old the world revolves around her.

"Hey, fatty!" Nick calls.

"Hey, long back," Lottie retaliates.

"Nick, look!" Abbie shoves the pictures at Nick who looks through them, beaming.

"All good?"

"Perfect!"

"All good," Lottie snorts. "Bitch please, I'm THE baby maker. This womb carried Tilly, your kid is no bother."

She has a point there.

Nick walks over, messing up Lottie's hair and kissing her crown. "Thank you for doing this."

"Don't go getting all soft on me."

"Trust you to ruin the moment," I snort.

"I don't do sweet well. Snarky I can do!"

"I won't debate that."

"Quiet you filthy little beast. Besides look at this dress, size 16! I was wearing it last week and it was a bit snug, it's loose now, woohoo! Shrinking!" Lottie picks up a digestive biscuit and starts chomping down.

"You lost weight and you're rewarding yourself with biscuits," Nick chuckles.

"Well yeah, I'm pregnant anyway, won't be fucking shrinking much longer."

"I fucking love you." I can't even with this woman. She's too random, much like her mother. She doesn't give a shit about anything and that's hot as hell.

Lottie may have been insecure when we first go together but since Ethan's come along, she has a confidence about her that's so alluring. She knows she's beautiful, finally start seeing what I've seen since day one. It took some time to reverse the damage Michael did to her, but she came around and I wouldn't change her or her ice cream cone nipples for the world.

Lottie grabs her belly and starts speaking in her baby voice. "I shall call you squishy, and you shall be mine, and you shall be my squishy."

"What happened to jiggly puff?" I ask.

"That was me on Tilly!"

"The Pillsbury doughboy?" Nick presses.

"Ethan."

"Snorlax?" Abbie giggles.

"Ellie! Couldn't stay awake on that child. Hey, Batman?"

"Yessums?"

"What's for dinner? I'm starving!"

"Lottie, it's like 12:30," Nick protests.

"Yeah, and I'm hungry. So, where's the food?"

"What do you want?" I ask.

"What have we got?"

"Burgers?"

"No."

"Fish?"

"No."

"Lasagne?"

"No."

"Pasta."

"No."

"For fuck's sake, what do you want, woman?"

"I don't know!" she looks at me like I'm the problem.

"Kebab?"

"No."

"McDonald's?"

"Nah."

"I'm going to skull you!"

Lottie shrugs, "maybe later."

"TGI'S?"

"No."

"Nando's?"

"Ick."

"Eddie's?"

"Ooh, yes! Eddie Rockets! Get in my belly! With garlic cheese fries, a big chocolate malt and my chicken burger! No onions! Extra sauce."

"No boneless chicken wings this time?" I tease.

"Well, if you're offering, I won't say no."

I turn to Nick and Abbie and ask, "do you pair want anything?"

"I'll rob some of Lottie's," Nick laughs.

"That's a good way to lose a hand," Lottie warns.

"I'll pick you up a slider basket," I offer.

"Make that two!" Abbie says.

"Satan!"

"What?"

"I'm going to Eddie's, what do you want?"

"Malt!" That's all I get before she vanishes.

"Ellie!"

"Yes?"

"What do you want in Eddie's?"

"Ooh, can I have the chilli pepper popper, please,"

"Of course you can, princess," where did I get this kid from? She's the only one with manners. "Ethan."

"M50 upgrade!"

"You were just waiting on the other side of that door for me to call you, weren't you?"

"Maybe."

"Good. Get your coat you're coming with me," I make a quick call, placing our order before getting in the car with Ethan and going to collect the haul.

"So, mam's having a baby?" Ethan asks.

"Yep."

"But it's not yours."

"Nope."

"It's Uncle Nick's."

"Yep."

"Did they have sex?"

Goodbye food, it was nice knowing you! I'm startled, I mount the kerb.

"No!"

"How is Nick's baby in her belly then?"

"The doctor put it in there. We had this discussion already, buddy."

"I know, it's just weird."

"Weird how?"

"Mam's going to have my cousin."

"Yep."

"So does that make her the baby's mam?"

"No," I groan and try and think of the best way to explain this. "Look, I get that this is all a bit confusing. The baby is all Nick and Abbie's just like Madison. Mam is just giving the baby somewhere to grow."

"Why can't Abbie do it?"

"It's complicated, buddy. Mam had you, Ellie, and Tilly, yeah."

"Yeah."

"So she's just giving the baby somewhere safe to grow because we know mammy can grow babies really well."

Wow, how do I get into these conversations?

"And Abbie can't?"

"It's not that she can't, it's just that it's much harder for Abbie to do it. So mam offered to do it in her place."

"Oh, ok," he squishes his lips to the side. "So no more sisters or brothers then?"

"No, buddy. It's just you three."

"Thank God."

I can't help but laugh, "why that reaction?"

"Have you met Tilly? She's enough without having another!"

I laugh harder. "That's your kid sister!"

"I know but she can still be a pain!"

"Get used to it."

When Nick and Abbie leave and the kids are gone to bed, I catch Lottie staring in the mirror.

"You alright, baby?"

"I'm going to be the size of a house again soon."

"You were never the size of a house."

"My big Bridget Jones pants will be making a return."

"Oh joy!" I chuckle.

She spins to face me, "at least my belly will give my boobs something to rest on."

I pull my shirt up overhead, kick off my shoes, push down my joggers and fall onto the bed. "You coming in or am I going to have to look at your arse for the night?"

"Complaining?"

"Not at all. I'd rather you come closer with it so I can cop a feel."

"You would think that you'd be sick of me by now."

"Never."

Lottie changes into one of my shirts, and then crawls up the bed to me, pouting.

I hate seeing her upset, "what's wrong?" I reach out, tilting her chin up to look at me.

"I miss you."

"Miss me? I'm right here!"

"You've been gone so much lately with the business and setting up the security place and then looking after Éabha. You're gone more than you're around."

I swallow the ball of guilt lodged at the back of my throat. "I'm sorry."

"Don't be. I'm proud of you. I'm glad that girl has someone looking out for her."

"It'll all be over soon, and I'll be around more often. I promise."

"Just be careful, please. Nick told me what happened with that witness..." she trails off, looking concerned.

"I'll be careful."

"What if someone comes after you?" fear sparks behind her eyes.

"Then I'll smash them through the pavement as I did with Michael," I sit up, pulling her onto my lap. "Baby, I'm not going anywhere, I swear." I lean in, kissing her tenderly. "I won't let anyone come between us."

"I know. Just hurry up already so I can have you back, yeah? I hate sharing you."

"Greedy," I tease.

"Possessive."

"I love you."

"I love you too, Batman. Now scooch over, it's my pick tonight." Lottie grabs the remote and starts flicking through Netflix, she told me to move and yet when I attempt it, she hauls me back to her, refusing to let me out of her sight.

She attempts to move into multiple positions, not able to get comfortable in any. By the end, she is reclining on me so I'm trying to watch the TV with Lottie between my legs and a face full of her hair.

CRAIG

Keys... keys. Where the hell are my keys?

Ah, there you are, you little bastards.

"Where you going?" Tilly demands.

"Gotta go to work, I'll be back later." I pull on my jacket and call up the stairs, "good luck today, princess! I'll see you later, ok?"

"Ok, daddy!"

She's got her first dance competition today and I have to miss it. I hate it. I try to be there for all the kids' big days but McIntosh is a particular breed of stubborn swine and refuses to change the day of the meeting.

I hear Lottie on the staircase demanding that Matilda put her shoes on asap.

Ellie's voice follows, "bye, daddy!"

I turn to Ellie and freeze. "What the hell is that?"

"What?"

Lottie huffs something colourful under her breath, "her outfit, what does it look like?"

"Where's the rest of it?"

"That's it," Lottie leans against the handrail, gearing for an argument.

"ALL OF IT?"

Ellie looks down at herself and asks, "what's wrong? Don't you like it?"

"It's not that, princess, I— ARE YOU WEARING MAKE-UP?"

"Calm down," Lottie growls.

"Calm down? *She's six!*" I spin, looking into the sitting room and then into the kitchen. "Where's my gun?"

Ethan snorts as he pulls on his jacket, "you don't have a gun, dad."

"Well, I'm going to fucking get a gun!"

"Ooh, you said it!" Tilly points an accusatory finger at me.

"Craig!" Lottie snaps. "You're being ridiculous. That's a standard outfit for these competitions."

"What paedo designed them? The outfit does not belong on a child! It belongs on a big titted barbie in a porno or sliding down a pole with the rest of her dreams!"

"Daddy," Ellie's lower lip begins to quiver.

Shit.

"Princess, I'm not mad at you, ok?"

"Ok," she sniffs and wipes her eyes.

"You'll be late for your meeting," Lottie growls.

I whip out my phone and find Jay's name.

"Yello!"

"Go on without me."

"What?"

"You heard!"

"You're not coming? What am I supposed to tell McIntosh?"

"Tell him I died of dysentery."

"I always knew you were full of shit."

I hang up, not bothering to hear Jason's crap jokes right now— no pun intended.

Ellie's face lights up, "you're coming to my competition?"

"Yes. Get your coat... a long one," a lightbulb goes off when I think of the Halloween outfits upstairs. "I'm sure I have a Teletubbies outfit up there somewhere, wear that!"

"Craig," Lottie rolls her eyes to the heavens.

"Charlotte."

"All the kids wear them."

"If all the kids decided to start wearing G-strings and nipple tassels would that be ok?"

"Wow," she finally comes down the stairs and I'm waiting for a clatter across the face. "You're that dad now?"

"Yes, I'm that fucking dad! Have you seen the news lately? Those attempted abductions at schools and playgrounds?"

"It's a dance competition!"

"That's performed in an outfit that is practically painted on!"

"Get. In. The. Car," Lottie snarls and I know I'm seconds away from a swift kick in the bollocks.

"With fucking pleasure!"

We all bundle in the car. I stick Tilly in her car seat. Ethan climbs in the middle, and I drape my jacket around Ellie and practically tie her in it before allowing her to walk to the car.

Lottie is pissed at me.

I attempt to climb into the driver's seat but she hits me with the door and hauls ass inside instead.

"You mad?" Tilly leans forwards, tapping me on the shoulder.

"No, Tilly."

"Mam's mad?"

"Yep."

"Why?"

"Daddy's being unreasonable," Lottie growls, putting the car in drive. If I really wanted to piss her off right now, I'd point out the fact that she can't drive a manual. She tried and failed her test four times before we got her an automatic and she passed on her first go. I'm sure if I mentioned that one right now, she'd stick my head through the windscreen.

"Why?" Tilly presses.

"Because he's a man."

"Because I'd like my child to be dressed appropriately for her age!"

"Stop fighting!" Ethan yells. "You're upsetting Ellie."

I turn around to see Ellie hiding in the confines of my jacket. Her eyes brimming with unshed tears.

"I'm sorry Ellie belly. Mom and I are just having a disagreement, this is not about you, princess, ok?"

"Ok."

Lottie glances in the rear-view mirror, "you look beautiful, Ellie. Doesn't she, daddy." Lottie says that last part through her teeth.

"Of course," I turn back to face my daughter, "that's why I have to hide you under there. I don't want anyone stealing you from me."

I just wish they wouldn't paint my daughter up like some streetwalker for a competition. I'll be watching like a hawk. If anyone so much as glances at her funnily I'll dance them into the ground.

Ellie is under explicit instructions not to remove the damn jacket until she gets called up to perform. The only other exception is her posing for pictures with her friends— I was outnumbered on that one. Jessica, Tiffany, and Lottie chewed the arse off me when I tried to object.

"Dad, look! Ellie's up next!" Ethan calls. I push forward, scanning the crowd, ready to hogtie anyone that looks remotely sketchy.

Then I see her. My little princess. She's up for her first solo dance.

She moves fluidly with the music. The room is silent.

Everyone, including me, watches as she twirls and leaps effortlessly in the air.

She looks so happy. Free. Perfect.

Ellie finishes her dance and waits for the judges' scores. It's no surprise that she comes out with one of the highest scores in her age group so far.

"Did you see me, daddy? Did you see me dance?"

"I saw, princess," I stuff her back inside my jacket. "You were amazing."

She beams with pride, tossing her arms around me. Lottie and Tiffy shower Ellie with praise, Jessica nudges me, grinning from ear to ear, "our girl can dance."

"Well done, sweetie," I hear William call. I spin around, surprised to see him here.

"Grandad!"

"You dance beautifully, Ellie."

"Thank you!"

When she scurries away to her friends and teachers, William steps up beside me, "you look like you're about to hit the roof."

"Tempted."

"Me?"

"No. Not for once."

He smiles then, "the costume?"

"You noticed," I grumble, keeping my eyes fixed on Ellie.

"Hard to miss. It's a bit... eh—"

"Wrong! Pervy! I'm sure that's breaking some kind of law!"

He chuckles lowly, "you sound just like your mother. She was always so protective over you. She would happily bludgeon anyone that looked at you funny."

"You think she was wrong?" Pulling my eyes from Ellie, I lock eyes with William.

"No. I think your mother was a better parent than I ever was," he admits, then turns away to search the crowd for Ellie. "Your girl is talented, Craig."

"I know."

"Unfortunately, the outfits are part of the piece. Jessica used to wear them. I hated it."

"She's happy... dancing that is," I follow his gaze back to Ellie and see her beaming. That smile could light up a room.

"She is. So, does this mean you're going to make peace with the outfits?"

"Nope. I'm just going to bring a shotgun to every future event." I spot Lottie out of the corner of my eye, talking to the other dance moms. Excusing myself, I go to her, draping my arm around her waist. "She looked beautiful up there."

"She did."

"Just like her mother," I kiss her crown.

"The stick slide out of your arse?"

"Nope. I'm not happy about the way they have her presented."

"But?" Lottie presses, turning to me, I notice an impish twinkle in her eye.

"But I'm not going to stop her from doing what she loves."

Lottie turns into me, and her bump finds me first, "you're too protective, you know that, right?"

"You love that about me."

"For the most part."

The day goes in quickly enough. Ellie leaves with four trophies, one for first place, one for second, and two for third. Each in different divisions and acts.

She's thrilled with herself.

I'm thrilled when she's done dancing and I can undercut her with a wet wipe and put her into normal clothes.

We celebrate her victories with a trip to TGI's on the way home. The kids are happier that Lottie and I are no longer growling at each other.

What can I say? That's my baby.

One of them anyway.

I'd rather be called an arse for being a helicopter parent than not know what the hell my kids are up to.

Little did I know that Lottie invited Ellie's friends over for a sleepover tonight.

Eight squealing girls in the house hyped up on sugar and adrenaline from their competition today.

I'm not fucking sleeping tonight, am I?

I'm in the kitchen, on the fifth tub of ice cream.

YES.

FIFTH!"

These girls are eating me out of house and home.

I haven't had a spoonful myself!

I'm charging their parents!

Lottie's ordered out three pizzas for the girls, has popcorn going 90 in the microwave and I swear to Christ if I hear another Bieber song I'm throwing myself out the fucking window.

The girls are inside, screaming out *Love Yourself.* Ironic that the little gerbil singing about loving yourself still looks like he's waiting for puberty to hit.

Sweet Jesus. I knew tonight would be bad, but I didn't know I needed to soundproof my house first!

Ethan thunders out of Lottie's office with his hands clamped over his ears, "Dad, make it stop!"

"If I knew how, I would!"

Lottie's sniggering at the table, munching on the last of the Pringles that again, I didn't see one of. "Calm down you two. Ellie's allowed to have some fun, you know."

"At the expense of our ears!"

Satan thunders down the stairs, wearing nothing more than her nappy and carrying her Mickey Mouse teddy. *"Shut up! I can't hear maself think!"* she slams the sitting room door with such force, she almost takes it from its hinges. "Cheese and rice!"

I now have a new favourite child.

Lottie has disappeared, most likely recording this and using the material for her next book. The one where the husband goes to the shop for cigarettes and never comes fucking back.

Ethan hops up on the stool at the kitchen island, "do we not get pizza?"

"Apparently not."

"What do we get?"

"MICKEY!" the puppy is thundering up the stairs after the child strutting around like a miniature sumo wrestler.

Thor is hiding under the table, pretending he's a chair leg so he isn't cornered by the oohs and ahhs of Ellie's friends.

"Want a Chinese?"

"Does it come with a side of chloroform?" Ethan whines.

He's definitely my child.

"Satan, do you want a Chinese?"

"Cuwwi!"

Ellie pokes her head around the door, "ooh, can we—"

"Feck off. You've got three pizzas and enough ice cream to kill four diabetics!"

"Craig!" Lottie appears at the doorway of her office.

"Me hole!"

"Craig..."

"Lockjaw! That's what you're getting after this, prepare yourself."

Lottie snorts, "tallying up a bill already?"

"You bet your arse I am. Speaking of... that's also on the list!"

"Huh?" Ethan tilts his head like a confused puppy.

I push the tub of ice cream at him, "shut up and keep scooping."

We finally have the gang fed and ready for bed after what

feels like decades. Ethan is hiding in his room, he barricaded the door shut after finding out that two of Ellies's friends have big crushes on him and he has yet to develop an interest in girls or anything that's not books, the Avengers or Sonic the Hedgehog.

He's huddled under his blankets with his books. Matilda fell asleep in our bed with Mickey, we moved both into her room. Thor was still hiding under the table when I locked up for the night. Meanwhile, the girls are cackling like a bunch of old crones.

How the hell am I supposed to sleep tonight?

"It's too warm," Lottie whines, dropping onto the bed in nothing more than her underwear.

That arse is getting skewered.

"Craig!" she gasps as I pounce on her. My body pins hers to the bed. I kiss and nip at her neck, grinding up against her. I can feel myself beginning to tent and I've barely touched her.

"We can't, not tonight."

"We'll be quiet," we've become experts at that.

"When are we ever quiet?" she pushes herself onto her knees and I go around her, repositioning her.

"When we have to be," I leave a trail of open-mouthed kisses down her back, then pull her panties off with my teeth.

"Craig..."

"I'll lock the door." I waste no time doing just that. I'm already straining against my joggers.

The laughter and squeals from downstairs drown out as I approach her.

"We can't—" her words are cut off as I palm her arse, lifting her high enough to taste.

Her fingers tangle in my hair as I dip my tongue inside, eager to please. Lottie bucks and wiggles, trying to break free. I'm having none of it.

I grab her by the hips, dragging her back down the bed. "Don't move while I'm feasting on you." My tongue soon finds its way back to her already-drenched centre. My lips wrap around her clit, sucking hard, just the way she likes it.

Sliding my hand up her body, I find her breasts and begin to squeeze, pinching the nipples, teasing the ever-loving hell out of her.

I bring her right to the edge; she's bucking beneath me like she's about to take off. Then I pull away and climb up the bed.

Grabbing her face between my hands, I kiss her hard. My tongue glides against hers. "I've got something for you. Open your mouth."

I push my joggers down, and she gifts me a wicked grin.

Lottie gives one long lick from base to tip, flicking her tongue over the slit then sucks hard.

I bite down, letting out a rumbling approving groan.

She takes me in slowly, inch by inch until she's taken me all the way to the base. Her mouth is warm and welcoming. I begin to thrust, slowly, allowing her time to adjust.

Lottie's gasps are muffled as I push down her throat, "that's it, baby. Take it all."

I feel her nails scraping over my lower back and arse. She looks up at me through lowered lashes, begging me to take her. To make her scream.

I pull away, leaning down I crush my lips against hers. "What way do you want me?"

"Any way you want," she kisses me hard.

"Turn around."

She grins, then turns, presenting that delectable arse. I kick my joggers off and grab the lube from the bedside table, slowly working a finger into her. Then another. Preparing her to take my full length.

Lottie fists the sheets as I line myself at her slick entrance, "are you ready?"

"Yes."

I press inside, one gratifying inch at a time. She feels

incredible.

Beginning a slow rhythm, slipping one hand around and down, rubbing her clit as I take her from behind, Lottie moans. She drops her head to the sheets to muffle her cries. She's clenching the sheets so hard that the blood pulls back from her knuckles.

"That's it, baby. You feel so fucking good," I growl, biting on my lower lip.

Leaning in, my mouth finds her shoulder and neck. I nip and suck at her exposed flesh while fucking her senseless.

Lottie's legs begin to tremble, her muffled moans grow louder. Her hips rock against me, she's close and racing towards her release.

I bring a hand around to cover her mouth as she comes, hard. Then spin her onto her back, hike her hips and slip back inside her arse.

She clutches my shoulders as I begin to thrust in long, deep strokes.

"Craig..." her teeth graze my neck. I toss her legs on my shoulders, stuff the pillow between the headboard and wall, and then capture her mouth in a possessive kiss.

My hips have a mind of their own, fucking her with abandon until I'm right on the edge, Lottie has one hand gripping the headboard, the other digging into my shoulder.

"Baby, fuck. Charlotte—" my vision goes white from the intensity of my orgasm. "Fuck!" I can't catch my breath, I'm seeing stars.

I look down and see Lottie's hooded, glassy eyes staring back at me. She has the look of a thoroughly satisfied woman.

"That was—" The door handle jiggles, followed by a hesitant knock.

"Daddy?" Ellie calls.

For fuck's sake, I haven't even pulled out yet!

Thank Christ I locked that door.

"What is it, princess?"

"The DVD froze!"

Stab me in the face and get it over with. "Can't you just turn on another?"

"But we want to watch Elsa!"

I'm gonna toe bog Elsa in the muff. "Turn on Disney Plus?"

"I don't know the password."

Have kids they said, it'll be fun they said. "I'll be right there."

"Thank you!"

I hear Ellie retreating downstairs, meanwhile, I'm still balls-deep in my wife.

"Well," Lottie grins, "that was interesting."

"This is your fault. You said she could have a sleepover."

"Are you seriously arguing with me while you're still inside me?"

I reluctantly pull out, get up on jelly legs, pull on my joggers, stumble into the wall and finally unlock the door. All the while Lottie is giggling her arse off at my misery.

I get halfway down the stairs when I hear a yelp, "for fuck's sake, Thor! Don't sleep on the poxy stairs if you don't want to get stepped on!"

Idiot dog.

I enter the battlefield of Disney princesses, turn on Disney Plus and suddenly I'm their hero.

Yippee for me.

"All sorted?"

"Thanks, Daddy," Ellie shuffles under her Elsa blanket.

"Right," I give one last glance around the room. I am not cleaning this tomorrow. "Goodnight, girls."

They all respond in unison… not the slightest bit creepy.

I walk back upstairs, avoiding the dog. Tuck Satan back in and stroll into my room to find Lottie passed out on the bed, cocooned in the blankets.

LOTTIE

Ok. The house is relatively clean. Dinner is on. The kids are still breathing. Dogs accounted for, all good here.

I hear keys in the door, and that can only mean one thing, Craig's home from his meeting. Hopefully, he sorted out the final details with McIntosh and didn't put his head through a wall.

I hear shoes on the floor as he approaches.

Glancing up, I catch sight of him. My beautiful man strutting in wearing a three-piece tailored grey suit, reminding me of our wedding.

It's rare to catch him in a suit and not his usual work gear. It suits him. He looks great.

It's only when my eyes trail to his face that I notice something is off. "Baby, what's wrong?"

His jaw is clenched, and his eyes are red-rimmed. He swallows, avoiding eye contact.

"Craig?"

I place the lid back on the pot of veg, lowering the temperature down to a simmer.

"We need to talk," he says after a pregnant pause.

Oh shit. What happened?

My eyes rake over his body; no busted knuckles, no blood spatter. He didn't kill anyone. There are no signs of a scuffle.

"Ok." I slowly lower myself into one of the kitchen chairs, wringing my hands while I wait for him to speak.

"I... eh... I haven't been entirely honest with you lately."

Oh shit.

Craig continues before I can think of a reply, "I've been keeping something from you. Something I'm not proud of."

What the hell did you do?

"I was afraid of you finding out—that if you found out, you'd see me in a different light."

What the hell is it?

Drugs?

Gambling?

Drinking problem? No, that can't be it; he doesn't drink enough for that.

Smoking. He's back to smoking again!

It better be that!

I swear to Christ, it better be that. If you tell me you're having an affair, Barnes, I will cut it off!

He reaches into his pocket and pulls out foil packaging.

Pills.

Oh God, it's drugs!

How the hell did he get hooked?

Right, deep breaths, Lottie. Counselling, rehab—we can get through this.

"Here," he says, passing me the packet. I turn it over in my hands to see the label. Sertraline 100mg.

Antidepressants.

He's on antidepressants.

Thank Christ for that!

Placing the packet on the table, I stand and go to him. Craig looks everywhere but at me.

I frame his face in my hands; he's still trying to avoid my gaze. "This is it? This is the big secret?"

He nods.

I haul him down, pressing my lips against his. His body relaxes in my hold after a moment. "Don't ever be ashamed to come to me with this."

"I didn't want to let you down," he says in a mere whisper. His eyes squeeze shut, and his forehead presses against mine.

"Craig, look at me."

His eyes drift open, and I'm left gazing into those stormy grey eyes.

"You can never let me down."

The sides of his mouth pull into a slight grin, and he lets out a sigh of relief. "I love you."

"I love you too."

He nuzzles into my neck and stays there for a short time. I won't budge. I hold him close, playing with the tufts of his hair.

"Eww!" Ethan grimaces from the hallway.

"If you don't like it, don't watch," I call back.

"You two are always kissing!"

"And I'm about to kiss Dad again."

He's gone running.

I turn to Craig and smirk, "kissies?"

"Gladly," he says, kissing me tenderly and looking more like himself now that he's spoken to me. "Am I still your Superman?"

"Always."

While the kids are at school, we drive to AJ's. Apparently, he has a gift for Craig and Jason. With James' assessment today, Jay couldn't make it, so I'm going in his place.

AJ's house is colossal. We are let in by a member of staff and find him sprinting on a treadmill in his home gym.

"Craig!" Aiden slaps the stop button, slowing the machine to a standstill. His broad, tattooed chest rises and falls in time with his rapid breathing. Reaching for a towel, Aiden brings it to his face and wipes away the beads of sweat from his forehead. "Charlotte," Aiden rasps, offering me a dapper smile, "it's lovely to see you again. Can I get you anything?"

"No, thank you."

"You're sure?" He cocks an eyebrow at me, taking my measure.

"Positive."

"Well, sit down, love. A woman in your state should be resting," Aiden says, ushering me to the couch and stuffing two sizeable cushions behind my back before turning to Craig. "You're a lucky man."

"I know; they're not ours." Craig points to my bump and snorts.

"Jason told me," Aiden admits. Reaching for a bottle of water, he spins the lid open with a mere flick before taking three long gulps.

"You said you had something for me." Craig looks around, his hands stuffed in his pockets. "I hope it's not an open grave."

"I'm offended." Aiden's hand lands on the tattoo above his heart.

"You're not."

"I'm not," Aiden grins. His grey eyes spark: "You looked after something very precious to me."

"Craig did?" I can't help but narrow my eyes at my husband. What the hell did he do? Hide a body?

As if reading my mind, Aiden scoffs. "Nothing illegal, Charlotte."

"I should hope not."

"What's the gift?" Craig presses.

"Come here," Aiden marches around his desk, taps a few keys, and I see Craig's brows furrow. "These are the right details, no?"

"They are." There is an air of suspicion in Craig's tone.

"Very good. Do me one little favour and sign yourself in there." Aiden walks around the desk to give Craig privacy or space. I don't know what the hell is going on; I'm about to get to my feet when AJ plonks his arse down on the armrest of the chair and says, "You might want to stay sitting for this part, love."

Craig's eyes grow wide like saucers. "Are you fucking serious?"

"What? What's going on?" I move for the edge of the seat, but Aiden places a firm but gentle hand down to stop me.

Craig spins the laptop around, showing me a seven-digit number in the bank account for his latest business.

"You did excellent work on your first case. It is only right that you get paid for the months of hard work you put in. Jason mentioned the banks are giving you some hassle; I'm sure that sum should make things easier. Cut out the middleman, so to speak."

"I can't accept this," Craig says, stepping back from the desk.

"Tough. It's already transferred." Aiden gets to his feet and, stepping up to Craig, whispers something to him that I can't make out. Whatever it is, Craig is left beaming.

"Now," Aiden says to me, gifting me a dazzling smile. "Make yourselves at home. I'm going to grab a quick shower, and then we can celebrate your new venture."

CRAIG

Everything has been going well for the last few months. Our new offices for our security agency are underway and should be finished soon. Nick has recovered from his stint with AJ, and Éabha is finally free and living with hot Joe.

She may have also robbed AJ blind and had him arrested, but that's a story for another day.

Jay and I have been juggling both businesses and family, and I've had extra therapy added to the mix since my talk with Lottie.

That woman is my rock.

She has supported me through everything. I made sure I took the pills, and I'm happy to say I finally got the all-clear to start coming down from them. Lottie makes sure I'm taking care of myself, even if that results in her chewing the arse off me for me to actually listen.

I'm in a much better place now. William is a constant for the kids, and, if I'm being honest, it's not horrible having him around. A major adjustment, yes, but he seems to be invested in the kids.

I've yet to meet Andrew, who is still off travelling, so that will be interesting when we finally meet face-to-face. In a little over a year, I've gained a sister, and the kids have gained a grandfather. I'm happy to leave the brother on the back burner for now.

AJ sent a massive baby bundle bumper pack to Nick's— his way of apologising for shooting him, I guess. What's even more impressive is that he managed to organise it all from a holding cell.

Lottie is due soon. I know this because she started devouring ice cream for breakfast; it was a dead giveaway that she is over the pregnancy and is in the final stages of not giving a crap.

She was the same on our three.

Ethan, not so much. She refused to wear a bra by the end of her pregnancy with him and lived in joggers and leggings.

With Ellie, her breakfast consisted of breadsticks and heaping amounts of Nutella. She also lived in slippers; I'm surprised she didn't give birth wearing them.

On Tilly, well, I practically lit a fire under her arse to smoke that demon out.

After meeting Matilda, I can safely say that was her attitude and not her mother's that I was getting at that time.

Now these babies

Yep.

You heard me right.

Babies.

Two of them.

One was hiding behind the other in the first scan picture because, come the second, they were there.

Nick passed out.

It was fucking hilarious.

I recorded that reaction and stuck it on TikTok; it's safe to say it went viral.

We have no idea what they are yet; they're keeping the gender a surprise.

I thought I had pregnant sex with my wife figured out until I saw how big that bump got with twins. I had to get creative. At one stage, it must have looked like a bad version of Leapfrog.

Lottie has created a wall of pillows at night, so I cannot find her in the bed under all the pillows, blankets, and duvets. She looks like the collector from the labyrinth in the mornings.

For anyone who does not get the reference, let me paint a picture for you—better yet, let me show you.

Are you ready for it?

There's no going back now!

Yeah, try waking up next to that!

That expression is usually received when I tell her that we ran out of ice cream.

I wouldn't go as far as saying that I kicked depression's arse, but I've got the fucker on the run. How Lottie has done this several times is beyond me.

We are ready for a fresh start. A new chapter in life, and I cannot wait to take this journey with Lottie and the kids. It's safe to say Matilda will keep us on our toes if nothing else.

Jessica is leaning on the table with Lottie's latest book in hand, "another best seller."

"What can I say, people just love Craig."

I snort, "I think Tilly sold that book for you, baby."

"I cannot deny that," Jessica laughs. "Will there be a

book three in the series?"

"I don't know. There wasn't even supposed to be book two, but I'll always give my readers what they want. We'll just have to wait and see." Lottie laces her fingers between mine, and I lean in to kiss her crown, only to step back as I feel a gush of water hit my legs.

"Your water just broke!" Jessica has the phone in hand and is already dialling Abbie.

Here we go again.

Follow Éabha's story.

Printed in Great Britain
by Amazon

25800140R00163